A CONSPIRACY OF MAGIC

Rod looked up, horrifi... two long, sharp fangs...

"Get away from me!"...

"But, Rod . . . I onl...

"Meant to stop by f... is this, a vampire horse?"

"Exactly," chuckled a rich baritone voice.

Rod whirled, and saw a tall, debonair devil lounging against a tree trunk, twirling its tail. "Go to blazes!"

"Oh, all right," the devil grumped. "But I'll find you later." He exploded into flame and was gone, leaving Rod trembling.

"Rod, if you were drugged, surely the correct antidote . . ."

"There *is* no antidote!" Rod leaped back. "Because there's no poison! You're in this with them! You're all out to get me—even you, my old tutor and guardian! Get away! Get out of here! Go!"

The vampire horse stood, glaring at him with eyes of fire.

Rod whipped out his dagger. "Turn into a sword!" The blade sprouted, grew three feet. "Silver!" Rod cried, and the sheen of steel turned to a mirror finish. He advanced toward Fess . . .

Praise for the WARLOCK series:

"Fresh . . . well written and entertaining."
—W.D. Stevens, *Fantasy Review*

"Enchanting adventures." —*Fanzine*

"It is refreshing to see a fantasy hero aided by his wife and children."
—Rick Osborne, *Fantasy Review*

Ace Books by Christopher Stasheff

A WIZARD IN BEDLAM

The Warlock Series

Christopher Stasheff

THE WARLOCK INSANE

ACE BOOKS, NEW YORK

This book is an Ace original edition,
and has never been previously published.

THE WARLOCK INSANE

An Ace Book/published by arrangement with
the author

PRINTING HISTORY
Ace edition/July 1989

ISBN: 0-441-87364-2

Ace Books are published by The Berkley Publishing Group,
200 Madison Avenue, New York, New York 10016.
The name ''ACE'' and the ''A'' logo are trademarks
belonging to Charter Communications, Inc.

PRINTED IN THE UNITED STATES OF AMERICA

10 9 8 7 6 5 4 3 2 1

With thanks to
L. Sprague de Camp and Fletcher Pratt,
whose *Castle of Iron*
introduced me to the
Orlando Furioso.

1

"Yeah, but *you* don't have to shovel it!"

"Oh, come, husband." Gwen tightened her grip on his arm, mouth pursed in amusement. " 'Tis beautiful by moonlight, naetheless. And thou hast no need to clear it by main force, in any event."

Rod smiled, watching the kids frolic up ahead, carefully avoiding the well-cleared road and slogging through the snowbanks, where they could get nice and wet. Geoffrey had started a snowball fight, and Magnus was retaliating with enthusiasm.

"Gregory's trying, anyway."

"He is merely distracted by watching the snowballs' trajectories, Rod, instead of their targets." The voice of the great black horse behind him sounded through the earphone implanted in his mastoid process. "He is a son to be proud of."

"Yes. He certainly is, Fess—he certainly is." Rod smiled down into Gwen's eyes, and she radiated back up at him. "They all are—each in his own way." He looked up with a sparkle of mischief in his eye. "Or hers."

Cordelia was standing by, watching her brothers with her nose in the air, pretending to be above such things—while she packed a snowball behind her back, waiting for a clear target.

The moonlight *was* lovely, throwing the shadow of the castle's turrets before them, glinting off the piled snow to either side of the hilly road, and frosting the village below. Not that Rod could admit that, when he was in the middle of a perfectly good banter with his wife. "But as to the shoveling—*you're* the one who's always saying we shouldn't use magic for daily tasks."

"Indeed we should not," Gwen said with prim rectitude. "Yet thou hast stalwart lads for the task, and thy lass . . ."

"Swings a mean broom, yeah. Okay, you win—I have to admit I like it. Of course, I'm still suffused with the glow of Twelfth Night. Tuan and Catharine throw a great party!"

"They are a most excellent host and hostess, aye—the more so on a feast day."

"Feast day is right! Talk about a royal banquet. You nearly had to roll me home." Rod smiled with nostalgic fondness, remembering the goose—and the ham, and the sausages, and the trifle . . . "Sorry there wasn't anything for you, Fess."

"On the contrary, Rod, there was a plenitude of oats and hay—and I had to pretend to eat, to avoid making the grooms suspicious. Still, there was ample interest in observing the infinite variation in their customs."

Rod frowned. "I would have thought you knew every habit of every groom in Gramarye by now."

"Knowing is one thing. Understanding is quite another."

"Oh." Rod pushed his tongue into his cheek. "Learn anything new?"

"There were some fascinating variations on courting rituals . . ."

Rod grinned. "That's right, it was a holiday for them, too, wasn't it? Of course, the banquet was over four hours ago." He frowned at the thought. "Y'know, I could've sworn I'd never have an appetite again."

Gregory came charging up, eyes and cheeks aglow. "Papa, Papa! A beldame doth linger by the roadside yon, hawking hot chestnuts! May we?"

"Oh, please!" Cordelia pleaded, appearing just behind him.

"I *was* talking about being a mite peckish, wasn't I?" Rod fished in his purse and pulled out a copper. "Okay, kids— but save a few for us, will you?"

"Thou shalt have the half of them!" Gregory snatched the coin and shot off, Cordelia hot on his heels.

"Glad we could do something." Rod could see the old lady now, shivering by the roadside in her shawl, popping chestnuts into Cordelia's kerchief.

"Aye." Gwen snuggled closer. " 'Tis beastly to have to stand in the chill."

"Tuan and Catharine have brought prosperity to the land," Fess observed, "but they have not succeeded in eliminating poverty."

"No one else ever has, either—all they do is redefine it. But at least she has a brazier—and I must say her wares are in the proper holiday spirit . . ."

"Thine!" Gregory popped up in front of them again, looking like a chipmunk. Behind him, his brothers and sister were cracking shells and gobbling goodies with more verve than neatness.

"Gee, thanks." But Rod was talking to air; his youngest was already en route back to his siblings. He sighed. "Well, left holding the bag, as usual. Care for one, dear?"

"I thank thee." Gwen accepted the chestnut, broke the shell the rest of the way, and nibbled at the meat.

Rod popped the whole kernel in his mouth and chewed.

His eyes widened. "My heavens! I didn't know chestnuts could taste so good!"

"They do, in truth." Gwen's eyes lost focus. "There are spices added to this. Let me see—there's rosemary, that's for remembrance . . ."

"Odd combination—but very good, I have to admit." Rod swallowed and took the last chestnut. "Share?"

"Aye." Gwen dimpled. "Three for us—and how many for them?"

"Half a dozen each, at a guess. Maybe we should buy some more." Rod looked up, just in time to see the old lady kicking snow onto her fire and turning away down the hill, pot in hand. "No, I guess we got the last of them."

"She had good custom, I doubt not, with all the folk of the village coming home from the castle."

Rod nodded. "Plenty of apprentices, and a ha'penny each adds up. Glad we happened by before she folded—it lent the perfect touch to a wonderful day."

Cordelia came up to them. She glanced back at the old peasant woman's retreating back, troubled. "What emptiness is that in her eyes, Mama?"

"Ah." Gwen exchanged a look with Rod. " 'Tis only that she is very simple, child."

"Simple?" Cordelia frowned. "Like to Their Majesties' fool?"

"Oh, no!" Rod looked up, shaking his head. "That jester is a very intelligent man, dear, with a quick wit and a sense of humor that borders on genius."

"Then why," said Magnus, "do they call him a fool?"

"Because some of the things he says and does are very foolish."

"Which is to say, they are things done by a fool," Gregory protested. "What sense is there in that, Papa?"

"A rather unpleasant sense, I'm afraid," Rod answered, and Gwen said gently, "Long ago, lords did take the simpleminded and keep them by, to laugh at their clumsiness and mistakes of judgement, which did amuse their masters greatly.''

"How cruel!'' Cordelia exclaimed indignantly, and all three of her brothers nodded in agreement. Rod felt a glow of pride in them as he replied, "It *was* cruel—and I'm afraid it wasn't exclusive to kings and queens. Most people have laughed at the mentally retarded, down through the ages.''

"E'en today, in a small village, thou wilt find many who do make mock of the village idiot,'' Gwen said softly. " 'Tis vile, but 'tis done.''

"So maybe it's just as well that smart people who had a gift for comedy convinced the lords that they were more foolish than the fools,'' Rod concluded.

"Aye,'' Geoffrey said through his scowl. "At the least, they do it willingly.''

"Yet I did hear some ladies discuss him as a 'madcap,' '' Gregory said. "Do they not mean that he is maddened, in his head?''

Rod smiled, a glint in his eye. "Very good, son! Maybe that's where the term came from. But even if that was its original meaning, it's not now—today it means that the man behaves insanely.'' Then he frowned. "Wait a minute . . .''

"That he doth do and say things that make no sense,'' Gwen explained.

"Then one who is 'insane' is senseless?'' Cordelia asked.

"Nay!'' Geoffrey said. "He who is senseless hath been knocked unconscious.''

"Yea and nay,'' Gwen said, smiling. "The term doth mean one who doth sleep so unwillingly, aye—yet it also doth speak of one who hath lost all judgement.''

"Or whose judgement has become so distorted that he has become completely unpredictable,'' Rod added. "He's as likely to hit you as to hail you.''

"Ah!" cried Gregory. "Then *that* is madness!"

"Well, yes, I suppose it would be," Rod said slowly, "in the way that Count Orlando was mad."

Magnus frowned. "I have not met him."

"No, nor are likely to, son," Rod said, amused. "Roland—or Orlando, as they called him in Italy—was nephew to Charlemagne . . ."

"The Emperor of the Franks?" Geoffrey looked up, round-eyed. "He is history, not myth!"

"Why yes, he is." Rod looked up at Fess with renewed respect; any tutor who could interest Geoffrey in history verged on being a magician. Of course, Charlemagne was *military* history . . . "But myths grow up around people who change the world, and Charlemagne did. Still, there's only so much you can say about a king, because he has to spend most of his time governing, which may be exciting in its own right, but is only occasionally dramatic—so the tale-tellers usually find somebody near him to build their stories around, and in Charlemagne's case, that person was his nephew."

"He did really live, then?"

"We think so," Fess said, "though he certainly did none of the supernatural feats attributed to him. He was an excellent focus for myth, however, and figures largely and luridly in a fairy-haunted world that never existed."

"And he went mad?"

"For a time," Rod said, "because he fell in love with a lady who didn't want anything to do with him—and when he found out she had married somebody else, he went into a nonstop rage, tearing up forests and slaughtering peasants, not to mention the occasional knight or two."

"Are the mad truly so?" Gregory asked, wide-eyed.

"Not 'mad,' Gregory—'mentally ill,' " Fess corrected, "and there are many kinds and degrees of mental illness. But one or two varieties do sometimes result in people going on rampages, beating and slaying numbers of people, yes.''

"Not *quite* on the scale that Orlando did, though," Rod said quickly. "In fact, I think his 'madness' was more probably a magnified version of someone suffering from rabies.''

"Oh! I have heard of that!" Cordelia shuddered. "Such poor souls do become like beasts, bereft of reason and seeking to bite and beat any who may cross their path!"

"Unfortunate, but true," Fess agreed, "and they are referred to as being 'mad.' ''

"But they are not, Fess! 'Tis only a sickness in the body, brought by a germ in the bite of a dog or rat!"

"True enough," Rod agreed, "but one of the symptoms is that the victim stops thinking, and turns homicidal.''

"There are many forms of mental illness that have physical causes, children," Fess said quietly, "even so slight a cause as an upset in the balance of the chemicals in people's bodies.''

"Now wait, wait!" Geoffrey held up a hand, squeezing his eyes shut. "Thou dost confuse me! Thou dost say that simple folk are fools, but fools are men of wit?''

"It is a problem in the language," Fess admitted, "brought by people using a word that describes one condition, and applying it to another. Let us say that a fool is a person of poor judgement, Geoffrey.''

Geoffrey looked doubtful, and Cordelia said, with hesitation, "That doth aid me somewhat in understanding . . .''

"I think it might cut through some of the confusion if you tell them the story," Rod suggested.

"A story?''

"Tell it!''

"Aye, tell, Fess! Matters are always made more clear by a tale!''

"Not if it has any true literary value," the robot hedged,

"but a fable generally does clarify matters, since fables are teaching stories."

"Then tell us a fable!"

"More pointedly," Rod said, "the fable of the Wise Man, the Jester, the Fool, the Simpleton, and the Madman."

"Aye, tell!" And they all stopped in the road and gathered around the great iron steed.

"As you will," Fess sighed. "*The Wise Man said, 'Gentlemen, the world will end tomorrow, if you do not save it.'*

"*The madman smiled with delight.*

" *'If we do not save it?' said the fool. 'Will you not share the risk?'*"

"Why, he was a fool in truth," Geoffrey snorted, "if he would cavil o'er fairness at a time of peril!"

"Thou hast been known to cavil so," Cordelia pointed out.

"Yet surely not when danger did threaten!"

"Perhaps not when it is imminent," Fess temporized. "Then you understand that the threat is more important than your pride—as the Wise Man satisfied the Fool by saying, *'I will go with you, to show you where to dig.'*

"*Then the fool felt shamed, and said, 'Do you really mean what you say?'*

" *'I really do,' the Wise Man answered.*

"*The Simpleton's brow furrowed with the effort of his thought. 'How can so great a thing as the world, be destroyed?'*

" *'There are tremendous fires within the earth,' the Wise Man answered. 'They burn too quickly; if we do not let them out, their smoke will burst the world.'*

"*The Simpleton stared. 'But how can there be anything within the earth? It is only dirt underfoot.'*

" *'It may seem so,' said the Wise Man, 'but it is truly a great ball, so vast that we are mere specks upon it—and it is hollow, with fires within.'*

"But the Simpleton only shook his head in bafflement, for he could not comprehend the notion.

" *'How then shall we save the world?'* asked the fool.

" *'We must dig a great hole,'* said the Wise Man, *'so that the fires may have a chimney.'*

" *'Why, that is too much work!'* said the fool."

"Too much work, and too great a folly," Geoffrey cried. "Did he not know he would breed a volcano?"

"He did, and so did the jester, for he said, *'Nay, Uncle—it is not the world that will be destroyed then, but us. It is bad enough to be smoked meat, but it is worse to be fried.' "*

"There is some wit in that," Gregory said judiciously, "but there is most excellent sense, too."

"Nay, there is cowardice!"

"Well, there was sensible caution, at least," Fess said, "but the Wise Man answered, *'If a few do not risk being burned to cinders, all will be blown to bits,'* and the Jester shivered and said, *'Alas the day, that I am one of the few who are made to see the need of it! But I shall go, then, for it is better to burn than to tarry.' "*

Gwen gave Fess a glare, and Rod murmured, "That's truly apauling."

Fess quickly went on. *"Then they all took their shovels and followed the Wise Man to an empty field, and began to dig where he showed them; but the madman only leaned on his shovel and watched them."*

"Is that all?" Magnus protested. "There is no madness in that, but laziness and blindness, and lack of concern!"

"Aye," Cordelia agreed. "When did he aught that was mad, Fess?"

"When the others went to dinner, Cordelia—for then he filled in the hole."

The children stared at him, shocked, while Gwen eyed Fess uncertainly, and Rod covered a smile.

"Was the world destroyed, then?" Gregory burst out.

"Nay, surely not," Geoffrey said, "for we stand on it now!"

"This was only a fable, children, and it stood on nothing but imagination," Fess reminded them. "But the world of the story was destroyed, yes."

"Why," Magnus gasped, "he *was* mad!" Then he stared, surprised by his own words.

"Why, indeed he was," Cordelia said slowly. "So that is madness!"

"But of only one kind." Gregory turned to Fess. "And thou hast said there are many, and of differing degrees."

"I have," Fess agreed, "but they all have this in common: that people who are mentally ill do things without reason—or at least, no reason that healthy minds can see."

Rod nodded. "So don't worry about it, children—and do try to help the simpleton and the madman when you can."

"What of the fool, Papa?"

Rod stirred uncomfortably. "I don't know if you *can* help a fool, children, except to save him from total disaster. But remember, it won't help any of them to go around looking gloomy."

Magnus grinned. "Aye, Papa. Let us help them when we can—but when we cannot, let us take what joy we may."

"Well said." Rod smiled. "And just now, it's the end of a perfect day."

"Aye." Gwen rested her head on his shoulder for a moment, then looked up at him, smiling. He returned the smile, gazing deeply into her eyes, hoping that she was really giving the promise he read there.

"You two really should be careful of your footing," Fess observed.

"Okay, I get the message. We'll watch where we're

going.'' Rod turned back to the road with a happy sigh. ''I can't complain, though. It's a perfect winter's night—clear as a bell, with the stars at their brightest.''

''Aye, and the greater moon nearly full.''

''Yeah.'' Rod looked up at the silver circle through the twigs of the branch above him. ''Funny how every decent-sized moon always has markings that look like a face.''

''Like a face?'' Gregory piped up. Rod looked down at his youngest. ''Thou hast told us some did see the whole of the man there!''

''Aye, and with a dog at his heels!'' Cordelia was still in the habit of behaving like little brother's shadow, just in case.

''And a lantern, too!'' Geoffrey wasn't about to be left out—and, suddenly, Gwen was surrounded with her whole brood again, as dapper young Magnus came sauntering back, smoothing his first moustache with a fingertip. (Rod had sworn he wouldn't teach him to shave until there was enough to make the effort worthwhile.)

''The man with the dog and lantern was a medieval European interpretation, children,'' Fess explained.

''Back on old Terra, kids, humanity's birthplace.'' Rod smiled down at Gwen. ''We did manage to find time to take a look at it, when we were there.''

''Tell us again how thou wert on that first Moon of Men,'' Geoffrey demanded.

Rod shook his head. ''Not tonight. But I will say that I never saw more than a face in it, myself.''

''Then is it in our minds that the Man in the Moon doth dwell, Papa, and not truly in his silver sphere?''

Rod nodded, looking up at the satellite again. ''Could be, Gregory. Of course, I suppose it depends on the viewer, too. For myself, trying to see what's really there and not what I've been told about, I'd have to say the Gramarye Moon looks like . . .''

"A pie!" Geoffrey cried.

"A shilling!" Cordelia caroled.

"A cheese!"

"A mirror!"

"I *was* going to say, an eye." Rod grinned. "See? It winked at me."

"Where!"

"Let me see!"

"Will it wink for me, too, Papa?"

"It would certainly be a very odd atmospheric effect." Fess looked up at the moon.

"*I* see not so much as an eyelash," Gwen informed them.

But the shape of the pupil and iris was becoming clearer, so clear that Rod couldn't doubt the resemblance. "It did. It winked again." Then he realized there was another eye beside it—and he froze. "There's two of them, and . . . they're narrowing!"

The branch above him moved downward, the twigs flexing, looking more and more like woody fingers on the end of a bark-covered arm, coming right down toward the family.

"*Look out!*" Rod grabbed Gwen in his right arm, Cordelia and Gregory in his left, and dove for the roadside, bowling down Geoffrey and Magnus on the way, as the enormous hand groped toward them.

The children howled with alarm, and Gwen cried, "Husband! What dost thou!"

"Battle stations!" Rod shouted. "It's coming for us!"

"What doth come for us?" Magnus scrambled to his feet, looking about wildly.

"Where? What?" Geoffrey sprang up, landing in a crouch, sword out, darting glances to left and to right.

Fess leaped out into the road, blocking them with his huge body. "Where is the enemy, Rod? I cannot see it!"

"There! It's a troll! That wasn't the moon, it was its eye—and that branch was its arm and hand!"

"Husband, calm thyself!" Gwen said. " 'Tis not a troll's eye, but truly the moon! And the branch is only a branch!"

"Can't you *see* it?" Rod dodged aside as the huge hand swept down past the horse, turning into a fist.

"Nay!" Cordelia wailed. "Oh, Papa, there's naught there!"

"Don't tell *me* what I don't see!" Rod leaped back, sword whisking out as the gigantic fist slammed into the snowbank in front of him and swung up again. "Quick, fly away! It's after us!"

"But there is naught . . ."

"Do you trust me or don't you?" Rod bellowed. "Run! I can't escape until you do!"

"Papa," Cordelia insisted through her tears, "there is no troll! 'Tis but a dream!"

"Then it's a dream that can hurt you! *Fly!*"

"Quickly, children!" Gwen cried. "Whatsoe'er he doth see, he cannot be calm while we're here! Up, aloft! Everyone!" Her broomstick appeared from beneath her cloak.

In a whisk, Cordelia was airborne, her brothers shooting up like skyrockets. Gwen spiraled up after them.

Fess came to Rod's side. "If there is a troll, Rod, it is invisible, and that is contrary to the laws of physics."

"Invisible? It's right *there*, for crying out loud! Fess, jump out of the way!"

But the horse stood still, so Rod leaped to the side, and the troll seemed to pause, unsure which target to aim at.

Gwen decided the issue by calling, "We are safe, husband!"

"No, you're not!" Rod shouted as the troll turned with a gibbering laugh, its huge hand reaching up toward Rod's daughter. " 'Delia, up to a hundred feet! He's after you!

You obscenity of a monster—get away from my child!''
And he leaped at the troll, slashing out with his sword.

The blade cracked against a leg hard as oak, but it
scored a long line, and ichor welled out. With a howl of
rage, the troll turned, huge fist smashing down at Rod.

He leaped again, and snow fountained where the fist
struck, while Fess's voice rang inside his head. ''Rod! Put
up your blade! There are none here but yourself and your
family! There is no troll!''

''Then how come he's trying to tear my head off?'' Rod
leaped again, but the troll's other hand caught him in a
crushing squeeze, driving the air from his lungs. He managed a sort of whinnying cry of alarm as the ground swung
away beneath his feet, and the troll's huge maw gaped
wide before him. Vision reddened as the viselike grip
pushed blood into his head, but a single thought swam
through the haze: even a troll had to have parts that were
soft—relatively, at least. He saw the huge lips soaring
closer and lunged out as hard as he could. His blade
jabbed into flesh that had the texture of balsa.

The troll let out a hoot that would have attracted a
female locomotive and threw Rod down, hard—he managed to think *Up!* barely in time to cushion the force of
the fall. He landed on his side and rolled up to his feet
as the troll roared and stalked toward him, its eyes crimson
in the night, huge foot slamming down at him.

Rod danced aside, and dodged the huge fist that
followed—then leaped as high as he could, rocketing upward with the full power of his levitation, sword spearing
toward the troll's belly.

It hit, with a shock that jolted Rod's whole arm—but the
troll howled in agony and doubled over. Rod managed to
shoot out of the way, then lunged in to skewer the monster's ear. The sword pierced the lobe, and the troll clapped
a hand over it with a roar that shook the hillside. It

snapped back upright—until the pain in its abdomen stopped it. Rod dove in at the inside of the elbow, feeling like a mosquito—but no insect ever brought out a bellow like that. The troll stumbled back, away, then away again, hands up to fend off the tiny demon that shot around and about it, darting in and stabbing. It turned away, burbling in alarm, and stumbled off into the forest.

The crashing of its passage faded, and Rod let himself sink back to the earth, panting and pressing a hand against the ache in his side, wondering if the monster's grip had cracked a bone. "Must have been—witch-moss," he gasped, "but a hell of a lot of it! What have we got—a whole village full of grannies telling ogre tales?" He turned to his family. "Okay, you can come down now."

They were down, all right—but Cordelia was huddled against her mother sobbing, and Gregory was clutching tight to her skirts, staring up at his father with huge, frightened eyes. Behind, Magnus and Geoffrey stood manfully, trying to hide their apprehension.

Rod frowned. "What's the matter with you? The *troll* was the monster—not me!"

Tears brimmed Gwen's eyes. "Husband, we saw naught! Thou didst dodge from no blows!"

"Come on! It plowed up a dozen snowdrifts!"

"The surface was completely undisturbed, Rod," Fess answered, "except by your own tumbles."

"Then thou didst rise up though naught did hold thee— yet thou didst struggle as though against a giant hand."

"Believe me, I *felt* it!"

"But we did not see it!"

"Not *see* it?" Rod stilled suddenly, feeling a chill of ice that had nothing to do with the winter. "You're all against me again, aren't you? Teaming up!"

"Husband, no!"—as though it were torn from her.

"Then *look*, will you?" Rod whirled, pointing at the

snow. "There're the footprints! Fess could stand in one! In fact, he *is* standing in one!"

The horse looked down. "I see only snow, Rod, disturbed by no more than my own hooves."

"Mayhap only thou couldst see it," Gregory offered. "Could it have been shielded by a spell that denied it to our eyes?"

That gave Rod pause, but Fess answered, "We would then have been able to see its effects, Gregory, and . . ."

"Save your breath, Fess." Rod's eyes narrowed as he looked down at the boy. "He's humoring me."

Gregory shrank back against Gwen's skirts, and for a moment, the whole family stood frozen, appalled at the memory of their father's rages, and bracing themselves for another.

"Hell's skulls," Rod moaned, "am I near lashing out at you all?"

No one answered him.

"I am," Rod breathed, "I really am! And there is no *way* I'm going to let that happen again!"

On the word, he turned and strode away into the forest.

"No, Papa!"

"Papa, come back!"

"Husband, thou hast not readied thyself for being long out of doors!"

"Sacred Blue!" Rod muttered to himself. "As though I hadn't slogged through sixteen-hour winter days before I ever met her!"

"On the planet Pohyola, as I remember, Rod," Fess said at his shoulder, "when you were helping the rebels to organize."

"Are you there, then?" Rod scowled up at the great black horse. "Go away. I'm of questionable mental equilibrium, remember?"

"No one but yourself has said so, Rod."

"No one but myself has had to live in my mind." Rod stopped stock-still, staring off into the night. "That's it!"

"What is what, Rod?"

"Why I could see a troll, and none of the rest of you could. Because it wasn't there."

You could almost hear the relief in Fess's voice. "That is, certainly, a logical conclusion, Rod."

"Yeah, but then isn't it equally logical that I'm hallucinating?"

"That is simply a matter of definition."

"No, it's a matter of scrambled brains. Face it, Fess—I'm insane." Rod stopped in the snow, a beatific smile spreading across his face. "Yeah, insane. Well! If *that's* all it is, then I can relax again."

"Would you . . . explain the basis for that attitude, Rod?"

"What's to explain? As long as I know what it is, I know what to do about it."

"Which is?" Fess asked, with foreboding.

"Stay far away from Gwen and the kids, for openers, so I can't hurt them. Stay away from everybody, for that matter, until I manage to get myself straightened out." Rod started walking again. "That forest looks inviting. I'm overdue for a vacation, anyway."

"Now, Rod." Fess hurried to catch up with him. "Surely you are exaggerating."

"No, I'm hallucinating. And if I'm hallucinating, I'm either starving, drugged, suffering from heatstroke, or insane."

"That is not a warranted inference . . ."

"Oh, yeah? Do *you* know any other causes of hallucination?"

Fess was silent a moment, then said, "An excess of religious zeal, perhaps, usually coinciding with deep meditation."

"Yeah, well, I sure haven't been praying this afternoon—and after that banquet Their Majesties fed us, I'm certainly not starving! If any of that food had been drugged, there'd be a hundred other people hallucinating, too!"

"Have we any proof that they are not?"

"Judging by the ruckus I've been making, we'd have heard them by now—or at least heard about them; Their Royalties always summon us when something unexplainable happens to somebody."

"That does seem valid," Fess said with reluctance.

"You bet it does! As to heatstroke, it's the middle of winter—and that leaves insanity!"

"The term is perhaps a bit extreme . . ."

"Sure—I'm just seeing things that aren't really there. Seeing them attack me, too—and will you really try to tell me that I haven't always been a little bit paranoid?"

"Your grandfather did perhaps exert too strong an influence on you, with his medieval fantasies . . ."

"Yes—my darling, beloved, but dotty grandfather. Is *that* an adjective you'd accept, Fess? Or how about 'mad as a hatter'?"

"I think I might prefer the last," Fess said slowly, "considering its association with the works of Lewis Carroll."

"Then it's heigh-ho! Off to Wonderland! Are you coming along, Fess?" But Rod didn't wait for an answer.

2

The trees closed behind him. Rod glanced back, and saw only a maze of bare branches, outlined by the snow clinging to them. At once, he slowed his pace with a sigh of relief. "They did it. They stayed."

"They do recognize your need for occasional solitude, Rod."

"Still there, Steel Steed?" Rod looked up at his old companion, and was surprised to see that the great black horse was facing front, not watching him. For some reason, this made the pressure roll off. "Well. So I'm on sick leave."

"It would seem advisable," the robot agreed.

"Great!" Rod stretched, then relaxed with a happy sigh. "No more emergency calls from Tuan and Catharine! At least, not for a while."

"Yet Gwen will have to manage the children alone," Fess murmured.

"She does, anyway, Fess, you know that. I'm just a security symbol for them all, a sort of animated teddy bear."

"Oh, no, Rod! You do them an injustice. You are far more, to all of them . . ." He stopped, seeing that his owner wasn't listening.

"Fess—what's that great big brown blob over there?"

"Where, Rod?" Fess followed Rod's gaze, but saw nothing.

Rod, however, saw a large, fat animal stand up on its hind legs and wave, a cheerful smile on its face. "It's a bear, Fess—six feet tall, if it's an inch. Very friendly-looking, too," he said, puzzled. "I thought bears were supposed to be hibernating."

"They are, Rod." There was a cautious note to the robot's voice. "Are its legs much thicker than is normal for its kind?"

"Yeah, and it has pink pads instead of paws . . . Hey!" Rod whirled, staring up at Fess. "You don't mean it's a teddy!"

"Yes, Rod—an animated teddy bear, such as you were just discussing."

"Odd coincidence." Rod waved back to the teddy, then watched it stroll away into the wood. It looked rather familiar. "You don't mean it showed up because I talked about it?"

"That is a distinct possibility, Rod. If you are hallucinating, anything that comes to your mind might appear."

"And anything that's there, waiting to surface, but hasn't come to the fore yet?" Rod frowned. "Don't know if I like the sound of that last part."

"It may turn out to be fallacious—but perhaps the visual images stored in your subconscious will not arise unless some random association triggers them."

"Like that thought about my role in the family." Rod glanced about him, suddenly apprehensive. "Right now, Fess, it looks to me as though I'm walking through a moonlit deciduous forest, with snow outlining the limbs of the trees.''

"You are, Rod."

"So the forest is real, anyway." Rod rubbed a glove across his chin.

A long, mournful cry echoed through the forest, and a shadow with eyes of fire detached itself from a nearby branch. "Fess! It's a vampire!"

"No, Rod—it is only an owl."

The huge bat dove at them, its jaws lolling open to show glistening fangs. Rod ducked, grabbed up a branch with a sharpened tip, and stabbed at the monster's breast. With a howl of dread, it sheered off and hurtled away into the forest. "Owl or not," Rod muttered, "I had to deal with it in terms of the fantasy it came from." Then a sudden thought struck him. "What am I holding, Fess?"

"A broken twig, Rod. ''

"It grew amazingly." Rod threw the sharpened stake away. "This is going to take some getting used to. Well, at least I have light." He looked up at the planetoid overhead. "Hey! It stayed a moon!"

"It would seem that the spell has passed," Fess murmured.

"Only temporarily." Rod shook his head. "Be nice if it would stay gone but I think I'd better wait a while, to make sure."

The moon reddened.

"Uh—strike that."

"What is happening, Rod?"

"The moon has turned crimson. A big, fat drop is collecting on its bottom . . . it's dripping . . ." Rod squeezed his eyes shut and shook his head. "No, I don't think I'm ready to go home."

"It is surely a chemical imbalance," the robot protested. "A blood analysis . . ."

Rod looked up, horrified. Fess had grown batwings; two long, sharp fangs protruded from his mouth. "Get away from me!"

"But, Rod . . . I only meant . . ."

"Meant to stop by for a quick sip! What the hell is this, a vampire horse?"

"Exactly," chuckled a rich baritone voice.

Rod whirled, and saw a tall, debonair devil lounging against a tree trunk, twirling its tail. "Go to blazes!"

"Oh, all right," the devil grumped. "But I'll find you later." He exploded into flame and was gone, leaving Rod trembling.

"Rod, surely the correct antidote . . ."

"There *is* no antidote!" Rod leaped back. "Because there's no poison! You're in this with them! You're all out to get me—even you, my old tutor and guardian! Get away! Get out of here! Go!"

The vampire horse stood, glaring at him with eyes of fire.

Rod whipped out his dagger. "Turn into a sword!" The blade sprouted, grew three feet. "Silver!" Rod cried, and the sheen of steel turned to a mirror finish.

"I will go," the vampire said slowly. "But I am grieved to find that your imbalance is so severe as to make you doubt me, Rod."

"Doubt? I'm sure of it! Now get out of here, before I run you through."

"I will go." The horse turned away—and as it went, the glow in its eyes died, the fangs shrank and were gone, the wings dwindled and flowed back into the form of a saddle—and only familiar old Fess plodded away through the snow, head hanging.

Rod felt a stab of remorse. "No! I mean . . ."

Fess paused and lifted his head, turning to face Rod. "Yes?"

"It's ebbing again," Rod explained. "It seems to come and go—and it makes me paranoid when it happens."

"I have heard of such phenomena," Fess answered.

Rod frowned. "Just reinforcing my natural tendencies, you mean?" Then before Fess could answer, "Never mind—it doesn't really matter. Whatever it is, I'll have to figure it out and learn to cope with it. You'll have to leave me alone to work it out, Fess. I know that's hard for you, but you'll have to."

"I have always endeavored not to be overly protective, Rod, in spite of my programming."

"Yeah—and I know how hard *that* is." Rod grimaced, remembering how he had to school himself to leave Gregory and Cordelia to fend for themselves—not always successfully. And Magnus and Geoffrey, when they were little. "No need to override that tendency completely, though. Don't be too far away, okay?"

The great black horse stared at him for a moment, while its eyes seemed to quicken again. Then it said, "I will come at your call, Rod."

"Thanks, old friend." Rod grinned with relief. "But you'd better not stay *too* close."

"I understand. I will be here, but not here." And the horse turned away, fading into the night.

Rod frowned, wondering if Fess had donned a cloak of invisibility. The thought alarmed him—he looked about in near panic, wondering how many invisible enemies might be looming over him.

"Magic spectacles." The devil was there again, a set of lenses dangling from its hand. "Guaranteed to let you see anyone wearing a cloak of invisibility, or even a Tarnhelm, anywhere nearby—and available only to you."

"Through this special offer, eh?" Rod glowered. "What's the price?"

"Only your signature, in blood."

Rod shook his head. "I couldn't read the fine print right now—it might keep changing on me. *Retro me, Satanus!*"

"Wrong devil," the demon scoffed, "but I take your point. Just remember, the offer remains open." It faded, and was gone.

"The offer is also empty," Rod snorted. Then he remembered that the biggest step in invention was realizing that something could be done—after that, research and engineering went faster. "Well, if I'm hallucinating, I ought to get *some* good out of it. Magic glasses! Appear!" He snapped his fingers, then held his hands out, cupped to catch.

Nothing happened.

"Might have known it wouldn't work when I wanted it to," he muttered, and turned away, plodding off into the night.

Rod hadn't gone far when he began to hear the piteous wail.

He broke into a trot—the fastest pace possible in the thick snow. The sound was that of someone in trouble and, his own natural inclination to help aside, he had to confront the hallucinations sprung from his secret fears, not flee from them.

Around a bend in the path, past a curving wall of trees, he saw a huge old oak tree, its trunk riven by some long-forgotten lightning bolt. The cleft in the trunk had closed fast around the arm of an old peasant woman who was moaning and shivering in the cold. She saw Rod. "A rescue, kind sir! Free me from the grip of this evil tree!"

And, so help him, the tree gave a menacing grumble.

Rod squeezed his eyes shut and gave his head a quick shake, then looked again. The oak and the crone were still there—of course. Still, what he saw might not be what she was seeing—or was she part of the hallucination, too?

One way to find out. He stepped up cautiously. "How did you come to catch your arm in that oak tree's trunk, grandmother?"

"I sought to grasp that sprig of mistletoe, sir, for the holiday!" A sprig dangled just beyond the woman's reach, for all the world like bait. "I reached, and the tree rocked toward me and caught my arm! Wilt free me, good sir? Oh, I beg of thee!"

A limb reached down twiggy fingers. Rod drew his sword in a slashing arc, and the twigs drew back with a shriek of stressed wood. The trunk rumbled angrily.

Rod looked up, eyes alight. "Doesn't like the steel, does it? Well, then, ma'am, all I have to do is . . ." He stretched out the blade, probing into the crack in the trunk. The tree moaned in horror, and the edges of the cleft shrank back. The old lady snatched her arm free with a shout of joy, and the tree rocked forward, rumbling in rage.

"Run!" Rod shouted, as a branch struck at him like a club. He dodged, but other branches began to wave and lash the air, reaching toward him, while the tree's groans rose to thunder—and nearby trees began to stir restlessly.

Well, if it hadn't liked the steel of the sword, what would it *really* fear? Rod remembered a six-foot-long, two-handed lumberjack's saw he'd seen in a museum once—and his sword fluxed and stretched, growing until he found himself holding just such a toothy blade in his hands.

The tree shrank back with a moan of fear.

"Sir, behind thee!" the crone cried, and Rod spun around to see a branch with a huge, knotted burl on its end, striking at him. He swung the saw about, holding the teeth up. The burl halted its swing and bobbed up while the trunk let out a positive wail. Rod turned back at the sound, brandishing the saw like a two-handed shield, and began retreating. "Stay behind me, Granny! We'll get out of here the slow way, but we'll get out!"

So they did, a foot at a time, away from the old oak and back toward the pathway. The oak thundered in anger, its branches lashing the air, and the nearby trees began to rock as though huge gusts were racking the forest. But the farther from the oak they went, the fewer the number of trees that were uneasy until, a hundred yards along the path, they were walking through a calm winter forest again, with trees whose branches moved only to the gentle night breezes.

Rod stopped in a patch of moonlight and wiped his brow. "Whew! That was a close one, Granny!"

"It was, in truth—yet we are free, and thou has saved me." The old woman's eyes were huge.

"Glad to help." Rod frowned at the saw, thinking what an inconvenience it was going to be to lug around—and it shrank back into a dagger again.

The old woman gasped. "Assuredly, sir, thou must needs be a puissant wizard!"

"Only a warlock, ma'am." Rod slipped the dagger away, trying to hide the trembling of his hand. "And to tell you the truth, I'm a little uneasy about that right now. I've never been able to make things change shape before. Unless they were made of witch-moss, of course."

"Thou art a crafter, too?" The old woman shrank back, raising a trembling hand to her lips.

"Hey, hold on, now! Nothing to be afraid of!" Rod's fright faded before his concern for someone else. "Don't believe all that nonsense you've heard about magic-folk! We're just like any other people—some good, some bad, and an awful lot in between. I'm one of the last ones—no saint, but basically a nice guy, as long as you don't attack me."

"Oh, I shall not, sir, I assure thee!"

"I believe you. But look, you've got to be freezing. How long were you standing there with your arm caught in that tree, anyway?"

"Since—since not long after noon, sir."

"You must be a lump of ice. Come on, I'll walk you home. Where do you live?"

" 'Tis but a cottage in the wildwood, sir. And you've no need to put thysen out for the likes of me . . ." But she glanced from side to side with apprehension.

Rod's resolve firmed. "It's no trouble, Granny—I wasn't going anywhere specific, anyway. Come on, let's go."

"Well . . . an it please thee, sir." She fell into step beside him, clutching her basket to her scrawny chest, eyes still flicking from side to side, wary of the night's dangers. "Pray the Wee Folk do not find us!"

"Why? We could use some help. Say, I can't keep calling you 'Granny'—we're not even related."

"Oh, do, kind sir, an it please thee! All other folk do—old Granny Ban, they call me, the Woman in the Wood."

"Not too many old ladies who opt for solitude, hm? Well, I'm Rod Gallowglass." He ignored her start of recognition, casually turning away to eye the forest. "Personally, I think you have a nice neighborhood."

"I do find beauty in it, sir." The old woman managed a timorous smile. "And the wild creatures do be good neighbors indeed, save the wolves and bears."

"You're just lucky one of them didn't come by while you were stuck in that tree." Rod frowned. "Or did it have them frightened, too?"

"I know not, sir—I ha' ne'er come near that oak aforetime. Yet I misdoubt me an . . ."

The conversation went on, her answers becoming longer and longer—and, bit by bit, he drew her out, until she was chattering like a power loom, months' worth of pent-up talk coming out in a stream, once she realized she had an attentive ear available. Rod listened and smiled, nodding and prompting her with the occasional question, usually having to do with which fork they should take; so he wasn't entirely surprised when, having reached her door, bade her good night, and turned away, he heard her cry, "Oh, no, sir, thou must not stay longer in this bitter cold! Come in and warm thysen by my fire, I prithee, until the sun hath risen to warm the air a bit."

Rod turned back and gazed at her, weighing his habitual reluctance to accept hospitality against his chilled feet and nose, and the possibility of frostbite. Then he shrugged and grinned. "Why not? If you don't mind my taking a nap. I can't do too much harm if I'm asleep."

"Assuredly, sir—yet thou must needs dine first; I doubt me not an thou hast gone hungry this night."

Rod was surprised to realize he actually could think of food again—in fact, he was downright famished. "Well, now that you mention it . . ."

"Thou hast as much hunger as one of those wolves we but now did speak of, hast thou not? There, I knew it!" Granny Ban hung her worn old cloak on a peg and bustled about the single, cozy room, much more relaxed now that she was home again. She lifted the lid on a pot that hung from a crane in the fireplace, and a heavenly aroma swirled through the cottage. Rod's mouth watered. "I don't mean to put you out . . ."

"Oh, there's stew enough for two, and more, sir! There, as if thou couldst put me out? When I owe my life to thee, belike. Here." A steaming loaf plumped down on the table before him, whisked out of the oven hole next to the fire. "Eat, and bide; the stew will be with thee ere long."

Rod didn't need urging. He munched on the crusty loaf, soaking in the warmth—he must have grown numb, not realizing how cold he was—and taking in his surroundings. No, this wasn't the only room—there was a door in the wall to his left. A scullery, probably, or an unheated pantry—good way to keep food the winter . . .

"And hast thou ne'er seen trees move of their own accord afore, sir?"

"Hm?" Rod hadn't realized he'd mentioned it. "No, never."

"Nor have I. 'Tis odd, for I've dwelt in the wildwood these twenty years and more—and so puissant a warlock as thysen must needs have seen all manner of magics."

"Well, I have seen a lot—but I must admit this land of Gramarye has continual surprises for me." From the aroma, he judged that the stew owed more to vegetables than to meat—but it was wonderfully seasoned, and smelled heavenly. Rod could hardly wait for it to be served.

" 'Tis a wicked spell woven by thine enemies, I doubt not. Thou hast enemies, hast thou not, sir? Nay, of a certainty thou hast—all do know that the enemies of the King are the enemies of the High Warlock, too." She shook her head with a sigh. "Our poor liege! Scarcely hath he dealt with one foe when a new doth arise. One would think . . ."

"Yes, one would." Rod frowned, his attention caught. "A spell? You think that tree coming alive could be the work of a sorcerer?"

"Might it not, sir?" She set a wooden bowl in front of him, a carven spoon beside it—more of a ladle, really. "Never hath it chanced aforetime, and I have paced the path past that oak twice a week or more, these twenty years."

"But I'm the only one who can see these sights! I'm hallucinating." Rod spooned up the stew, held it to his lips, then shook his head at the notion. "No, that's impossible, Granny Ban! Hallucinations that other people can see, too? How could that be?"

"Art thou not a warlock, sir? Canst thou not send thy thoughts into others' minds?"

"Well, yeah, but . . . No, doggone it! My wife and kids would have picked up on it, and they didn't see anything!"

"Well, belike 'tis some other work of thine enemies," Granny Ban soothed; but Rod froze at the first taste of the stew. She had almost managed it, had almost distracted him enough for him to eat the stew without noticing the oddness, the strange quality of its flavor . . .

Paranoia, the objective part of his mind said, so he knew he should hold off, should insist on proof . . .

But she was watching him closely, much too closely, too intently, so he said, "Your stew certainly has a unique taste, Granny Ban. Is there some secret herb you use?"

She smiled as though she were flattered, but her eyes were wary—or was that just his imagination, now? "Scarcely secret, sir—only herbs that any wife may find in the forest. Though I will own, not many have my trick of blending them."

It was the word "trick" that really sent the alarm bells clanging in Rod's head. "Odd word for it. Certainly a secret blend, wouldn't you say?"

"Well . . . aye . . ."

"And a secret blend of herbs betokens a *lot* of experience with them." Rod lurched to his feet, bumping the table out of the way. He could have sworn that the mere aroma of the stew was making him light-headed. "That door, Granny—this is a very small cottage. What's so important that you'd go to the trouble of putting up an inside wall, even putting in a door?"

"Naught, sir!" She caught at his arm, trying to hold him back. " 'Tis naught but my storeroom, my pantry! Oh, sir, wherefore waste the fire's heat on those things that are only stored away?"

She ended in a wail, as Rod thrust the door open.

For a moment, the objects inside seemed to flux and flow; then his eyes adjusted, and the light from the fire behind him showed bunches of dried grasses and plants hanging from the rafters. Below them stood row upon row of earthenware jars, each with its pictograph, characters whose meanings he was sure were known only to Granny Ban—and, below them, a long worktable, cluttered with a mortar and pestle, a small brazier and tripod, breakers, bowls, and a pint-sized cauldron; even—yes, primitive, but definitely there—an alembic and a distilling tube.

"A stillery," he said. "A complete, thorough, very well equipped stillery."

" 'Tis but for aid of the poor village folk, sir," she wailed. "Oh, have pity! I know not the brewing of any potions that might bring harm!"

Rod gave her a look that had been stored in dry ice. "There, you lie—for no one can learn many medicines that will help people, without learning a few that will cure in small doses, and kill in large doses."

"Oh, never would I abuse such knowledge, sir! Never have I given man or woman any dose that might bring harm!"

But a glint caught Rod's eye. "You haven't, hm?" He stepped over to the corner, wishing for light—and a torch was there in his left hand, glittering on the gold coins visible through the open top of the bag. He pulled at it, letting the coins run through his fingers, then looked up and saw the small chest, lid open, showing pearls and rubies among more gold and silver. Odd that he hadn't noticed it before. "Doing rather well for yourself, aren't you, Granny?"

"Nay, sir! I only hold these goods in trust for a traveler, whose donkey hath taken ill!"

"The traveler took ill, you mean—very ill, once he'd

tasted your stew. How often have you pulled that trick with the oak tree, Granny? How did you work it—witch-moss? Telekinesis? How many gallant young men have you murdered, for no worse sin than seeking to help an old lady?''

"None, sir! Oh, none! Nay, never have I slain! Only robbed, sir, that is all—only taken their purses!''

"And those of their wives, to judge by this haul. What was in the stew, Granny? Belladonna? Angel-of-Death? Deadly nightshade?''

"Poppy, sir! Only the juice of the poppy! Ah, sir, never did I seek to slay!''

"No? Then why didn't your victims come back for their valuables once the drug had worn off?'' He whirled, drawing his sword. "Here's a quicker death, Granny, and a cleaner!''

"Nay, thou wouldst not!'' she howled, shrinking away from the point—but the wall was at her back, and she dared not move, staring fascinated at the blade. "Not a poor widow-woman, sir, with none to defend her! Thou couldst not lack honor so!''

"Honor doesn't mean that much to me. Justice does.''

No, Rod!

It was Fess's voice, inside his head—and Granny Ban, staring in horror over the sword at him, couldn't hear a whisper. Rod frowned. "You're the sort that FESSters in this wood.''

Thank you for responding. I confess to eavesdropping, Rod. I have been concerned for you.

"Concern is a good thing. Betrayal is not.''

"I have never betrayed any, sir!'' Granny Ban wailed.

Nor have I, Rod. But think—justice requires proof.

"Gold coins in a peasant hut? That pile of loot is all the proof I need!''

"Sir, 'twas only a fee," she howled, "a fee for a task I shunned, yet had no choice in!"

Gold coins might indeed be proof of something, Rod—if they are truly there.

Rod hesitated. Had he really seen gold coins? Or had his mind manufactured them, out of a few pennies?

For that matter, was this stillery really here? Was this cottage? For all he knew, he might be talking to a crazed old lady in a hovel, guilty of nothing but talking too much.

He lowered his sword. "No, I won't kill you, Granny."

The old woman sagged with relief, and Fess's voice said, *I commend the wisdom of your decision, Rod.*

"Oh, bless thee, sir!" Granny Ban blubbered.

"Don't bother—because I *am* going to leave you bound hand and foot. Go lie down on your bed."

The old woman stiffened, appalled. "Nay, sir! Slay me, rather—for I'd liefer a quick death than die of starvation and thirst!"

"You won't starve, though you might get a little chilly I'll send word to the shire-reeve, at the next village I come to. Tell *him* how saintly you are! Go on, now, lie down—and you'd better pull up your blankets, too. I'll leave more wood on the fire, but it might take the reeve's men a while to get here."

A few minutes later, he stepped out the cottage door, closed it firmly behind him, and wrapped his cloak about him again. "Fess?"

"Here, Rod." A darker shape detached itself from the shadows among the trees.

"Thanks for interfering," Rod said grudgingly. "You may have just saved me from committing a heinous crime."

"It is ever my honor to serve you, Rod. Still, may I suggest that you do indeed summon the authorities as quickly as possible? I have seen a keeper's cottage not far from here.''

Rod nodded. "Yeah, good idea. He'll know Granny Ban personally, I'll bet, and will know whether she's a candidate for the stocks, or for the gallows.''

"An excellent point. Shall we seek him, then?''

Rod frowned up at the horse, weighing trust against suspicion.

Then he nodded again, and slogged through the snow to mount the steel steed. "Sorry I doubted you, old retainer. Things don't always seem what they are any more.''

"Yes, Rod. Trust is difficult when you cannot be sure of the validity of your perceptions.''

"True. But that's what logic is for, isn't it? To discover which perceptions are real, and which aren't.''

"That is one of its uses, yes. However, logic is difficult to achieve in a highly emotional state.''

"Yes—and the world does seem to be picking on me at the moment. I'm clear-headed enough, just now, to realize that's only my perception—but when the emotions take over, I forget.''

"Of course, Rod. If you did not believe your perceptions to be true, you would not be paranoid.''

"How's that again?'' Rod frowned down at the back of the horsehead, then shook his head. "No, don't tell me. I'm happier in my ignorance. Or do you mean that if I weren't paranoid, I would doubt my perceptions—at least, when it seems as though everything's out to get me?''

"That is the converse of the proposition,'' Fess agreed.

"Glad I got it right,'' Rod responded. "But the main question is still there, Fess—how come I'm having spells of paranoia, all of a sudden?''

"They are not totally new to you, Rod,'' the robot said slowly.

"Thank you for your tact, Mr. Hammer. But I don't

usually have such intense feelings of persecution, with such *total* certainty that I'm right.''

"That is new, fortunately—and, since it was accompanied by the beginning of hallucinations, I can only conjecture that . . .''

"It's a chemical problem, yeah. But, Fess—is the chemical imbalance generated in me, or brought in from the outside world?''

"Whatever its source, Rod, it is in you now.''

"Much more of this, and you'll have me believing it,'' Rod grumbled.

"That would definitely be a more desirable condition,'' the robot mused.

"All right, so we'll go with the working hypothesis that what I see isn't real,'' Rod grumbled. "But how am I supposed to know what's real and what isn't?''

"Of more immediate concern, perhaps,'' Fess said slowly, "is: when does it truly matter?''

Rod sighed as horse and man headed deeper into the forest.

3

Sometime later, Rod had dismounted and was walking slowly behind Fess, when his foot hit an icy patch. He slipped, skidded, and just barely managed to regain his balance. He looked down at the side of the trail and saw a river's sheen below him. It was frozen solid. In the distance, he could see a sled moving away, laden with bundles, pushed by an ice-skating merchant. Half-timbered buildings fronted on the water, their stucco dyed in pastels. Rod stared—it was an incongruously gay and light-hearted scene in the midst of the winter's grimness.

Then he heard the crunch of a footstep behind him.

He whirled, blood pounding in his ears, panic stringing him as taut as a trap. The lurker stepped out from behind a huge old oak, and Rod found himself staring at . . .

Himself.

It was him to the life—hatchet face, eagle-beak nose, wide mouth, and glower. He was even wearing the same clothing—doublet and hose, boots, gloves, cloak, and sword, though in different colors.

Rod decided to keep an eye on the sword. "Who are you?"

"Who are *you*?" his double demanded.

"Rod Gallowglass," Rod snapped, "Lord High Warlock." The reminder of magic lent insight, and anger. "And who the hell do you think *you* are, to go around wearing my face?"

"It's *my* face! Who do you think *you* are, to be wearing it?"

At least the double didn't have Rod's voice, too. "The man who was born with it, damn it!" Well, that wasn't quite true—Rod had grown into the face. "What the devil do you mean, impersonating me?"

"*Me* impersonating *you*! The audacity, the effrontery of it!"

"I notice you don't deny it!"

"All left, I deny it!" the doppelganger bawled. "*You're* copying *me*! Just what the hell do you think you're trying to get away with?"

Rod frowned, looking the man up and down. It was possible, it was just possible . . . "What does $E = MC^2$ mean?"

"Energy equals mass times the square of the speed of light." The stranger frowned, too. "Which is to say, energy and mass are just different aspects of the same thing. What the hell kind of question is *that*?"

"A very clear one. If you know the answer, it means you're from off-planet."

"Yeah, sure, and you're from off-planet if you can ask it! So what does *that* prove?"

"That you're an imposter."

"Imposter! What are you talking about, you fool? I'm *Rod Gallowglass*!"

Rod stared, shocked—and the whole scene swam in front of his eyes. He staggered, putting out a hand to brace himself against a tree trunk, afraid he would faint. Then his vision cleared, and he saw the doppelganger clearly again, glaring at him with hostility, and the clarity of inner insight hit him: he remembered. *He was crazy*!

Well, of course. If he was crazy, he might see anything, mightn't he? I mean, if he was having delusions, why couldn't his own self be one of those delusions?

Apparently, it was.

Rod leaned back on one hip, folding his arms. "Let me get this straight. You claim that *you're* Rod Gallowglass?"

"The very same." The doppelganger was looking wary now. "And who do you think *you* are?"

"Rod Gallowglass."

But the doppelganger didn't squawk in outrage. He stood quietly, brooding—which sent a chill shivering up Rod's spine; it was exactly what *he* would have done, at this juncture.

What he *had* done, in fact.

Rod shook himself back into gear. Denial hadn't worked, so it was time for thinking.

Why not?

"There's two of us," the doppelganger pointed out.

"Sh! Don't tell!" Rod glanced around furtively. "They'd banish us, you know."

"Banish us?" The doppelganger stared. "Who?"

"The sane people."

"You know some?"

"Well, yes, I think so," Rod admitted. "And just in case I don't, there's always my touchstone, Fess."

"*My* touchstone." But the doppelganger's heart wasn't in it any more; he was too busy studying the great black robot-horse. "Do you see two of us, old boy?"

"There is only one of you, Rod."

Rod shuddered—Fess had heard the doppelganger!

"But you do seem to be talking to yourself," the robot amplified. "A fascinating conversation, no doubt."

No doubt? But Rod didn't stop to ask. "We could try to figure out which one of us is real . . ."

"Yeah, and after that, we can try to figure out what 'real' means." The doppelganger's lip curled. "Can't you think of something a little more productive?"

"Well," Rod said, "the sensible thing is for us to join forces. I mean, if we can't tell ourselves apart, we should certainly make one hell of a unit."

"Makes sense," the doppelganger said judiciously. "But how are we going to coordinate?"

"Very easily, I should think. You take the left side, and I'll take the right."

The doppelganger seemed dubious. "How come *you're* willing to take the right?"

"I just see you as sinister, I guess. Try it the other way—I'll be glad to have you as my squire."

"*Me* be *your* squire? You can be *my* squire!"

"What, and try to live with your idea of tactics? I'd die first! No, amend that—I'd die trying."

"Not much faith in yourself, have you?" the doppelganger snorted.

That brought Rod up short. He thought about it for a minute, but didn't succeed. "Afraid not. You're obviously left."

"And will be in everything, clunkhead! You'd better take me up on my offer, and be *my* squire!"

"Not if you're me, bucko! If I want dumb ideas, I can make up my own!"

"Ridiculous," the doppelganger snapped. "At least *I* trust my own instincts!"

"Oh, yeah? How about mine?"

"Of course not!"

"Then you can't trust your own."

The doppelganger started to answer, shoaled on the logic, and froze with his mouth open. After a few moments, he closed his jaw and nodded. "Point to you. How's it feel to *be* one horn of a dilemma?"

"Makes me feel like wanting to blow," Rod admitted.

"Not a bad idea." The doppelganger turned away, brushing past Rod and hurrying on down the trail. "Let's go."

Rod lifted his head with a smile. "Yeah. Not a bad idea is right." He jumped to catch up.

As they plodded along through the snow with Fess behind, Rod offered, "This is going to get a little confusing. What're we going to call each other?"

"How about, 'Hey, you'?"

"Well, it certainly beats 'Hey, me.' Look, I could be Rod, and you . . ."

"Hold it left there." The doppelganger stopped, holding out a hand, palm up. "*I* could be 'Rod.'"

"I see your point." Rod frowned. "Won't work, will it? Well, we have twenty middle names—can't we manage something with that?"

The doppelganger nodded. "Nice idea. Any preference?"

"Yeah." Rod grinned. "I'll be 'Rod,' and you can be 'Rodney.'"

The doppelganger winced. "You *know* I always hated that name!"

"But you did like your ancestor's version."

"True," the doppelganger mused. "I've always been partial to 'Roderick.'"

"Fine by me—you can be 'Roderick,' and I'll be 'Rodney'—but 'Rod' for short, of course." He turned away down the road.

The doppelganger gave him a dubious look as he fell into step beside him. "How come I feel like I came out on the short end, this time?"

"Just overly sensitive," Rod said breezily. "You know we've always been a little paranoid."

"True enough," the doppelganger said. Then his face cleared. "I know! Tomorrow we'll change names! How's *that* sound?"

"If you must." Rod sighed, then came to a halt, frowning. "Hey! How come we're walking when we could ride?"

"Good point." His other self turned back to Fess. "You don't mind carrying double, do you, old horse?"

"Not at all, Rod," the robot said, and stepped forward.

"We'll take turns in the saddle, of course," Rod noted as the doppelganger mounted.

"Oh, of course." The doppelganger shook the reins and clucked to the horse, and they rode off down the road, with the saddle empty and Fess speculating on the exact nature of the delusion that was causing Rod to ride pillion.

The trail led along the river, then forked. Rod stopped. "I'd just as soon not go into town right now."

The doppelganger grinned. "Don't trust yourself, eh?"

"Not at all. I mean, it looks like a very nice, quiet little village from here, but who knows what it'll appear to be once I get there?"

"I could go ahead and scout it out," the doppelganger offered.

"Great!" Rod saw a chance to get rid of his other self. "I'll ride around and meet you on the far side."

"Fine. And speaking of meat, I'll stop by the tavern and get you some lunch."

"There's a tavern there?"

"Well, I saw a green bush hanging from a sign bracket, and I don't think it was a florist's."

Rod was tempted, but the thought of dumping his unwanted companion was stronger than the urge for hearth and ale. "I'll be obliged."

The doppelganger grinned. "I know." They both dismounted; he turned away and struck out toward the town.

Rod turned, too, toward the woods—and stopped, one foot in the air. He looked back to see what was holding him, but couldn't see anything—except for his doppel-ganger, stuck in the same pose, apparently straining against it with all his might. Rod lunged toward the wood, exerting every iota of willpower in an attempt to put his foot down—but he couldn't move an inch. "Fess—how come I can't go on?"

"There is no physical cause, Rod."

"Meaning it's psychosomatic. But I need to keep going." Rod turned back to the doppelganger, just as he turned to look at him.

"Something there is that does not like a stall," he said.

Rod winced. "Don't talk about Fess that way."

"I didn't," his double assured him. "It's pretty obvious that something doesn't want us parted."

"Have a heart!"

"I do. So do you, in fact. And something wants the union of true hearts to be preserved."

"You mean I can't get rid of you."

"Hey! Look at it from *my* side—*I* can't get away from *you*!"

"Well, what must be, must be." Rod sighed. "I guess we travel together, or not at all. Come on, let's go."

"And I had my skin all set for heat," the doppelganger griped. "But I have to admit, a hike through the woods is safer than letting you into a town."

Rod scowled. "And are you so much safer than I am?"

"Oh, infinitely safer! You think I'm a figment of your subconscious, don't you?"

"Well . . ."

"Right. And whoever heard of a mere figment doing any damage?"

"Ever hear of Willy Loman?" Rod jibed. "But I take your point—hopefully on my shield. Come on, let's go."

They did.

• • • •

They'd been traveling about half an hour when they heard the roar. They jumped for cover, but it was too late. Pounding feet came thundering up to their thicket. "I see yuh, I see yuh!" bellowed a sub-basso. "Come on out and fight like a man!"

"Oh, don't be so tiresome!" a more mellow voice said. "They weren't hurting you in the slightest."

"Shut up, goody-goody! Awright, come out with your hands up!"

Rod came, sword first.

The monster backed away from the point, its snout wrinkling in consternation. "Hey, now! You ain't supposed to fight back!"

"No more than you can expect," the other voice said.

"You shaddup!"

It was a two-headed monster, like a very fat dragon with a rhinoceros's tail and elephant's feet—and it was puce with yellow polka dots. Rod took one look at it and was *certain* his hallucinations came courtesy of his subconscious.

"I will *not* shut up," the other head said. "After all, you're trying to threaten them with my body, too."

"*My* body! You only control the right half!"

"So I do." The right-hand head turned to the two Rods. "I'll have to ask you to pardon this intrusion; I didn't really have much choice in the matter. You can call me 'Dexter.' "

"You don't look very dextrous," the doppelganger pointed out.

It didn't, but the right-hand head did have a pleasant, though bothered, look about it, in spite of being mostly snout and teeth. Its companion head, though, managed to have a sneaky, predatory look with exactly the same features. "Don't you dare call me 'Sinister'!!" It swiveled to glare at Rod. "I'll bite off your head! I'll roast you alive!"

"It's been tried." For some reason, Rod was taking a

dislike to Sinister. He hefted his blade. "If you think you can argue with cold steel, go ahead and try."

"Cold steel! I'll melt that tin toothpick down into slag!" But Sinister didn't seem eager to try.

"I take it you had some reason for coming up to us," the doppelganger said.

"Reason! Yeah! I'm hungry!"

"Now, Sinister," Dexter murmured, "you know we discussed this."

"Disgusted, maybe! Now, look, Dex, you're gonna follow my lead this time, or I'm gonna fry you to a crisp!"

"I'm sorry, Sinister," Dexter said in a very low voice, "but I absolutely will have nothing to do with this charade." He turned to the two Rods. "You really should hurry on by. This can't be very pleasant for you."

"Right." The doppelganger turned to go.

With a roar, Sinister slapped out the left foot, and the doppelganger leaped back.

"Sinister! You *know* these people haven't done anything to deserve . . ."

"They came into my territory, didn't they?" Sinister roared. "They walked down my road, and they didn't even offer to pay for it!"

"Oh!" Rod said, startled. "Did you build the road?"

"Build? What the hell difference does that make? I'm *standing* on it!"

"I know it's confusing," Dexter said to the doppelganger, "but you really shouldn't let this little scene keep you from . . ."

"You shut up, jelly-back! If I wanna make these little bastards pay, then . . ."

Dexter winced. "Please! You really have no reason . . ."

"Reason!" Sinister bellowed. "You want a reason? I'll give you . . ."

Rod caught the doppelganger's eye and nodded toward

Dexter's side. The doppelganger sidled toward him, and together, displaying great interest in the argument, they moved slowly around the right side of the creature. On the other side, Fess whinnied and stamped to distract Sinister.

It almost worked; they almost got past him. But at the last moment, Sinister saw them and bawled, "Hey! You come back here!" It charged.

"Back!" Rod shouted, and he and the doppelganger sprang away. Not far enough, though—the huge head was soaring toward him, fangs first.

Dexter dug in the right-side legs and shoved back for all he was worth.

Sinister's head came to a sudden jarring halt; inertia slammed the great jaws closed an inch from Rod's head.

"Back!" Rod snapped, and jabbed Sinister's nose with the point of his sword. The huge head whipped up with a howl, and Rod lowered his blade, just in time for his arm to start trembling.

"Poor Sinister! Are you hurt?" Dexter cried.

"He maimed me!" the dragon wailed. "He cut me!"

"A pinprick!" Rod snorted.

"Understandable," Dexter said reluctantly, "but unnecessary. He's really quite harmless, though he is a bit of a bully."

"Bully? I am not! You take that back!"

"Now, Sinister . . . you know you . . ."

"*You're* the one who's always picking on *me*!"

"I never!"

"Oh, yeah? Then why won't yuh . . ."

"They were improper in using force after the danger was past, true. Still, you must admit you . . ."

"Lemme *at* 'em!"

And Sinister hurtled toward the Rods again. Dexter dug in, of course, and the result was that Sinister slewed around in a circle, bawling and cursing at his better half—

and around and around they went, churning like a pocket tornado, with roaring accusations underscored by firm, quiet counterstatements.

Rod nudged the doppelganger and pointed down the trail in the direction in which they'd been going. The doppelganger nodded, and together, they inched away from the arguing heads, sidling farther away and more toward the side of the road, with Fess pacing them at a discreet distance.

They almost made it into the thicket where the trail curved, but just before they reached the cover of the evergreens, Sinister looked up, saw how far they'd moved, let out a howl like a freight train whose cars had been kidnapped, and charged them.

"Run!" Rod shouted, and did so. But he heard a roar of fury behind him and skidded to a stop behind two evergreens, turning to look, with the doppelganger right beside him.

They had stopped too soon; Sinister was lunging toward them full-strength, with Dexter digging in his heels and pulling back—and their whole body pivoted, swinging around in a huge arc with Sinister's head at the end of it, jaws open wide, shooting right toward Rod.

Rod still had his sword out. He brought it up to guard position—and the huge head flinched away, trying to avoid the blade. Sinister overbalanced, and the body stumbled forward a step; Sinister's head caught Rod side-on, slamming him head over heels into the fir tree.

"Let that learn ya!" Sinister crowed. The effect was somewhat spoiled by the tremor in his voice, though, possibly occasioned by Fess leaping in between the creature and his masters with a screaming whinny, rearing back to lash out with his hooves. Sinister flinched away.

Which was just as well, because Rod came scrambling back out of the fir tree with blood in his eye. "You chuckle-headed lumpish fugitive from an overloaded night-mare! You crumb! Of ill-digested cheese! You . . .''

"Please!" Dexter protested, wounded. "I tried my best!"

"Not you—your . . . Well, him!" Rod aimed his sword at Sinister, who flinched back.

The doppelganger had his sword up, too, but gave Rod a knowing look and lowered his blade. Reluctantly, so did Rod. Fess saw, and snorted as he stepped aside.

That was all the opening Sinister needed. "Scared, huh?" he cried in glee, and leaped—or at least, the left-hand side of the body did. The right-hand side planted itself firmly—and the monster tripped over its own feet. Bellowing, it rolled heads over heels down the slope beside the trail, crashing through twigs and underbrush, and caroming off tree trunks.

"The poor beast," Rod whispered.

"Poor, my aunt Fanny!" his doppelganger snapped. "He's rubber—he bounces! *Our* job is to get out of here before Sinister manages to get his side moving enough to drag Dexter back up to the trail. Come on—run!"

They stopped after a mile, staggering up against tree trunks and wheezing for breath. The chill winter air stabbed their lungs like tiny knives. Fess slowed and stopped behind them.

"Must be getting—outa shape," Rod gasped. "A mile never did this to me . . . before."

"Yeah, but this mile . . . was through foot-deep snow," the doppelganger answered.

"I would have carried you, Rod," Fess reproached him.

"I didn't want to take the time to . . . mount." Rod forced himself back to his feet, looking around. "Well . . . better keep . . . going. Which way . . . now?"

"Good . . . question," the doppelganger puffed, pushing himself away from the tree.

They found themselves staring at a fork in the trail.

"Which branch?" Rod murmured.

"Dexter, or Sinister?" his doppelganger responded.
"You have but to ask."

They looked around, staring.

A trunk detached itself from the trees and stepped forward between the two arms of the fork. They discovered, with starts of surprise, that it was a man. He was a foot taller than either of them, and his clothes were the dark gray of bark. The same fabric shrouded his head in a cowl.

Rod exchanged a wary look with his double. The doppelganger nodded and sidled around the stranger, loosening his sword in its sheath.

The bark-man folded his cowl back.

Rod stared—the man's whole face seemed to curve upward on the sides. His mouth was a grin, and the corners of his eyes tilted up. His bunched cheeks were so red they could have been spots of paint. He looked as though the mere idea of sadness had never even touched him.

"He's a happy-face," Rod said.

"No, he's not," the doppelganger contradicted. "You should see him from the back! He's a sad-face."

"Gentlemen, gentlemen!" The stranger lifted both hands in appeal. "I am both—Comedy before and Tragedy after!"

Rod didn't like what that said about the man's view of life. "And I'm supposed to ask *you* which path to take to my future?"

The stranger shrugged and said gaily, "Why trouble yourself with the future?" From behind, the same voice said, with dire tones, "To me, all futures are past."

Rod decided the man would have done well in commodities.

"Wherever you go," counseled Mirth, "there is much to enjoy; for there is beauty in all things, and vividness in every experience."

"Experience is a history of pain," answered Tragedy, "for ugliness and squalor prevail."

The doppelganger cocked an eyebrow in skepticism. "You boys really can't agree on anything, can you?"

"Aye," said Mirth, "on Unity!"

"We concur on Duality," Tragedy explained.

"They can't even agree on what they agree on," Rod said to the doppelganger, exasperated.

"Oh, they do, if you look at it the right way." The doppelganger tilted his head way to the side. "I mean, after all, the Duality is just the two aspects of Eternity."

"Not you, too," Rod groaned. "Look, can we get down to basics here?" He turned back to the two-faced man. "Which way should we go?"

"To the right," said Mirth; so of course:

"To the left," said Tragedy.

"Got a coin?" Rod asked the doppelganger.

"Why?"

" 'Cause I'm ready to flip."

"Chance brings disaster," Tragedy intoned.

"Chance may bring happiness," Mirth responded.

"Why did I know that was coming?" Rod muttered. He looked up at Fess. "Can you make sense out of all this?"

"Not readily," Fess answered. "However, I do detect a slight depression in the snow between the two paths of the fork."

Rod whirled, staring. "I don't see anything."

"It is a matter of averaging the bumps in the snow, Rod."

"I'll take your word for it." Rod stepped forward toward the center.

"Back!" cried Mirth.

"You must not go there!" cried Tragedy.

"At last," muttered the doppelganger, "something they agree on."

Both faces whirled toward him at the same moment—or tried to. The only real result was that the two-faced man lurched aside, and Rod dodged past him.

"Stop!" shrieked Mirth.

"Avoid moderation!" lamented Tragedy.

But Rod was kicking the snow aside, and discovered a very faint, but discernible, track. "Come on," he said to the doppelganger, who jumped to follow him.

The two-faced man lumbered into motion, following them with the ungainly stride of a man who is of two minds about an issue, reaching out with clumsy arms. "The Middle Way is forbidden!" "There is nothing amusing in synthesis!"

Fess took two leaps and stood astride the trail between the two Rods and the two-faced man, who blundered into him with a loud "*Oof!*" and rebounded, falling over his own feet and collapsing. He was scrabbling back up in a minute, but Fess had turned away, and the guardian of extremes found himself facing a horsetail.

With a sigh and a shake of his head, he turned back to face the single trail again.

Rod had to kick his way through leafless ground vines, last year's leaves and fallen sticks, to find the path. He was glad he favored stout boots, and kept them heavily waxed. "I assume this will take us someplace."

"Someplace not overly favored by those who search for fame and fortune, at a guess," the doppelganger returned.

"Well, yes," Rod agreed, "but not too many of those find either one, do they?"

The doppelganger shrugged. "Myself, I wouldn't know. I keep trying for obscurity."

Rod nodded. "I know the feeling. All I want is a calm, peaceful, quiet, contented existence."

"Wonder why we never get it?" the doppelganger mused.

"Because we want it, of course . . . Whoa! What's this?"

Rod had parted a screen of brush, and they found themselves staring out at a broad road on top of a ridge.

"It's the King's Highway," said the doppelganger softly.

Rod grinned. "Of course. We go looking for a quiet life, and what do we find?"

"I'll take the low road," the doppelganger said quickly.

"But you'll get the high one," Rod answered. "Come on—let's see what tranquillity and solitude await us here."

It was out onto the highway then with Fess scrambling up behind them. They mounted the great iron steed and set off down the middle of the road.

The chill deepened as the sky darkened. To make matters worse, the trees began to crowd in at either side of the road.

"Maybe we ought to stop and consider digging in for the night," the doppelganger suggested.

"Just what I was thinking." Rod shivered. "A nice campfire and some roasting pheasants . . ."

A huge snarling yowl tore the stillness, and six strapping figures leaped out of the woods, three on each side, muscles rippling under fur. They stood upright like men, but had the heads of cats. Their feet were encased in boots, but their arms ended in genuine hands, albeit fur-covered and clawed; and they wore knee-length mail-shirts, criscrossed by weapons belts.

They attacked with feline screams, two of them leaping for Fess's bridle; but the great black horse tossed his head, knocking one of them aside, and struck the other away with a hoof.

Rod spun around on the horse's rump, drawing his sword and dagger, setting his back against the doppelganger's. A huge cat-man sprang up on the horsehair, scimitar swinging down. Rod parried, just barely managing to keep his blade intact, and riposted. The point struck a leather belt, skidded, and scored through fur. The cat shrank back, screaming—and slipped off the rump. Another landed in its place, splitting and snarling, sword flashing around in a flat arc. Rod ducked and lurched forward, hooking upward with his dagger. A tremendous shock jarred him, but he held his place, and the cat screamed, its eyes beginning to dull even as it slipped back and away.

Then, suddenly, it was over. Two dead cats lay staining the snow with their blood, and the other four were fleeing back into the trees, spitting and snarling. Rod stared in surprise, then turned with a grin. "I don't know what you managed to do to them, O alter ego, but you . . ."

The doppelganger slumped, slipped out of the saddle, and sprawled on the ground.

Rod stared in shock.

"Rod?" Fess asked. "What has happened?"

"Can't you *see*?" Rod leaped down and knelt beside his own huddled form. "Where'd they get you? Quick! Maybe I can staunch the flow!"

"Too . . . late . . ." the doppelganger gasped. "Carotid . . . cut . . ."

It was true. The whole front of his doublet was soaked in blood.

"What happened? No, don't answer—one of them got past your guard. With those claws, one swipe would do it." Rod leaped up and dug through the saddlebag frantically. "Got to be *something* in here! Fess, I *told* you we should have packed some plasma!"

"Don't . . . trouble . . ." the doppelganger gasped.

"Don't *trouble*?" Rod whirled back down, staring at his own wan visage. "I can't let you die!"

"Do," the doppelganger urged. "Don't . . . trouble . . . I'll be back when . . . you need . . ."

His voice trailed off, and his eyes dulled.

Rod stared, kneeling, frozen in the snow.

"Rod."

"Not now!" Rod glanced up at Fess in irritation, but when he turned back to the doppelganger, he was gone. There wasn't even a hollow in the snow to show where he had been.

Rod stared.

"What has happened, Rod?"

"Six cat-men just attacked us," Rod heard himself explaining. "We killed two . . ." He glanced around. "I don't see them, either . . . And we chased off the rest. But one of them slit my double's throat."

"I had surmised as much," the robot sympathized. "But how shall we bury him, when the ground is frozen?"

Rod glanced up at him in irritation. "Come off it! You know he wasn't really there."

Then he stopped, startled by his own words.

"Neither were the bandits," Fess told him. "There were only two peasants, dressed in remarkably well kept brown jerkins and leggins. You drove them off."

But Rod wasn't listening. He was staring at the barren, unstained snow and muttering, "All the monsters we meet can't do more damage than cat-men do. Damn! Just when I thought I was getting to know myself, too!"

He sighed, mounted Fess, and turned away from the road, riding deeper into the forest.

4

It was one of those nights that seem to last forever. As soon as Rod realized that, he developed suspicions. "Fess, how long has it been since I left the family?"

"Approximately three hours, Rod."

"Is that all?" Rod was appalled to realize how much had happened in so short a time. "Is something wrong with my time sense?"

"Perhaps," the robot said slowly, "since you have experienced a multiplicity of events during that period."

"Well how long has it been since I found Granny Ban with her arm stuck in that tree?"

"Was that her difficulty? From the sound, I thought perhaps she had been ensnared by a troop of bandits."

"Not that I saw." Rod frowned. "Or should I say, 'That's not what *I* saw.' Anyway, how long?"

"Two hours and forty-three minutes have elapsed, Rod."

"You're kidding! That was two hours, if it was a minute!"

"It was more than a minute, Rod, but considerably less than two hours. It is nearly midnight."

"I could have sworn it was the wee hours, not the hours of wee folk. Y'know, I should be feeling sleepy by now."

"Perhaps you will be when the adrenaline ebbs."

" 'If,' not 'when.' What's that light up ahead?"

Fess expanded his video image. "I see no light but the moon's reflection, Rod."

"Not another hallucination! Well, I suppose I might as well get it over with." Rod dismounted. "Stay close, okay? And don't let me hurt anybody."

"I will endeavor to prevent damage, Rod—but I believe there is no cause for concern. I see absolutely nothing."

"Wish I could say that." Rod turned away, gathering his cloak about him, but he still shivered as he plowed his way through the snow toward the glow ahead.

In the distance, the bells of the Runnymede cathedral chimed midnight.

Rod stopped on the edge of a little clearing. In its middle, a campfire burned—a tiny campfire, its flames guttering. A man knelt before it, his back to Rod, wearing a cowled cloak. Rod wondered what a monk was doing out at this time of night, then remembered that foresters' cloaks looked very much like monks' robes—especially when you couldn't make out colors. Whoever he was, he was racked with shivers as he groped in the snow. At last, he brought up a small branch, knocked the snow off it, and threw it on the fire.

There had been enough light for Rod to see the boniness of the hand. There was no doubt that the man was old, quite old. Rod felt a surge of sympathy and stepped out into the clearing, kicking up the snow, bending to pick up fallen branches and sticks. "Here, Grandfather!" He stepped past the old man and knelt by the fire, holding one of the smaller sticks in the flame till it caught, then laying it carefully on the coals and setting a small branch over it. "We'll have it burning merrily in no time."

"It is good of you," the old man whispered, sitting back on a fallen tree.

"Glad to help. Glad of the warmth, too." Rod put a three-inch branch over the others, then turned to the oldster. "There you go, Grandfather."

He froze, staring.

"Thank you, Grandson." From under the hood, the old eyes glinted with amusement. "But then, you always were a generous, warmhearted boy. I am glad to see you have grown into so fine a man."

"Grandfather," Rod whispered again. "My *real* grandfather."

And it was—Count Rory d'Armand, in the flesh. Or seemingly.

"You can't be real." But Rod stretched out a hand anyway. "You died twenty-six years ago."

Count Rory winced. "Hardly generous of you, my boy."

"Oh, I'm sorry, Grandfather! But how did you get here? I mean, Gramarye is light-years and light-years away from this solar system!"

"Why, I came with you, Rodney." The old eyes glowed into his. "In your genes—for surely, as long as you live, so does part of me. And in your heart and mind, too, I would like to think!"

"Oh, be sure of that! If the foundation of my personality is Mother and Father, you're the foundation of the foundation!"

"The sub-basement, eh?" Rory smiled, amused. "And all that I have thought and dreamed, Rodney—what of that?"

"I can't say 'all,' " Rod said honestly, "but a large part of it—yes. I think your ideals are within me, too—for they're embedded in the stories you told me, and those stories will always be with me."

"Ah. My stories, yes." The Count nodded, turning his

gaze to the fire. "And if you live within my stories, then Rodney, you certainly can have no question as to how I came to be here."

"What?" Rod frowned. "I think I missed something."

"Why, I am Rory, Lord Chronicler." The old man lifted his gaze to Rod's again. "For surely we are in the realm of Granclarte."

Rod stared at him.

"Yes, surely," he said softly. "Why didn't I realize that?"

"Because you had not thought of it," the Lord Chronicler said, smiling. "Yet did I not tell you the tales of this magic kingdom would ever be your shield and your refuge?"

"Why, so they have been, in metaphor," Rod said slowly, "but I never thought they could be so, in actuality."

Rory tossed his head impatiently. "There is a sickness of the soul upon you, my boy, a darkness of the spirit. Where else could you shelter from that night, except in the Courts of Great Light?"

"Yes." Slowly, Rod sat down beside the old man, on the log. "God bless you, Grandfather, for giving my soul a shield against its own lances."

"Be not so sure they are its own, my boy, for you have many enemies, with many weapons. Yet do be sure that, in the realm of Granclarte, you shall find a magic guardian to shield you from any of them."

"I'll remember that," Rod said fervently. "But Grandfather, I've gone mad on Gramarye. How can I be in the realm of Granclarte?"

"Because you inherited it from me, Rodney, inherited it within your soul, just as your body inherited my genes. The events and ideals within its Chronicles are part of the sub-structure of your personality, of the way you see the universe around you. It is yours now—I bequeath it to you."

"I'm not worthy . . ."

"On the contrary, you are eminently worthy; you have proved yourself so. Even as the Four Kings strove to avoid war, so have you—and even as they strove mightily when war could no longer be avoided, so have you."

Rod was quiet; he couldn't deny his accomplishments, but was too modest to speak of them. Granclarte, after all, had been founded as a neutral meeting place by four kings who sought to spare their subjects the devastation of war; they had reigned all from the same palace over their adjoining realms. How could he compare himself to any one of them? "The Four Kings were enlightened, Grandfather, and all inspired with the same idea at the same moment—to have a common court, and thereby bring knowledge, wisdom, and peace. I have had no such moment of enlightenment in my life."

"Perhaps you had, but did not recognize it. Perhaps you are having it now. Or perhaps this is the beginning of the greatest period of your life."

"Now, when I'm forty-seven? That's too late for the glory of youth, too early for the wisdom of age."

"Yet it is also the time when wisdom and energy most thoroughly blend—just as the pinnacle of the Courts of Granclarte came in its middle years, when the knight Beaubras set forth in quest, and returned with the Rainbow Crystal. Its light suffused the nobility and, aye, all the folk of the court, with harmony and generosity."

"And its effect spread out from them through all the Four Kingdoms, yielding a Golden Age of peace, prosperity, and happiness. But Granclarte endured only through the generation of the Four Kings, Grandfather. In the time of their sons, the sorcerer Obscura stole away the Rainbow Crystal."

"Yes, in vengeance for King Alban's refusal."

Rod nodded. "The King refused to grant Obscura the

hand of his daughter Lucina, the most beautiful damsel of the court—for he knew Prince Dardinel loved her, and that she loved him.''

''He knew also that their union would more tightly bind his kingdoms with that of Dardinel's father, King Turpin. But Obscura did steal the Great Crystal, and cast a death-spell on King Alban—and without its light of harmony and grace, the king sickened and died. His son Constantine became king in his place—but the young kings, whose hearts knew not the importance of Glancarte, fell to vying with one another in richness and pomp, then in their champions' passages at arms.''

''And tournament gave way to battle,'' Rod said, remembering, ''and the confederation fell apart. But why did the young kings have to tear down the palace, Grandfather?''

''Because each feared that the other might use it as a stronghold, reaching out to conquer all three other kingdoms. Thus is it ever—the center suffers the greatest strain, when balance is lost. As it was, certainly, when Obscura ingratiated himself with King Agramant, and persuaded him to attack King Turpin.''

''And King Turpin died in battle, so Prince Dardinel became King before he had learned restraint,'' Rod mused. ''Then Obscura planted a rumor that Lucina had been imprisoned by her brother, so Dardinel declared war on King Constantine. But the knight Beaubras awoke from his enchanted sleep, and came forth to rid the earth of the evil sorcerer.''

''Yes, Grandson, but he was slain himself in that battle. Oh, do not grieve, for I promised you that Beaubras shall rise again; Beaubras shall ever rise again. Yet in his death, King Dardinel realized his folly and made peace with King Constantine. But their realms had been devastated, so King Agramant allied with King Rodomont, and invaded.''

"They conquered," Rod said, remembering, "but their own lands were devastated in the process, for Dardinel and Constantine fought like demons, to protect fair Lucina."

"Aye, and though they died, they sold their lives dearly. Agramant and Rodomont held dominion, but then began to vie for power."

"And their armies were too weak to both guard their castles and maintain law and order—and there were many, many soldiers who had fled defeat, and were desperate for food and shelter. So banditry became rife."

"Then the contest of diplomacy failed, for Rodomont thought himself strong enough to conquer Agramant."

"But he was wrong."

"Aye; they were evenly matched, and tore one another to bits. Thus the Golden Age ended, and the Four Kingdoms sank into the barbarism from which they had risen."

Rod sighed, gazing off into space, his head ringing with the shouting and cries of great battles, with the thunder of hooves and the clash of weapons. He was shocked to feel tears in his eyes. "Can it not live again, Grandfather?"

"Aye—every time we tell its tale. I have begun it for you this time, my grandson. You are now on the verge of its greatest of days, for the knight Beaubras has but now set forth on his quest, and the Rainbow Crystal is yet to be found."

"Yet to be found?" Rod whirled, eyes widening. "But that means that Ordale hasn't come forth to show him the Faerie World yet—and Olympia still waits at the crest of Mount Stehr! It's all still to come—the glory, the wonder, the enchantment!"

"Aye, all yet to come." The old man nodded, his eyes aglow. "And we have talked away the night, my grandson, and the east is burgeoning with the sun. The hour is come when poor, tenuous ghosts, wandering here and there, must troop home to churchyards."

"No!" Rod cried in a panic. "Don't go! We have so much still to talk about!"

"All that truly matters has been said." The count had risen and was backing away. "The history of Granclarte, and the good it sought to bring."

"But I need you! I can't be without you!"

"Nor will you be." Mist was rising from the clearing, all about the old man. "I am within your heart and your mind, Rodney—you cannot be without me. None can take me from you."

"But what of Granclarte?" Rod cried. "How will it endure without you?"

"Through you, mine heir. I bequeath it to you, root, stock, and branch. Let it rise again, Rodney. Let it grow, let it ever grow." And his voice was fading now, as his outline softened and his substance blurred into the mist, suffused with the golden light of dawn. "The night has gone, and the day comes—your day, my grandson, and your realm now. Live in it; fare well in it.

"Farewell . . ."

Rod stood, petrified, scalp prickling, seeing the ghost diffuse and fade, hearing his voice dwindle, speaking again, but so softly that it might have been the cry of a distant songbird: "Farewell . . ."

Then it *was* the cry of a bird, far away, calling, summoning . . .

Rod turned away from the clearing in the glory of the newly risen sun and plodded back through the forest, his heart leaden, but his soul exalted.

"He was there, Fess," he said softly. "He was really there."

"So I judged, from the words I heard you say, Rod," the great black horse answered. "It is inspiring."

But he didn't sound joyous. Rod frowned, peering closely,

then understood, with a surge of sympathy. "Hard on you, isn't it, Old Heart, to be reminded of your former master?"

"Robots do not grieve, Rod."

"Nor computers delight. Sure." Rod swung up into the saddle again. "But how could the time pass so quickly all of a sudden?"

"It did not really, Rod. The passage of time was no faster than in the evening."

"It just felt like it." Rod shook his head. "Well, then, I'm safe in a way, Fess. I'm in Granclarte."

"Yes, Rod, safe in many ways—but remember the perils the good knight confronted."

"How could I forget them?" Rod replied. "But how did I come to be here, Fess? Why did I go crazy so suddenly?"

"I have given you *my* best answer," the robot said softly. "You must find your own now."

"I think I have." Rod nodded. "Yes, I think I have."

"In your grandfather's stories?" The robot sounded surprised.

"Yes. After all, it makes sense, doesn't it? The knight Beaubras, I mean. He's just beginning his quest now. He must have sent for me, must have called me here. There must be some way in which I can help him."

The robot was quiet for a second, evaluating the statement. Then it said, "Beaubras rode alone, Rod."

"Yes, but there were mighty deeds wrought by other knights in other places, and their accomplishments helped him find the Rainbow Crystal, Fess. Maybe he needed one more." Rod's eyes glittered. "Just think—somewhere in this magic land, the knight Beaubras is riding his good steed Balincet, right this minute!"

Fess was silent, weighing, planning for contingencies.

Lucidity pierced for a gritty moment. "Fess—I'm really far gone in delusion, aren't I?"

"There is always a way back, Rod," the robot said quietly.

"Yes." Rod nodded. "Yes, there is, isn't there?"

He turned the horse's head toward the east. "And if it's always there, then it won't matter if we go a little farther in before we turn back out. Right, Fess? Yes, of course right. We'll give it a chance to wear off, at least. Shall we go?"

5

Dawn turned the winter forest into an enchanted realm of crystal trunks with glittering branches, a cathedral of ice carpeted with fleece.

"But then, it *is* an enchanted realm," Rod mused. "This is Granclarte."

Fess maintained silence.

"Ow-w-w-w-w-oo!"

Rod reined in, startled. "What the hell was *that*?"

"It did not have the sound of an animal," Fess answered.

"Then it's a man in trouble." Rod turned Fess's head toward the sound. It came again, and Rod shivered. "If it's a man, he's more angry than hurt."

"Howling in rage?" Fess asked.

He was, and he was a man. But Rod stopped in amazement, because he was one of the few dwarfs Rod had ever seen in Gramarye, besides Brom O'Berin.

And Brom was half elven . . .

The dwarf glowered up at him. "Am I so rare a sight, then, that thou must needs stare at me?"

"Frankly, yes." Rod backpedaled quickly, trying to

find a way to cover his rudeness. "Sorry. I'm Rod Gallowglass."

He waited for the reaction, but there wasn't any, other than a sardonic, "And I am Modwis the Smith. Now that we are met, wilt thou cease to gawk?"

"Sorry. It's just that you don't usually see people caught in their own traps."

" 'Tis not mine, dolt! Would a *dwarf* lay a trap like to this?"

"Like what?" Rod leaned forward, peering. "I can't even see what that thing is, much less how to undo it."

" 'Tis but a forester's snare, like any other." The dwarf leaned against a nearby tree trunk, lifting his right foot. A length of glitter stretched up from the snow to his ankle. "Yet 'tis laid with a silver chain, and mine efforts to part it have yielded naught. Were it Cold Iron, I'd have broke its links with scarce a thought—but over silver, I've no power."

Rod frowned: Brom alone, of the elf-folk, could handle Cold Iron with impunity—but he could work silver and gold, too.

"You are in Granclarte, Rod, not Gramarye." Fess might have read his thoughts.

Rod lifted his head—that made sense. "Well, silver can't stand against steel." He dismounted and stepped over to Modwis.

"What dost thou mean to do!" the dwarf cried with alarm.

"Cut the chain off your ankle. Be careful, now."

"I'll not stir." The dwarf held his leg rock-steady, eyeing Rod strangely.

Obviously, Modwis hadn't expected help. It made Rod wonder about his relations with other people. For that matter, why was the dwarf out here, alone, in the forest?

Not that it was any of Rod's business. He slipped the

point of his dagger through a link, then twisted. The link bulged, thinned, then parted, and the chain fell off the dwarf's leg.

He put his foot down with a sigh of relief. "A blessing on thee, now, for timely aid!"

"My pleasure." Rod rose, sheathing his dagger and sizing up his new acquaintance. Modwis was about three feet tall, broad in the shoulder, chest, and hips. He had arms as thick as Rod's thighs, and thighs as thick as tree trunks. His long hair fell loose to his shoulders; it and his beard were ginger, sprinkled with gray. He wore buff-colored leggings, green boots and tunic, a red cloak, and a red cap with a fur brim. He carried a dagger the size of a short sword, with elaborate carving on the hilt and scabbard. He returned Rod's gaze with a frank stare, up and down.

Rod took the hint. "Who would set a silver snare?"

"One who wished to catch elf-folk, belike."

"Guess so . . . *Hey!*" Rod felt something clutch at his own ankle.

"What moves?"

"Something under the snow." Rod kicked out—and his leg jolted to a halt. A length of silver stretched up from the frost. "You didn't tell me there were more of them!"

"In truth, I did not know." Modwis caught up a broken branch, stepped toward Rod—and fell flat on his face. " 'Ware!"

"Don't worry, I will." Rod reached down to take Modwis's arm—and silver links shot round his wrist, pulling taut. "Not wary enough! Quick, get up—before they tie you down."

Modwis was scrabbling, trying to push himself up—but silver chains held down his forearms. "I cannot!"

"Why didn't you tell me—no, strike that. *You* weren't foolish enough to go reaching down, were you?"

"Nay, though I came near to falling when first the chain pulled at me. *Nay!* Forfend!"

More chains were snaking out of the snow to wrap around his chest and torso.

Rod sliced the links holding his wrist, then severed the chain around his own ankle. "Well, Cold Iron works against them . . ."

"But thou canst not cut them more quickly than they rise against me! Nay, leave me! Save thyself!"

"I, uh, don't think that'll be necessary." Rod turned to his mount. "Fess?"

"Yes, Rod—my hooves are of steel." The horse strode into the patch of writhing chains. Silver strings snaked around his fetlocks—and parted, as the robot's strength snapped their links. He trampled carefully around Modwis's torso, one hoof to either side, standing over him. "Tell the gentleman to grasp the cinch."

"That's right, he can't hear you. Yo, Modwis! Reach up and grab the horse's bellyband! That'll get your upper body out of range, at least."

Modwis lunged, and caught the strap under Fess's belly. "Yet what of my legs?"

"Oh, he's very precise." Rod watched as Fess kicked through the chains beside Modwis's hip and right side. "Now! Get your right leg up!"

Modwis kicked high, and Fess scythed the chains along his left. "Get ready—and hold *tight*!"

Fess leaped away into the trees, Modwis hanging on for dear life. The horse landed, and Modwis scrambled free. "I thank thee, good folk!"

"Up!" Rod called. "Into the saddle! If there're any more near you . . ."

But Modwis was already in the air, landing in the saddle in one clean bound. Fess turned back, and Modwis wrapped one hand in his mane, reaching out with the other. As they swept past, Rod caught Modwis's forearm and swung up behind him, onto Fess's rump. The horse cleared the patch of snares and slowed, turning back toward the glitter of broken links as he stopped.

"Nay, fear not," Modwis rumbled. "We are clear of them, and they cannot follow."

"Still," Rod said, "we can't be sure. Better make tracks, Steel Stud."

"Rod, you should not refer to biological impossibilities . . ."

"Okay, Manganese Mule! Just go!"

"Well, if you insist on being rude about it," Fess huffed, but he turned and trotted away down the trail.

Modwis turned his head to look back at Rod. "I ken not who thou art, Rod Gallowglass, but thou art most assuredly well met. I thank thee, mortal, and thine horse."

"Always glad to help a fellow being in distress." Interesting that he wasn't known here, Rod thought—a relief, in a way. "Just return the favor to the next person in trouble you meet—if you can be sure it's not a scam. What were you doing out in the forest, anyway?"

"Gathering hazel branches, to make charcoal for mine forge. And thou?"

Rod squirmed uncomfortably. "Deserting, I suppose you could say. Who do you think set those snares?"

"I've little doubt," Modwis returned. "It must needs be a sorcerer, for who else could hold sway over silver, to make it strike like a snake?"

Rod nodded. "Makes sense. I was kinda hoping chains didn't behave like that by themselves here."

"Here?" Modwis frowned. "Whence comest thou, mortal?"

"From another world," Rod explained. "It happens, now and then."

"An thou sayest it, I'll believe thee." But the frown deepened. "How didst thou come to Granclarte?"

"By magic—and not entirely reluctantly, I'll admit."

At that Modwis smiled. "Nay, surely—for who'd not wish to sojourn in Granclarte, an he could? Yet whom didst thou desert?"

"My wife and children," Rod answered honestly. "I've gone a little crazy, see, and I never know when I'm gonna turn mean—so I took myself off where I couldn't hurt them. Which is by way of serving you warning, too."

"Well, I am warned." The frown settled back into place. "And 'tis this madness which hath brought thee hither?"

Rod nodded.

"Then must I bless it, for thy coming was timely for me—yet I'd fain return thee to thy wife and babes. Assuming thou dost wish it." Modwis scowled. "Dost thou?"

The question took Rod by surprise. He suppressed the natural assent, unsure whether it was genuine or conditioned. Instead, he pursed his lips, stared up at the forest canopy, and searched his feelings. "I do," he said slowly, "but I must admit I wouldn't mind taking my time about it."

Modwis rumbled; Rod assumed it was amusement, but he couldn't tell through the whiskers. Either amusement or a nervous stomach. "Then let us seek a means of returning thee, for 'tis like to take long enough in the finding. Was the magic that brought thee here good or ill? There lies the nubbin."

"Well, whoever did it, I don't think he had my good in mind."

"Yet perchance did have ours. Yet I think it may be that he who laid the snares for me laid another sort for thee."

"I'm limed, then. Have any particular trapper in mind?"

"Aye." Modwis looked grim. "He dwells to the east,

in a ruined castle perched high on a crag, and all the countryside about him abides in corruption and putrefaction. Vultures are his nightingales, and carrion jackals his dogs.''

"Sounds like a real charmer. Does this nice guy have a name?"

"Gormlin is he called, though few dare say his name openly." Modwis glowered off to the east. "Yet I do, for I'm sworn to find his bane! Gormlin, an thou canst hear, do thy worst! For I'll yet find a means of bringing thy foul castle down on thy head!"

Modwis was silent, taut, as though expecting an answer. Rod found that he was, too, and shifted in his seat just to break the mood. "Any, uh, particular reason why you've got it in for him? Or do you just have an obsession about destroying evil?"

"There is that, but there is the other, too," Modwis growled. "There was a maiden, Rod Gallowglass, and though there was no chance that she might smile upon me, yet I ached to do all that I might to bring her happiness."

"And she was stolen away by Brume?"

"Aye, and none know her fate. I will tear that castle down stone by stone if I must, I shall free her or learn of her death! That, though it take all my life!"

"Valiantly said," Rod said softly. "Can I help?"

" 'Tis not thy coil, Rod Gallowglass."

"Maybe not," Rod said slowly, "but weren't you working your way up to telling me Gormlin might have been the one who brought me here?"

Modwis was silent.

"Or that someone else might have brought me here, to fight him?"

Reluctantly, Modwis nodded.

"So," Rod said, "if he brought me here, I have to persuade him to send me back, somehow—and if he didn't, the wizard who did might let me go when I've done what he brought me here for.''

"Mayhap," Modwis said, "and 'mayhap' again and again, and thrice more. I can promise thee naught, Rod Gallowglass."

"That's okay—I can't, either." Rod shrugged. "Either way, sounds like a good way to see the country. Let's go.''

Modwis whirled to stare at him, thunderstruck. "Art thou mad?''

"Frankly yes.''

"Assuredly, thou must needs be, an thou wilt speak so easily of marching down the throat of the dragon! How dost thou think to come alive to his walls?''

"I'll have to develop a plan of attack when I've seen his castle. As to getting there, well—I have this hobby, you see . . .''

"Summat to do with enchanted horses that can break ensorcelled silver?''

"Oh, you noticed Fess isn't the average stallion, eh? Yes, I had something like that in mind—he and I have a few weapons we're too modest to show. And some of mine never show at all—only their effects.''

Modwis stared directly into his eyes. "Dost say thou art a sorcerer?''

"No, an esper. It isn't magic, but it sure looks like it.''

"How doth it differ?''

"Well," Rod said, "I don't get my magic from evil.''

"From God, then?''

Rod shrugged. "It's a talent I was born with. In itself, it's neither good nor bad.''

" 'Tis in how thou dost use it, then?''

Rod nodded. "And for what purpose. Yes.''

"And thou hast ne'er met one who could best thee, eh?" Modwis's voice was flat with sarcasm.

"I'm still alive, aren't I?"

Modwis turned thoughtful. "There is that."

"It's my most convincing argument. So what do you say? Feel like giving me a tour of the road to the east?"

Modwis grinned like a shark. "Aye, and right gladly! If we die, we die!"

"It wasn't really on my agenda—but if we have to go, do you suppose we could go with full stomachs? It's been a while since I ate."

"I have a small house, not far from here." Modwis turned back toward Fess's head. "Mystical horse, set forth! Turn to the south on this next branch of the trail, and we will come to a warm stable, and sweet hay!"

Fess dutifully took the next southward fork. After all, one had to keep up appearances.

6

Modwis propped Rod on a bench by the fire with a mug of ale while he clanged and pottered about the stove. It was noisy enough for Rod to have a quiet discussion with Fess.

"So what do you think, Iron Id? Was it a setup, or what?"

"There was certainly some element of hallucination involved, Rod," Fess answered, his tone cautious.

Rod frowned. "Care to expand on that?"

"No."

Rod pressed his lips thin. "All right, I'm making it an order. What did you see?"

Fess sighed. "The person you perceive as a dwarf, Rod, is in fact a leprechaun."

"Leprechaun! Who—Kelly?"

"No, Rod—a stranger. He seems to speak truly when he says his name is 'Modwis.' "

"Not terribly Irish."

"Neither is Kelly's last name."

Alarm bells rang. "So what have I got now? Brom assigning me a baby-sitter?"

"There is no evidence of prior arrangement," the robot answered. "The elf was indeed snared in a silver chain when you found him."

"Who would do such a dirty trick? No, strike that—anyone who wanted a crock of gold. But why wasn't the trapper there to watch his snare?"

"Perhaps he fled at your approach."

"Do I look *that* bad?"

Fess was silent, and Rod decided not to press the point. "How about the attack of the chains?"

"I saw only ground vines, Rod—but they were green, which is odd for winter, and they did entangle both you and Modwis."

"Odd, to say the least." Rod said. "Maybe the trapper is a telekinetic, and didn't run all *that* far away?"

"That is possible . . ."

"Or it's possible that Modwis staged the whole thing." Rod began to feel prickles of suspicion along the back of his scalp.

"The leprechaun might have some psi power, yes."

Rod grimaced, beginning to wonder if the robot was humoring him.

"Be careful not to drink too much of the ale, Rod," Fess cautioned. "You have not eaten in some time."

That, at least, was reassuring.

Then the time for speculation was done, because Modwis set a platter heaped with eggs and meats and a basket of rolls on the table. Rod returned to more important matters.

Modwis's hospitality was cozy, but lavish—if Rod had eaten everything offered, he would have been comatose. But strangely, he found that his appetite vanished with a few bites, leaving him edgy and nervous. "It was very good," he said. "Thanks for the hospitality, Modwis, but I need to get back on the road again."

The dwarf peered at him. "How long is't sin thou hast slept?"

Rod considered, and decided that the question wasn't relevant. "I couldn't stand to sleep right now. Thanks, but I'll be off."

(Come to think of it, he was.)

Without a word, the dwarf carried the dishes to the door, gave a fluting birdcall, swept the crumbs off, scoured the plates with sand, and removed a pack from the wall. He put the dishes in it, then wrapped up each of the items of food from the table. He scraped more crumbs into his hand from the table, walked to the door and tossed them out, shouldered his pack, and took down a large iron key from a hook on the wall. Then he bowed Rod out the door.

Rod suddenly realized what the ceremony meant. "Hey, wait a minute! We don't have to look for Gormlin—and you don't have to come along!"

"True." Modwis turned the key in the great lock, hung it around his neck, and took up a walking staff from its place by the jamb. "Yet surely thou'lt not deny me thy companionship upon the road?"

"Well—no, of course not. Glad of it, really. But where are you going?"

"Down the road some miles. Whither goest thou?"

"Uh well . . . down the road a way, actually."

"Well met!" Modwis beamed and clapped him on the arm. "By some fair chance, we journey toward the same destination! Then thou wilt not be amazed an I keep pace with thee for the full length of the journey."

And they set off into the forest, with Rod having that old, nagging feeling that, somehow, he'd been conned. Again.

After an hour, Rod reined in and dismounted. "Okay, your turn to ride now."

Modwis looked up, amused. "Dost think me so weak as to need another's limbs?"

"Well . . . No, not when you put it that way. But it is more restful. And faster."

"It shall take more than a day's walk to tire me. And as to speed, set thy pace, and I'll match it."

Rod wasn't about to test it—but he was in no hurry, anyway, so he kept Fess to a walk. Modwis would not relent, so, after a while, Rod quit trying. But when they stopped to rest at a village, Rod bought a donkey, leaving a peasant blessing heaven for the good fortune of a real gold crown, and offered it to Modwis. The dwarf still would not ride, but only led the donkey, until Rod let his embarrassment begin to show. Then, finally, Modwis relented and climbed onto the donkey. So, both mounted, they rode on toward romance and adventure.

By late afternoon, they were out of the forest and in open country again, coming down from the Crag Mountains into the northern plateau.

Plateau? Runnymede was on a plateau, not the northern baronies! Rod realized, with a sudden sense of vertigo, that he really *was* in Granclarte, not just a thinly disguised Gramarye.

At least, he seemed to be . . .

Well, you couldn't tell it by the look of the rider who was coming up the road toward them. He was clad in black armor, and rode a horse that would have done credit to a beer wagon. It was hard to tell who wore the better armor, horse or rider . . .

The knight reined in alongside and lifted his visor. "Hail! Art thou knight or yeoman?"

"Neither, really," Rod said with a smile. "No one ever got around to knighting me, but I was raised to the peerage. Born to it, too, but I was a second son of a second son."

"Then assuredly, thou art a knight born!"

"Seemed that way to me, too, but nobody ever made it official." Then Rod saw the device on the knight's shield, and froze.

It was a silver arm with a closed fist, slanting across a black field—and Rod knew that plain, severe sight as well as he knew the form of Fess. "My pardon, Sir Knight. You are a man of virtue rare!"

"Thou dost me too much honor, good sir. Yet thou hast the advantage of me, an thou knowest me by repute. Say who thou art."

Rod swallowed. "I am Rod Gallowglass, Lord High Warlock of the Kingdom of Gramarye."

"A warlock!" The sword's point was at Rod's throat. He didn't remember the knight drawing it, but it was there. "Is thy magic white or black?"

"Neither, really—it just is." Rod ignored the sword (while sweat trickled off his brow) and looked steadily into the sky-blue eyes beneath the noble brow. "Is your sword crafted by white magic or black?"

The point didn't waver, and the face behind it turned more flinten than ever. "Smiths do own magic, aye—they chant strength as they forge the blade, and carve runes down its length. Yet whether the magic is white or black depends upon the smith."

Rod nodded. "So it is with me. I am no saint, and I cannot work miracles—but neither am I devoted to Satan; I abhor him, and all his works."

Still the sword did not waver. "Magic must be from either God or Satan. Which is thine?"

"It's certainly not from Satan—and I do live in hope of Heaven."

The knight held his gaze a moment more, then sheathed the great sword. "Thou art a white warlock."

"If you say so." Rod felt a surge of hubris coming, and somehow knew better than to squelch it. "But if you want to make sure, why don't you test my mettle? I'll withhold my magic, if you withhold your sword."

The knight still gazed at him, then smiled just a little. " 'Tis apt. With what weapon shall we contend?"

Rod jerked his head toward the willows bordering the stream by the road. "I suspect two enterprising gentlemen could find a couple of six-foot staves in there."

Now the knight grinned. "Even as thou sayest. Sin that I lack a squire, wilt thine choose my weapon for me?"

"Well, he's not really my squire . . ."

"Nay, be assured that I am!" Modwis was off his donkey in an instant, his eyes huge. "A moment only, good knights!" And he vanished into the copse with remarkable speed.

The knight frowned. "An he is not thy squire, who is he?"

"Only a friend," Rod said, "and a new one at that. But he strikes me as reliable."

The knight nodded. "The dwarves are known for their hearts of oak. Their loyalty is rarely given, yet when 'tis, 'twill stand like a mountain."

Modwis was back, holding up two green poles, sliced through at each end, twigs trimmed to smoothness. "Thou dost me honor, sirs and knights."

"As thou dost for us," the knight said, in the best tradition of chivalry. He dismounted. Rod couldn't help staring—any man who could get on or off a horse with a full load of plate armor and no derrick was fantastically strong.

But of course, this was fantasy . . .

"I would prefer not to take advantage," he said, nonetheless. "Your armor must weigh you down, sir."

The knight tossed his helm with impatience. "What matters such weight to a true knight? Yet to yield *mine* advantage, I must bare my pate for thee." He set hands to his helm, unfastened and removed it. Golden locks flowed down to his shoulders; a flat, sloping forehead ran up against a brace of bony brow-ridges, somewhat camouflaged by bushy blond eyebrows. They overhung two large deeply-set blue eyes, thresholded by high, prominent cheekbones, divided by a blade of a nose. Beneath the nose was a wide, thin-lipped mouth above a strong, squarish jawbone and a jutting chin. Rod felt his heart skip a beat—the knight was just as he'd always imagined him.

Of course, said his monitor-mind.

The knight took up his staff, twirled it around his head to warm up, then brought it down. "At thy convenience, milord."

Rod grinned, feeling the joy of battle start—and against such an opponent! He knew he'd be lucky to manage a draw, but that didn't matter—the thrill was equivalent to singing at Covent Garden with Domingo.

Modwis stood by, fairly bursting with excitement.

They circled each other, both grinning, eyes alight, quarterstaves held slanting, on guard. Then the knight cried, "Avaunt!" and his pole tip shot through the air so fast Rod could scarcely see it. But he managed to get his own stick up just high enough, somehow, and the crack of their meeting echoed off the rock face a hundred yards behind them.

It also left Rod's hands stinging so badly he could have sworn his bones were vibrating.

No time to think about it—the bottom of the knight's staff was sweeping toward Rod's kneecap. He barely managed to block, and the blow knocked his own staff into his kneecap. He stepped back, alarmed to feel his knee buckle, and blocked the knight's next blow from a great defensive position on one knee. At last he realized that he had to go on the offensive, and the low position was handy for a knock at the shins. It landed, but it was more like a clang, with a rebound Rod didn't believe. He used it, though, to aim the top of his staff at the knight's head. The knight's staff swept up to block, of course, and Rod seized the chance to shove himself back upright. He found his balance just in time, for the knight's staff was shooting right at his sinuses. He blocked and, getting the rhythm of it (finally!), swung the lower end of the staff at a joint in the knight's armor. The tip hit chain mail between the plates, but it jolted the man momentarily, long enough for Rod to slam a knock at his helmetless head.

He actually connected! Nasty hollow sound, too. Not that it did much harm. Oh, the knight fell back a step, but he simply gave his head a shake and waded back in.

But it had been time enough for Rod to get his own speciality back in play. He whirled his staff around in a circle, so fast it was a blur, describing a plane that was angled at forty-five degrees—it was supposed to be upright, but a quarterstaff was really too long for single-stick play.

The knight frowned; this was apparently new to him. But he slammed a blow bravely at Rod's head.

Crack! The knight's stick snapped itself out of his hands. "*Parbleu!*" He wrung his hands—they were stinging, too; pretty good, since he was wearing gauntlets. He leaped back, catching up his staff, and his lips firmed with impatience.

Rod stopped his whirligig, limped to the nearest tree, propped his back against it, and set himself, staff up between both hands. It was coming now.

It did. He was the center of a tornado of blows, cracking about him like lightning bursts. He plied his own stick frantically, blocking blow for blow and countering when he could, down low, up high, up high again, down low, up high . . .

But the knight's staff tip came in down low again, somehow, and caught Rod right in the midriff. The breath whooshed out of his lungs; he gasped, gulping for air, not gaining any, fighting against the pain that racked him as the day darkened about him, and fell.

Then it was light again, and he could actually breathe, and Modwis was running a cool, damp rag over his face. He pulled in a long breath, deciding it was the sweetest draft he'd had in a long time, and struggled to sit up. The dwarf's arm was around his shoulders in a second, helping, and he saw the golden-haired knight leaning on his staff, smiling enigmatically. "My thanks for a worthy bout, milord. Thy skill is great."

"Not quite as great as yours." Rod grinned, and shoved himself painfully up, saying. "Not that I expected it to be."

"Still, you comported yourself most excellently." The knight clasped his forearm and hauled him to his feet. "I would be glad of your company in my travels, milord."

Rod stared, unable to believe his ears. *He* travel with this hero? This man who always rode alone? "I—I'd be honored." He was suddenly aware of Modwis's arm under his own hand. "But I couldn't leave my squire."

"So faithful and stalwart a companion must needs be of inestimable value. Wilt thou both aid me awhile?"

"Why . . . of course," Rod said, overcome. "Whatever we can do."

"Aye," Modwis rumbled.

"Thou mayest be of great aid indeed, the more so an thou knowest the land hereabouts." The knight turned to survey the valley below with a frown.

"I have dwelt here all my life," Modwis answered.

"There's not a stump nor a stone for ten miles that I know not."

"I have need of such knowledge," the knight conceded. "I oppose a fell sorcerer, dost thou see, and he hath cast a glamour over my sight, which doth so change the appearance of all the country hereabouts that I can no longer find my way."

"A foul spell in truth," the dwarf muttered.

"Even so. Three times now have I fallen into a bog, and once fallen from a height, when I could have sworn naught lay before me but open land. I could not even be sure that thou wast truly nigh, when I saw thee."

"Vile," Rod agreed. "I'm under something of the same enchantment, myself."

Modwis stared at him in sudden surprise, which was reassuring, as did the knight. "Thou hast a glamour about thee?"

"I wouldn't have thought so," Rod muttered, "but I do seem to be seeing things that aren't there." For a moment, the spell thinned, and he saw only an open road before him, bound with fog under a leaden sky, with deep ruts in the snow heaped high upon it.

" 'Tis the sorcerer hath cast this dimness o'er thy sight," Modwis averred, "the foul sorcerer, who doth seek to blind thee to such things as are real!"

The sun shone again, on a dusty road amid summer greenery, and the knight was back. Rod relaxed and explained, "But the only illusions I see are of people and monsters." A lingering regard for truth made him add, "And seasons. I don't seem to be having trouble with geographical features."

The knight grinned and clapped him on the shoulder. "Then we are well met, thou and I! I shall see the folk aright, and thou shalt see the terrain! Come, let us march against this fell sorcerer, and root him from the land!"

The grin was infectious; Rod couldn't help but return it. "And just in case I'm fooled, Modwis will check us. And my horse, of course—he's very good at discerning reality." He ignored the buzz behind his ear. "What sorcerer is this?"

"Some country churl, and a weak-kneed 'prentice of a magic-worker, I doubt not," the knight answered with disdain. "None have e'er heard of him aforetime, nor shall after, I warrant."

"But his name?" Rod insisted.

"He doth call himself 'Saltique,' " the knight answered, "and I trust we shall salt him indeed."

It was a strange name, right enough, which was odd, because Rod knew all the Chronicles of Granclarte by heart.

"Your grandfather's ghost did say that you were to continue the saga, Rod," Fess murmured behind his ear.

"Salt him away for future use?" Rod pretended dismay. "Why not just put him out of business permanently?"

"I warrant we'll send him to his just reward," the knight answered. "Yet first, we must needs discover his lair."

"I have heard summat of him," Modwis grated. "We must track him to the Wastelands, milords."

"Why, we are nearly there!" the knight cried, and clapped Modwis on the shoulder. "How can we fail, with a true guide before us? To horse, milord! And away!"

They mounted and rode out, heading down into the valley—and Fess couldn't avoid the realization that his master was riding back into his childhood.

"Fess, just think of it!" Rod burbled. "I'm riding with him! I'm actually riding with him!"

"It is a rare honor indeed." Fess was growing increasingly concerned, even more so now that Rod had begun talking to himself. That was bad enough, but it was worse that he was making perfect sense.

Rod sobered, some of his exuberance absorbed into the robot's caution. "Where's the worm in the apple, huh? Y'know, he looks almost familiar . . . hauntingly familiar . . ."

"Should he not?"

"Well, yeah, he should look the way I've always pictured him." Rod frowned at the tall, broad figure riding straight in the saddle in front of him. "But then he should look familiar, period. Why this niggling reminder of someone I once knew?"

"It is entirely natural."

"Yeah, I guess my childish mind built him after some adult I'd met."

Fess kept silent.

"Just think—riding with him, on his quest!" Rod felt his spirits bubble up again. "I may never go back to the real world!"

"That," said Fess, "may be exactly what your enemies are hoping for."

"Oh, don't be a killjoy! Ho, for adventure! I ride in quest of the Rainbow Crystal, with the great knight Beaubras!"

7

They had traveled some time before Rod thought to ask, "Where do you wish to go, Sir Knight?"

"To the rescue of my fair lady Haughteur, Lord Gallowglass," the knight replied.

Great. But not quite as helpful as Rod needed. "Where is she imprisoned?"

The knight shook his head in sorrow. "Not bound in a prison, Lord Gallowglass, but in a glamour. She dwells within the keep of High Dudgeon, in the sway of Lady Aggravate."

A new one again, an element not in Grandfather's saga. Rod frowned.

"Where is High Dudgeon?" Modwis asked.

Nice to know it was new to him, too.

"Hid within the clouds at the top of Mount Sullen," Beaubras answered. " 'Tis a keep nigh eighty feet tall—yet for the first sixty of those feet, it hath not one single opening. Nay, not so much as an arrow-slit."

"Quite secure," Rod said. "Yet not the most sensible

arrangement for defense, to say nothing of aesthetics. Any particular reason for the lack of windows?''

"So that all within may look down on those beneath them—as they believe everyone to be, who doth not view the world from High Dudgeon.''

Rod said slowly, "I take it they like to have *everyone* beneath them.''

"Aye. None come there who do not—sad to say.'' The knight hung his head. "My lady is the fairest in the land, but many among us hath a weakness—and this is hers.''

"But you don't seem to think going there was entirely her doing.''

Beaubras rode in thought for a while, then nodded. "There may be truth in that—for, though she may have come willingly, the glamour may also have been wrapped about her aforetime.''

"Therefore she may have wished to come, because she had been enchanted.'' Rod nodded; it was ever the way of young girls and high living. Still, he took Sir Beaubras's point—the lady had to find the glamour tempting, for the glamour to ensnare her. "The chatelaine, Lady Aggravate— she is something of a magician.''

"She is a sorceress entire, sir, who doth gain her strength by sapping the vitality of the young folk she doth call to her. The mark of her corruption may be seen in her abhorrence of the cleansing touch of water.''

"No water?'' Rod stared. "What do her people drink?''

"Only wine, and brandywine, which doth render them the more susceptible to her whims.''

"Good grief!'' Rod turned away, shaken. "How can they stand to be near each other?''

"Oh, she doth ever fill her halls with sweet aromas, by the burning of fragrant gums and resins, so that those who dwell within her courts cannot sense the corruption about them.''

"You mean the people who dwell in High Dudgeon are always incensed?" Rod gave his head a shake. "No, what's the matter with me? Of course they are." He shuddered. "A grim and awful keep indeed, Sir Beaubras! You must not go alone against such a horrible castle!"

"I cannot ask thee to accompany me into so fell a place, Lord Gallowglass."

"You didn't—I volunteered. Unless you think I'll be in the way, of course."

The knight turned, a smile making his countenance radiant. "Of a certainty, thou shalt not! Thou art a wizard, art thou not? And assuredly, thou shalt be of most timely aid against this sorceress Aggravate!"

Rod hoped he was right.

The sun was just past noon, and Rod was on the watch for an inn, when Modwis brought them up with a raised hand. They reined in, and the knight frowned. "What stirs, friend?"

"I mislike the sense of this place." Modwis scowled at the roadway ahead of them. The farmlands narrowed, then gave way to tall, dark oaks and elms that overhung the road. "There have been bandits here in times gone by."

"Like enough; 'tis well suited to an ambush." Beaubras lifted his head, baring his teeth in a grin. "So much the worse for them, then. How good of thee, Modwis, to find that with which to cheer me! Lord Gallowglass, an there do be bandits, I doubt me not they warrant punishment. What sayest thou?"

"Mostly surely," Rod said bravely, but his spine crawled with apprehension as they rode under the boughs. He wished he could be as delighted at the prospect of . . .

A roar like a score of locomotives let loose at once, and a handful of bandits leaped out from the trees. They were scruffy but stocky, their clothes as ragged and dirty as their weapons were bright. Two of them had halberds; two had swords; one had only a club. But the club was huge and had a spike, and the spike was swooping toward Rod's temple. He ducked, shouting a totally unnecessary warning to his companions. Fess dodged, and between the two of them, he only got hit with the side of the club as it shot past. But the blow hit a lot harder than a five-and-a-half-foot malnourished thug should have been able to manage; Rod flew from the saddle and landed, hard, on his back. It knocked the wind out of him and paralyzed his diaphragm; he struggled to pull in a breath at the same time as he struggled to get up. Fess screamed a threat and warning, and leaped to stand over him, shielding Rod with his own steel body from the ministrations of the club-wielder and a sword-swinger who swerved over to join in. Fess tried to lash out with a front hoof and a back hoof simultaneously, and promptly had a seizure, legs locking stiff over his master, head dropping to swing between his fetlocks.

But he had given Rod enough time to thrash his way up on one elbow and get a look at the bandits, through the tears in his eyes. They looked wobbly and out of focus— but they also looked to be moving inside vague, hulking, translucent outlines that were half again as tall as they were, and much more misshapen. Then he blinked away the tears, and saw only bandits again—but the clue was enough. "Trolls!" he shouted to his companions. "They're really trolls in disguise!"

It was enough for Beaubras. He changed his style of attack on the instant, aiming a ringing blow two feet *above* the head of the nearest bandit.

The blow rang indeed, and struck sparks, too. The bandit gave a scream and fell back a pace, shocked.

As well he might be. Beaubras's magic blade, Coupetou,

had carved a gash out of the troll's granite hide. For all
that Rod could see, the sword hadn't come anywhere near
the bandit—but a gash had opened in the air above him,
welling bright green ichor, and Beaubras was slashing at it
again.

Not that Rod had time to look. He had spared a quick
glance before he turned to block the next blow, dodging
aside from it as he thought *Long!* at his dagger. It sprouted
amazingly, shooting out like a switchblade.

Behind him, Coupetou rang like an alarm bell, and
Modwis underscored its melody with a percussion of dull
thuds as he laid about him with an iron club.

Rod thought *Hard!* and his sword's edge glittered like a
diamond.

In fact, it *was* diamond, as the next bandit found out
when Rod sidestepped and chopped right through his club.
The "man" stared at the sheared stub in surprise, and Rod
scored a line across the air directly above his head.

The bandit screamed and fell back, but his mate with the
sword stepped in—and toppled as Modwis straightened up,
holding the bandit's ankle. Rod didn't pause to debate
points of chivalry—he chopped while he could. The blade
clanged and rebounded, vibrating so hard it stung his
hands. Bright green lined the air above it and the bandit
screamed like a factory whistle, rolling to his feet and
pelting back toward the forest. His mate with the stub of
club joined him, and Rod started to run after them, then
thought of confronting them on their home territory, and
slowed to a halt. He turned back, and saw right away that
Beaubras and Modwis had done considerably better than
he had. Two bandits lay writhing on the ground; another
gave one last shudder, and lay still. All three were growing hazy around the edges, but the dead bandit was the
first whose form blurred completely, then re-formed into

an eight-foot monster, wide in the shoulders and chest, absurdly short in the legs, that looked somehow like a turnip—with arms five feet long, muscled like steel cables, and hands that had claws, not fingernails.

Rod stared, appalled. He had had the temerity to fight a thing like *that*?

He looked up quickly—and, sure enough, the other two bandits had turned into the same type of monster. They thrashed about on the ground, moaning and howling.

"We must aid them." Beaubras took a flask of brandy from his saddlebag.

Modwis nodded, and found a roll of bandage in his own saddlebag.

Rod felt very much at a loss. He disguised it with protest. "Wait a minute! We were just trying to chop these things into pieces!"

"Only for that they sought to injure us, Lord Gallowglass." Beaubras looked up, then went back to trying to wipe up ichor and pour in brandy.

Rod couldn't help thinking that the brandy would do more good in the creature's mouth—especially since it roared at the burning of the alcohol and slammed a huge fist at the knight, who adroitly stepped back. "I bid thee hold thy peace, poor creature. The brandy doth sting, aye, but 'twill prevent infection."

How considerate of Grandfather to construct the land of Granclarte with a rudimentary, but accurate, knowledge of medicine! "Look, I hate to sound like a heel, but wouldn't it be a bit more practical to put them out of their misery?"

Beaubras stared, appalled. "Only they themselves can do that, Lord Gallowglass, by repenting of their evil ways and turning to God."

"Revenge," one of the fallen monsters snarled. "Kill slow!"

"Well, not slowly." Rod fingered his sword. "I have a *little* mercy, after all."

The knight protested, and even Modwis paled. "Thou canst not mean to do it, Lord Gallowglass!"

"No, I can, actually. Look at it this way—these aren't civilized beings you're dealing with, or even ones that *can* be civilized. They're sadistic monsters who enjoy nothing so much as watching people suffer. Heal 'em, and they'll come right back to attack us—and if not us, then the next traveler who comes down this road."

"We must do our Christian duty," the knight responded sternly, "no matter the cost!"

"With respect, Sir Knight, it won't be us who have to pay that cost."

"If we treat them with mercy, Lord Gallowglass, they may give mercy in their own steads," Modwis explained.

"Fat chance!"

"He doth speak truth." Beaubras frowned. "Works of charity may ope the hearts of others to God's grace, Lord Gallowglass. Yet whether they do or not, we can but do our part, and be merciful toward fallen foes."

Rod had it on the tip of his tongue, but he bit it back. This was, after all, his grandfather's universe, and a realm of complete fantasy. Here it was quite possible that blood-thirsty monsters could be reformed and recruited. In fact, wasn't there a story, in his childhood, of the giant Blunderthud, who became one of the Four Kings' most ardent supporters?

He sighed and turned away to grope beneath Fess's saddle for the reset switch, then in one of the saddlebags for the medical kit. As he knelt beside a moaning troll, a thought of reality intruded for a moment, and he seemed to see a genuine peasant rolling in agony, not a troll.

Then the moment was gone, and the troll was back.

Shaken, Rod sponged up ichor and sprinkled in antiseptic powder. He pressed down firmly as the troll roared and tried to rise, murmuring, "Yes, I know it hurts, but that's the medicine burning up all the nasty little germs that would try to give you gangrene and make your arm fall off. Just hang in there, and the pain will fade."

Suddenly, he was very glad that Beaubras had been such a stickler about chivalry. If his flash of insight was accurate, he was treating a human being, and the troll was only a hallucination.

Or was the troll real, and the peasant a hallucination? He went to reset his horse. "Fess?"

"Uhhaaaeee . . . chadd . . . uh seizurrre, Rrrrodd?"

"Yeah, you did." He'd have to wait a little while for the truth; it took Fess's perceptions a few minutes to clear.

When they were back on the road, the moaning trolls staggering to their feet behind them, Rod asked, under his breath, "What did we fight back there, Fess?"

"Five peasants, Rod—though they were remarkably tall and well fed for Gramarye field hands."

"Futurians?" Rod wondered. "What're *they* doing here?"

"More probably local agents brought up by the Futurians. But high-technology intervention is quite likely—the heads of those halberds were strangely free of the slightest trace of rust, and the shafts were tipped with lenses."

"Lasers?" Rod frowned. "Good thing they didn't get a chance to use them."

Then the shocking thought hit—if Beaubras wasn't really there, who had finished off that one bandit, and wounded the other two?

Fortunately, Modwis spoke up before Rod could try to answer that question, and Modwis was real—within limits. "Sir and lord, trolls own little magic, and assuredly cannot change their shapes."

Beaubras and Rod were both silent, digesting the point. Then Beaubras said, "Thou speakest sooth, good Modwis. What dost thou infer from this impossibility?"

"Why, that a sorcerer must have aided them."

"The Lady Aggravate?" Rod asked.

"More likely the crazed old sorcerer who set silver snares for me, and caught thee in glamours—the wicked Saltique."

Rod tried that one on for size, and didn't like the fit. "What's he got against us, anyway?"

"Mayhap he doth see the future," Beaubras said slowly, "and doth know that we shall be his bane."

"He doth fear us for some reason, that's certain," Modwis qualified, "and doth seek to prevent our coming to his lair."

Beaubras grinned, with a toss of his head. "Why, then, let us not dispute his sagacity, my companions! Ride, for the death of sorcerers!" And he kicked his horse into a trot.

Modwis and Rod had perforce to hurry to keep up with him.

"Do I detect a certain lack of logic there?" Rod sub-vocalized.

"If you do, your perceptions are fallacious," Fess assured him. "Modwis's logic is correct, the more so since he is careful to state his inference as a hypothesis. It is Beaubras who leaps to the conclusion that what Modwis infers must be fact."

"Yes, Beaubras was never in doubt," Rod said with a sardonic smile. "But you don't think there really is a genuine sorcerer involved here?"

"In Granclarte, Rod, anything may be real."

"Right. Uh . . . how about in Gramarye, Fess? Or isn't that an issue, at the moment?"

"The coincidence of both worlds is desirable," Fess admitted. "In Gramarye, there well could be an esper, allied with the Futurians, who is somewhat unbalanced."

"So instead of a mad scientist, we have a mad warlock. Just great. Is he really out to get us, do you think?"

The robot was silent as he plodded ahead.

"Fess?" Rod pressed. "Am I just being paranoid? Or am I really being persecuted?"

The horse said, with reluctance, "I do not think your hallucinations were naturally induced, Rod."

Rod knew better than to ask him to explain.

8

They didn't stop for lunch, but for some reason, Rod didn't miss it. He was growing a mite peckish, however, as the sun declined toward teatime, and asked Modwis, "Are we apt to come to an inn before nightfall?"

"Nay," the dwarf replied. "We have taken the road less traveled by, Lord Gallowglass, and come into lands rarely visited. There is not even a keep 'twixt here and High Dudgeon."

Rod sighed. "We get to rough it, then. How romantic."

Both Beaubras and Modwis frowned at him as though he'd said a very strange word and, all things considered, he was just as glad the opportunity to explain himself vanished with the appearance of another pair of travelers.

"Hail!" cried Beaubras. "Wilt thou break a lance with me?"

"Gladly," came the muffled reply, and the other knight spurred his great golden war-horse into a gallop, leveling his lance as he did. He wore gleaming silver armor, but his helmet winked golden in the rays of the setting sun. Rod strained to make out the device on his shield, but couldn't.

Beaubras, of course, had taken the position of disadvantage, and had to ride with the sun in his eyes. He kicked his mount into a gallop, and the two juggernauts rode down on each other with all the grace and deftness of a matched pair of tanks.

Rod pressed his hands over his ears.

Even so, he could hear the crash as the knights slammed into each other—and, sure enough, the stranger's lance broke. He reeled in his saddle, then regained his seat, and was almost to Rod as he reined in and turned his horse. "A brave joust!" he cried, unshipping his sword. "Wilt thou do me the honor of measuring thy blade against mine, good knight?"

"I thank thee," Beaubras answered, riding up, "yet must I decline; for I must save my steel to deflect the spells of an evil sorceress."

"A sorceress!" The knight lifted the visor of his golden helmet, revealing a gaunt face with white eyebrows and moustaches, lined by the cares of years. Yet there was fire in those farseeing eyes, and a zeal for living that lit his whole countenance. "How marvelous an adventure! Assuredly, thou wilt not be so pinch-fisted as to hold all chance of glory to thyself alone!"

"Why, nay." Beaubras looked as though he would have liked to do just that, but chivalry forbade such selfishness. "Wilt thou join with us in this gallant battle, Sir Knight?"

"That will I gladly!" cried the Knight of the Golden Helmet. "Ho, squire of mine! Glory awaits!"

His squire approached, a short, compact man with a smile, riding on a donkey and carrying a spare spear. He proffered it, but the knight waved him away. "Nay, nay! One passage at arms must suffice; we have true foes to conquer now!" And he took his squire aside to explain the new mission.

Beaubras turned to Rod, his eyes alight, his voice low

with suppressed excitement. "He is the paladin Rinaldo, grown old!"

"One of Charlemagne's heroes?" Rod looked after the old man, frowning. "What makes you think that?"

"He wears the golden helmet of Mambrino!" Beaubras whispered to Rod. "Only to Rinaldo was that enchanted helm given!"

"No," Rod said slowly, "I can think of another who wore it, eight hundred years after. Except that he didn't really have it, actually, he only thought he did . . ."

And he ran down. Who was he, to criticize someone else's delusions?

Beaubras turned away, opening his helmet, and fell into an animated discussion with the old knight, comparing notes about weapons and monsters. From the occasional scrap of conversation that floated his way, Rod gathered that they were taking turns telling of their adventures, each one eagerly prompting the other. The stranger's squire looked up at him with a smile and a shrug, but he didn't really seem to mind at all.

Nor did Modwis. He rode leaning forward a little, eyes bright, ears straining, and began to edge closer and closer to the two knights, hanging on their every word.

The other squire kicked his feet, leaned back in the saddle, and began whistling a little tune.

Rod rode after them all in a daze, wondering into what sort of world he'd ridden. Or perhaps what sorts of worlds.

However, some compromise with reality was necessary, especially after the sun went down and the two knights kept riding blissfully through the gloaming, still rattling on with shop talk. "Enough is enough," Rod muttered, and kicked Fess into a trot. The robot-horse swerved around in front of the two armored ones, and Rod said, "O valorous knights, I blush to intrude upon your lofty conversation, but I really do think we might do well to rest through the hours of darkness."

"Eh? Why, it has become dark!" said the stranger, looking about him in surprise. "Bless me! We must indeed halt!"

"Aye, evil walks at night, and we must be ready in defense," Beaubras responded. "We must make a camp, indeed."

Rod noticed that neither of the knights said a word about sleeping. He also noticed that neither of them lifted a finger to pitch the tents; they left that to Rod, Modwis, and the squire.

"Leave this to us, Lord Gallowglass," Modwis rumbled. "Sit thee with the other knights, and talk of matters befitting thy station."

"A little rabbit stew or some roasted partridge would fit my station just fine, thank you," Rod grumbled. "*You* go listen to 'em, Modwis."

The dwarf looked up at the two knights, sitting unhelmed on a log chattering merrily away, and for a moment, his longing showed naked in his face. Then he mastered his feelings, turning away and grumbling, "Nay. 'Twould not befit my station."

Rod disagreed, but he knew there wasn't much point in saying so. So he moved as fast as he could, and at least had the campfire burning merrily by the time darkness fell.

He woke to the sound of conversation, followed shortly by the cry of a distant rooster. He scowled, looking about; the sky was just barely beginning to turn rosy behind the two knights, who sat where he had left them, comparing notes on villains dead but hopefully not deathless. Rod squeezed his eyes shut, gave his head a shake, and looked again. No, they were still there, just as fresh as they had ever been, with just as much to talk about.

Could you call it boasting, when they were both doing it, and each fascinated by the other's accounts?

This really *was* a fantasy world, wasn't it?

Which reminded Rod of reality. "Fess—it's really the dead of winter, isn't it?"

"Yes, Rod. The night's temperature was close to zero."

"How'd I make it through?" Rod frowned; he had some memory of having conjured up a sleeping bag. He looked down and, sure enough, he was in one. "Where'd *this* come from? In the real world, I mean."

"From your spaceship, Rod, buried though it may be."

"That's right, it *is* navy issue, isn't it?"

"Designed to maintain an interior temperature of seventy degrees Fahrenheit, down to an exterior temperature of negative twenty degrees, Rod, and using the temperature differential as . . ."

"Yeah, yeah, I read the instruction manual, too. But how'd it get here?"

The robot hesitated.

"Go on, tell me. I can take it."

"It appeared with a small thunderclap, Rod. Modwis and the other squire found it quite impressive."

Rod glanced at the fire; the squire gave him a cheery smile. He already had a kettle hanging from a tripod over the flames. Modwis was folding up his blankets. "No doubt that's why they slept on the far side of the fire. But *how did the sleeping bag get here?*"

Fess was very slow in answering. "Only you and I knew of its existence, Rod."

"You mean that, even in the real world, I conjured it here?" Rod asked.

"No doubt an exercise in teleportation."

"Yeah, but I've never been able to do much in that line before." Rod frowned. "Except projecting myself, and anything I'm holding on to . . ."

"Your talents continue to amaze me, Rod."

"You're not the only one. Well, let's start the day."

The knights were induced to stop their conversation long enough to partake of some porridge Modwis concocted, and some quick bread the squire produced. Not much, though—Rod didn't see how they could fuel enough muscle to support all that steel, on so few calories. On the other hand, he could appreciate the difficulties of becoming obese inside a suit of armor.

With camp struck and the fire doused, they hit the road again, Rod riding right behind the two knights, whether he wanted to or not, the squire and Modwis bringing up the rear—whether *they* wanted to or not. Rod was wondering whether he was really hearing a new story coming from the Knight of the Golden Helmet, or whether the old man was beginning to repeat himself—all the battles began to blur together, after a while—when there was a mad cawing, and a featherball struck out of a cloudless sky.

It may have come cloaked in feathers, but it had sharp claws that tore through his clothing—and it *stank!* Rod batted the thing away, and it squawked, "Well, I never! What a way to treat a lady! Take *that!*" And a wing slammed into his face. It didn't hurt much, but it blinded him enough to keep him from fending off the claws—and this time, they took out a chunk of his chest. Rod bellowed in fury and shoved the thing away, pulling his sword.

"Oh, that's right, use a blade on a poor defenseless female!" his attacker cackled. "Well, if you want to use *weapons . . .*" It swooped away from him, and something cracked into the top of his head. It didn't hurt, but he felt a warm fluid oozing down through his hair—and it stank at least as bad as the bird!

What kind of fowl laid *rotten* eggs?

He pushed the mess back away from his forehead, shuddering at the feel of the goo, and got a good look at his attacker. It was indeed a foul fowl, a huge female bird, the size of a condor—but she had a woman's head, and pendulous breasts. Her hair had never heard of a comb, much less shampoo, and her feathers were filthy. Rod obviously wasn't smelling her natural odor, but that of her food—several years' worth of it.

A harpy.

Beyond him, the two knights were thrashing about, knocking harpies out of the air—but they weren't using their swords, so the birds just kept swooping back.

Rod could understand. Somehow it didn't feel right, using a sword on something that looked like a woman.

The harpy was screeching back to the attack like a dive-bomber, and Rod suddenly saw the advantages of a shield. Not having one, he glared at the egg that plummeted toward him and thought *Feedback!* at it. The egg halted, looped up, and began chasing the harpy. She saw it coming, gave a squawk of dismay, and swerved out of its way.

It swerved to follow.

"*He's* doing it," her buddy called. "Distract him, and it'll drop!" She suited the action to the word; her idea of distraction was aiming for the eyes, claws first.

Rod ducked, came up fast, and caught her under his arm, managing two good swats on the tail feathers before his nose couldn't take any more. She went off in a flutter of fluster—but the egg was still chasing her buddy.

"Take it back!" she cried, arrowing straight for Rod and swerving aside at the last minute. He saw it coming, with horror, and ducked, but not fast enough. The shell broke on his forehead and his head filled with the sulphurous reek. He swatted at his face, trying to clear the mess, and intercepted the talons that were reaching for his eyes. He caught them, and rage boiled up. Chivalry countered it, but chivalry was wearing thin. He swung the harpy around his head. She cried, "Don't you *dare!*" so he did—he tossed her right into her colleague, and the two of them went down in a squawking, milling cloud of pinfeathers.

Rod barely had time to see Modwis and the squire flailing about them with quarterstaves, swatting at harpies. They didn't hit them, of course—the harpies sheered off, squawking, "You're not supposed to do that, boys!" "You've got to play the game!"

Then the two who had chosen him were on him again, clawing and screeching. "You think it's time to stroke him, Phyla?"

"Don't be silly, Chlamys—he's not in a position to do you any good!"

Rod decided it was time to be offensive. "Charge!"

Fess leaped straight at the two harpies.

They got out of the way in time, with squawks of indignation. "Stay away from him, Phyla—you've got to associate with the right people."

"Yes, it's all in who you know."

"Where to, Rod?"

"Around in a circle, Fess. Get 'em chasing their tail feathers."

The heinous hens were right behind him. "Oh, so you think you can get away with it, eh? He doesn't know much about harpies, does he, Phyla?"

"Let's show him!" her mate cackled, and they peeled off into the blue, going for altitude.

Now! while they were away for a moment. Rod leaned down and caught up, not a staff, but a whole fallen branch, late of a pine tree. As the female Fokkers roared down at him, he swirled the branch around his head in a *moulinet*.

"Oh, isn't that nice! He's sweeping up for us!"

"No, wait, Phyla! He's . . ."

The bough crashed into her, sweeping them both out of the sky with a flurry of indignant screeches.

Modwis and the squire advanced, with determination and upraised staves.

"Get out, Chlamys! They look like they've got their mouths set for fried drumsticks!"

And they were off and running, flapping like albatrosses, barely managing to get into the air a few feet in front of the quarterstaves.

"Enough is enough!" Rod fumed.

One of the harpies banked back toward him. "Don't talk that way! You can't be honest and hope to get ahead!"

Rod swirled his bough at her, then squeezed his eyes shut and thought hard.

The squires shouted in surprise, and the knights exclaimed.

Rod looked up and saw three cats with twelve-foot wings sailing toward the flock with happy yowls.

The harpies shrieked with horror and flew for the coop.

"Art whole, Sir Knight?" Beaubras cried.

"I am well, though reeking." The old knight was trembling with rage. "How dare such filthy creatures so befoul a belted knight!"

"Be mindful of thy chivalry, brave paladin!"

"Why, so I am." The old knight finished wiping yolk off his golden helmet and unlimbered his lance. "Those brave felines are sadly outnumbered, Sir Beaubras! See! Even now, the birds of foul feather turn upon them!"

He was right. The whole flock had pulled together and were wheeling back with caws of delight, straight for the winged cats.

The cats yowled and dove straight on.

"What brave creatures!" Beaubras exclaimed.

"The cats are females, too!" Rod called. And they were; he'd had a last-minute inspiration.

"Then we must give them rescue! Charge!" And the old knight galloped off, lance spearing straight up toward the flock. His squire kicked his donkey and galloped after him, staff whirling.

The harpies saw them coming and changed their minds;

this looked too much like an even fight. With squawks of dismay, the whole flock wheeled and headed back toward its roost in an old windmill.

The old knight streaked away in pursuit, his squire riding frantically after.

"I shall be sorry to lose their company," Beaubras mused, watching knight and squire depart, "though I cannot deny they are needed here."

"They've got the right stuff," Rod demurred, "but they weren't really all that great as fighters, you know."

"Nay—though who knows what doughty deeds they may once have done?"

Rod privately thought that Beaubras should know if anybody did, after all that talk, but he was polite enough not to say so.

The flock of harpies dove into the old windmill. It was dilapidated with the years, its sails torn and dusty. With a high, clear call, the old knight charged straight at it, his squire close behind him.

"Yet their faith in chivalry is inspiring," Sir Beaubras said.

"Oh, yes," Rod said softly. "Oh, yes."

Modwis nodded. " 'Tis such as they who will ever cheer the hearts of those who suffer for the doing of the deeds they believe to be right."

9

The sun was directly overhead, and Rod was beginning to think about lunch when something roared. He noticed a Doppler effect and looked up, just in time to see a nine-foot-tall man with a hideous face and six arms charging down at him.

Beaubras shouted, reining his horse around and couching his lance. Modwis blanched, but he pulled out his iron club.

What else could Rod do? He drew his sword.

Then the ogre struck like an avalanche.

Rod went down under the first onslaught; he had a brief vision of huge legs churning past, of Fess's steel body flying through the air. Then he managed to fold his arms over his head, roll, and come up, his sword somehow still in his hand, bellowing with anger.

Not that he could hear himself. The ogre was bellowing loudly enough for all of them, and Beaubras, who had somehow managed to stay mounted through the first charge, sailed into him with sword and shield. Modwis was picking himself up, casting about for his iron club, and Fess was scrambling to his feet on the far side of the ogre.

Relief shot through Rod, with anger in its wake. He charged the huge humanoid, howling like a banshee. The ogre immediately assigned two of his arms to take care of Rod with shield and sword, slashing and feinting—and Rod was startled to find himself giving ground, slowly but surely. So, even more surprisingly, was Beaubras, and Modwis had found his club but was having trouble avoiding the cuts of another sword on the ogre's far side. Rod couldn't understand how the monster could coordinate three fights at the same time—but, then, he was too busy blocking and parrying to give it much thought.

"I cannot prevail!" Beaubras shouted. "He is enchanted!"

Well, that was as good an excuse as any.

" 'Tis more work of the foul sorcerer Brume!" Modwis howled.

Within Granclarte, he had a point—nothing short of a duke could fight Beaubras to a standoff.

Which meant it *was* magic.

But what kind of magic?

Fess slammed into the ogre's back, screaming; nice that one member of the party didn't need to worry about chivalry. But two of the ogre's arms immediately grabbed the horse and shoved him aside, almost as though they had a sub-brain all their own.

This *was* magic, and of no mean order! But how could it really work?

A huge foot sent Modwis flying, and a blade scored Rod's forearm. The hot, bright pain brought a surge of rage that somehow made Rod instantly clearheaded, and he realized that in the real world, the ogre must be made of witch-moss.

Change! he thought at it grimly, and pictured a huge ball of bread dough rolling down the road.

The ogre obstinately remained an ogre. Rod was floored—nothing in Granclarte had refused to change when he wished it to. He'd done some numbers on Gramarye witch-moss constructs, too.

He was so astounded that he was late blocking as the huge broadsword slashed straight at his face. Panic clawed as he yanked his sword up, knowing it was too late, knowing he was going to feel agony as the steel cut his head in two . . .

Then the sword jolted aside, and the huge mass of muscle toppled, leaving Rod seeing clear sky, with a roaring in his ears.

He looked down. The roaring was coming from the ogre, but that was his left ear; the right ear was picking up even more noise, coming from a normal-sized man who was holding one of the ogre's feet, face contorted with rage.

Fairly normal-sized, anyway—he was only six feet tall, maybe a few inches more. But he had the most fantastic build Rod had ever seen, outside of a health-spa catalogue. His shoulders were at least thirty inches across with slabs of muscle a foot thick, and his arms bulged like a normal man's thighs. His legs were virtual tree trunks, and he was naked except for a filthy rag of a loincloth. Not that it was easy to see—his whole body was encrusted with dirt. His hair was either brown or coated with grime, and it was so stringy that Rod favored the latter hypothesis. His beard was matted and mangy, hanging down onto the huge slabs of muscle that passed for his chest. His face was all staring eyes and snarling mouth, and Rod could have sworn he had fangs.

Even Beaubras had sense enough to step back and let this stranger do his work.

The ogre was on his feet again, thundering like a volcano erupting. Four boughs of arms grabbed for the wild man, but he leaped inside the squeeze and slammed a fist into the ogre's belly—way in. The ogre hooted in pain and doubled over, and the wild man slammed an uppercut into his jaw. The ogre snapped upright—but even as he did, one huge foot lashed out, catching the wild man in the midriff. He went flying and slammed into a thicket. The ogre jumped on that thicket with both feet—but the wild man squirmed out behind his heels, flipped over on his back, and kicked the ogre's legs out from under him.

The ogre fell—backward.

The wild man moved fast, incredibly fast. The ogre landed on hard ground, and the wild man jumped on *him* with both feet. The ogre's breath whooshed out, but he caught the wild man's ankles and threw him away into the forest.

"We must aid!" Somehow, Beaubras had come up with a new lance.

"No, wait!" Rod set a hand on his arm. "The wild man's not out yet!"

No, not a bit. He came charging back out of the brush, bellowing like a bull, and hit the ogre like a fullback, shoulder into the monster's hips. The two of them went sailing ten feet before the ogre smashed into a tree. The tree went over, and so did the ogre.

"Whence came this champion?" Beaubras gasped. "Olympus?"

"No," Rod answered. "Ariosto."

The fighters were all thrashing legs and grabbing hands, but somehow, the ogre was on his belly, and the wild man was slamming the monster's head against a rock, again and again, actually shouting something that sounded like numbers.

The rock was splitting.

The wild man had mercy on the granite and tossed the ogre down with something that certainly had the right intonation for an oath of disgust. The six arms twitched feebly, and the wild man kicked the huge ribs with contempt. He spat, and turned away.

And saw Rod, Beaubras, and Modwis.

For a long moment, they stood there, staring at each other, while prickles of apprehension flitted their way up Rod's spine.

Then the wild man bellowed and charged.

"Split up!" Rod yelled, and Fess leaped to the side. Modwis took him at his word and jumped away into the thicket—but Beaubras leveled his lance and charged straight ahead.

Rod moaned, then stared. If he hadn't seen it, he wouldn't have believed it—but the wild man caught the knight's lance, turning as he did, and heaving—and Sir Beaubras went sailing through the air to slam down into the thicket.

Rod couldn't let him be killed! He shouted and rode straight for the wild man.

On the other side, Modwis came at full donkey-gallop.

The wild man turned to grapple Rod, ignoring Modwis— and found himself facing flashing steel hooves as Fess reared, whinnying. But he dodged adroitly, caught Fess's fetlocks, and was turning to heave when Modwis crashed into him headfirst.

His head had a steel cap on it.

The wild man said "Hunh!" very clearly, in that tone that indicates a tightening of the stomach muscles, and was immobile for just a moment.

Rod seized the moment—also the wild man's hair.

He almost dropped it in disgust, and he could have sworn he felt something crawling over his fingers—but he called, "Reverse!" and Fess kicked free of the wild man's hold, slamming his forehooves down and pushing back hard. The wild man bellowed in anger, but he was off balance for another second, as Modwis dismounted and yanked up his ankles. The wild man fell with a roar. Rod dropped his hair (thankfully) and shouted, "Roll him, Fess!"

As the wild man tried to get an arm under himself, the great black horse pushed with a hoof, rolling him over, and shoved hard between the shoulder blades. The wild man went down hard.

Rod knew that sheer strength couldn't hold this superman, not even the strength of Fess's relay reflexes and servo-powered "muscles." But they *were* in the domain of fantasy, and it was Rod's universe now, after all—hadn't he inherited it? So he thought of a force field, and saw the air thicken around the wild man.

Incredibly, he still moved. More slowly—he was slowed down to normal speed for a man with quick reflexes—but he still thrashed, roaring, and probably would have toppled Fess in another second. But the spell delayed him just long enough for Beaubras to leap in, grabbing at the wild man's left arm. Rod jumped out of the saddle to grab his right. The wild man kicked, roaring, and Modwis went flying, but Rod caught the ankle on the rebound and yanked it up to the buttock. "Cradle hold!"

Beaubras got the idea, if not the term, and managed to catch the other leg and shove it up in similar fashion. The wild man thrashed and roared, but there really wasn't much he could look forward to from that position, except possibly a hot shower.

Beaubras looked up at Rod. "What can we do with him now, Lord Gallowglass?"

How did Rod become the expert, all of a sudden?

It was a good question. It was a very good question. If they let go, one very angry wild man would be on his feet in a second, pounding their heads in—but if they tried to hold on, sooner or later they'd tire, and he'd kick loose on his own.

"Only hold him a moment longer, good sirs!"

Excellent idea. Rod renewed his grip and wondered who had said that.

It was a new knight who had said that, a knight who had dropped in on a flying horse—well, no, not a horse, really; its wings and head were those of an eagle. He leaped to the ground and came running—never mind that he wore full plate armor; none of the chroniclers had ever minded—and knelt by the wild man's head while he pulled out a very large test tube. There was a label on it, but Rod couldn't make it out; he was a little busy at the moment. The new knight ignored the wild man's roaring and popped the wax cap off the vial right under the wild man's nose.

What was it, his grandmother's smelling salts?

Whatever it was, it worked like a charm, which it probably was. The wild man stilled instantly, utter astonishment on his face. Then he looked back up over his shoulder at Beaubras and Rod, took in the situation, nodded slowly—and, wonder of wonders, spoke. "I thank thee for thine aid, kind sirs—yet my wits are of a sudden restored to me. Thou mayest loose me now; be assured, I'll not attack thee."

Rod looked the question at Beaubras. The knight nodded and, very carefully, they loosed their holds—then jumped back.

The wild man rolled to his feet in a single, sinuous movement, looking down at his body with a mortified expression. "Alas! Am I become a savage beast, then?"

"Thou art returned to us now," the new knight said tactfully. "Yet are thy wits all of a whole again, lord Count?"

"Aye." The wild man looked up with a pensive frown. "And now that I mind me, that first sickness of the brain is vanished also—that spellbound desire for the maid Angelica." His voice took on a note of wonder. "She is naught to me now—only another woman that I have met, and not a pleasant one, though still must I acknowledge her beauty. Yet I could not care less for her, though 'twas the news of her marriage that did drive me mad. Is't not wondrous, my lord Duke?''

"It is, surely," the duke answered. "Thou dost remember, then?''

"Remember! Ah, would that I did not!" The count squeezed his eyes shut. "Every wild, senseless act of utter destruction that I have wrought—the flocks scattered, the cattle torn limb from limb, the trees uprooted, the fields laid waste! Ah, the poor folk who have suffered from my madness!" A tear glittered on his cheek.

" 'Tis done, my lord Count," the new knight said softly. " 'Tis done; thou hast regained thy wits, and are restored to thy lord and uncle, Charles.''

"Aye, thanks to thee, brave Duke." The wild man raised his head with a frown. "But mine uncle? What of him?''

"He is in Paris, my lord, besieged by a Saracen host.''

"Why, we must go to him, then!" the wild man cried. "Come, my lord! Away!" But he remembered to turn to Beaubras, Rod, and Modwis, inclining his head. "Knight and gentlemen, I thank thee. Most gracious aid hast thou given, and at no small peril to thyselves. This act of charity shall be numbered among thy glories; the minstrels shall sing of it.''

Rod and his companions could only return the bow in mute acknowledgement.

Then the count turned and marched away, clothed in dignity and grime, grim resolution in every line of his filthy body.

The duke hurried after him, whipping the cloak off his own shoulders and throwing it over the count's.

The hippogriff took wing, circled once over the new clearing (the ogre and the wild man had knocked down a lot of trees in their fight), and flew off after his master.

"A most noble count," Beaubras murmured.

"As noble as yourself," Rod agreed, but inside, he was wondering just how a classic epic and a classic parody had both become mixed up in his grandfather's romance.

He shrugged and turned away—it had been a thrill, anyway, and he'd manage to sort it out someday.

The ogre groaned and stirred.

"Oh. Yes." Rod turned, frowning. "We still have this little problem to dispose of, don't we?"

"Aye." Beaubras drew his sword, just in case. "What shall we do with him, Lord Gallowglass?"

Rod shrugged. "Why take chances? We know he's got to be guilty of something." And he whipped out his blade, poised for the death blow.

Inside him, someone was screaming and protesting, but the world seemed to be reddening, Rod could feel his pulse pounding in his temples, and suddenly, he knew that if he let this creature live, it would hunt him down and kill him, it and all its ilk, tracking him down day by day until finally, exhausted, he could run no more . . .

But there was a hand staying his arm, a hand that didn't push or grab, just rested there, and a voice that filled his head, saying, "Nay, Lord Gallowglass. To slay in cold blood is a woeful transgression 'gainst chivalry!"

Rod wanted to put down the sword, but the image of the ogre stalking him still made his heart race, the dark, misshapen thing tracking him through a moonless night . . . "If we don't kill him in cold blood, he'll kill us in hot blood!"

The ogre suddenly stirred, muttering something that sounded like agreement. Rod lifted the sword a little higher, but another voice filled his head, Fess's, saying, "Remember, Rod, that what you see may not be what truly exists."

The sword wavered, and beneath its point, as though mist were clearing, the ogre's shape became translucent.

Rod seemed to see inside it, see three men heaped one atop another, jostling each other as they regained consciousness. Not filthy half-beasts, either, but clean-shaven men dressed in neat tunics and hose, made of good cloth—far better than real peasants wore, though they resembled peasant styles.

Rod's voice shook. "Ogre or assassins, they're still enemies who will kill me if I give them the chance!"

"Then we will not give him that chance," Beaubras said simply. "We will leave him bound hand and foot, and will be long gone ere he can work himself free."

And it *was* an "it," not a "them"—it was only a single ogre again, thrusting himself up on one elbow.

The sword trembled as Rod lowered it with a single, short nod. "All right. All right, we'll show mercy. But let's be quick about it, eh? Before it can fight again."

On the instant, Modwis cast rope about the ogre, and Beaubras bent to push, rolling the monster over and over until he was wrapped in rope from shoulder to hip. It roared and gnashed its teeth, but Beaubras and Modwis stayed clear of its kicking feet as they tied the knots, the knight supplying the strength, the dwarf shaping the rope into a devious puzzle that only a wizard could unravel. Then they cast loops about the feet, tightening them so as not to prevent circulation, and bound the ankles together on the other side of a thick old tree.

As for Rod, he was feeling too sick to even wonder where Modwis had found the rope. His stomach was churning, and his head was rent with a stabbing pain. He turned away, hands trembling too much to even sheathe his sword, and held on to a tree, hoping the world would stop whirling.

"Rod," said Fess's voice, "are you ill?"

"Yes," Rod croaked, "and I deserve it. I would have run that ogre through if you and Beaubras hadn't prevented me, Fess."

"But you have relented, and it will live long enough for the foresters to find it and bring troops. You have done well, after all, Rod."

"But why do I feel so . . . ill, all of a sudden?" Rod let himself slide down to the forest floor, leaning against the trunk. "My pulse is hammering, my head is splitting . . . Look, Fess! I'm shaking all over!"

"It will pass, Rod."

"You . . . sure about that?"

The great black horsehead dipped down, nuzzling Rod's neck. "Your temperature is elevated, and your pulse is erratic. Your blood pressure is high. But there is no cause for concern if these symptoms do not persist."

"I'll . . . take your word . . . for it . . ." Rod swallowed. "But . . . why, Fess? So suddenly . . ."

"It could be an adrenaline reaction, Rod. You are feeling the effects of exposure, you know, and your body is weakening."

That was a horrifying thought. "What do I . . . need to do?"

"Come in out of the rain, Rod—or the snow, in this case."

"I . . . can't. Not till I'm sure I'm . . . safe. To be around, I mean."

"I appreciate the double entendre, Rod. I assure you that you do need shelter, though."

"But not just my body! Where'd that . . . homicidal fear come from? *That's* why I can't come in!"

Fess was quiet a moment, then said, "You are aware that you have always had an element of paranoia in your personality, Rod."

"An element, yeah, a streak—but what's letting it run wild and take over? I mean, if I had some warning, I could deal with it, maybe, but . . . No, don't give me any of that 'chemical analysis' business again—especially since it might be true!'' There was a little anger now, born of indignation, and it was helping, his pulse was beginning to steady, but his head still felt as though it were built around live coals . . .

"You need proper medical facilities, Rod.''

"Well, medical facilities mean medical people.'' Rod clawed at the tree. "And the condition I'm in, I'm likely to think they've turned into monsters, and go berserk. No, I have to weather it as well as I can, Fess. Please! I'm just going to have to, that's all!'' Rod staggered to his feet and turned back to Beaubras and Modwis, who stood by, watching him with concern. "I'm—all right, guys. Just a . . . bad spell, there.''

"Let thine heart be at peace,'' the knight assured him. "Thou hast done aright.''

"Because the ogre may not be as evil as I see it, yes. At the least, it deserves a trial by somebody objective—which I am definitely not, right now.''

"Thou art wise to see it so,'' Modwis rumbled.

"Wise, and gracious,'' Beaubras murmured. "I must commend thee for thy chivalry.''

"Thanks—but it's really just chronic self-doubt. Right now, I can't really believe in my own good judgement.''

"Then believe in me,'' Beaubras returned, and Rod said, "I do. I always have.''

Then he wondered what he'd meant by that.

10

High Dudgeon was high indeed. It stood atop a cliff that thrust out from the foothills in a sort of peninsula, surrounded by lowlands instead of water, connected to the hills by a narrow causeway. The cliffsides rose a sheer hundred feet from the fields below, and the keep soared straight up from the edges of the cliff.

They, however, were still in the mountains, just coming out of the pass above. Beaubras pointed at the causeway. "We may work our way down to their bridge unseen. Then, though, we must charge directly, and quite quickly, too, ere they can lower the portcullis, or send a party of monster footmen out to grapple with us."

"Where shall we grapple with them, then?" Modwis rumbled. "For certes, thou dost not wish to avoid this conflict."

"Nay, assuredly not." Beaubras grinned. "As to where, I care not, so long as 'tis within the castle."

"Well, it won't be," Rod said with complete certainty. "That causeway is a good three quarters of a mile if it's an inch. If they keep any kind of watch at all, they'll have plenty of time to drop the portcullis. Then they can sit there and laugh at us—or throw rocks, more likely.''

"Naught can stand 'gainst courage and valor, Lord Gallowglass!''

"Yeah, but anything can stand against stupidity. With respect, Sir Beaubras, we might do better to consider a more indirect approach.''

Beaubras turned, frowning at the impatience in Rod's tone. "Thou has ne'er spoke in such fashion to me aforetime, Lord Gallowglass. I must needs think thou dost know more of this craft than thou dost tell.''

"What—invading a castle? Well, I've been in on it once or twice, and I've found that courage and valor are no excuse for not using common sense.''

"Why, how wouldst thou come within, then? That keep is impregnable!''

"An interesting hypothesis,'' Rod said, nodding, "but you can always attack any hypothesis by questioning the assumptions on which it's based, Sir Knight.''

"And on what is this castle based?''

"Why, on the cliff,'' Modwis rumbled.

"Exactly.'' Rod pointed. "And unless my eyes deceive me, Sir Beaubras, I see a crack in that foundation.''

The knight and dwarf looked and, sure enough, there was an irregular line zigzagging down the side of the cliff.

" 'Tis but a hairline,'' Beaubras protested.

"Aye, but is not the whole castle only a child's toy, from this distance?'' Modwis asked. "From the ground nearby, that hairline might be a crevasse.''

"Assuredly, they who built the keep would have known of it!''

"And decided to build, anyway.'' Rod nodded. "So either their escalier doesn't go all the way to the top, or it's just as strongly guarded as the gate. This way, though, they can't see us approaching—at least, not if we wait for nightfall.''

Sir Beaubras looked dubious, but he shook his head with a sigh and dismounted. ''Thou art haply in error, Lord Gallowglass, yet if thou hast the right of it, thou dost offer a more sure road to my lady than the more obvious. Come, pitch our tents again! An we are going to work o' night, we must sleep while we may.''

It was times like this that Rod was glad Beaubras wore black armor and rode a black horse. The lowland lay still and dark; even an overcast obligingly hid the moon. But high above them, the keep of High Dudgeon glittered with late light. Snatches of song and laughter drifted down to them.

''Even their laughter sounds nasty,'' Rod muttered.

''None can rejoice with a light heart in such a place,'' Modwis agreed. ''They must ever be probing to discern at whom they may sneer, and to whom they must bow— ever, for this ranking may change at any moment.''

'' 'Tis at Lady Aggravate's whim,'' Sir Beaubras agreed. ''Who shall be Queen of the Hill an she is overthrown?''

''Let's try the experiment, shall we?'' Rod said. ''As soon as we can get up there. Let's see, now—where is the base of that crack in the cliff?''

''Off to your right, Rod, and around the bend of the rock face,'' Fess answered. ''My light amplification is boosted to maximum, but the contrast is causing difficulties.''

Rod sighed. ''Ah, wouldn't it be nice if we could see sentries in the dark.''

Beaubras gave him a peculiar look, but Fess answered, ''I have activated my infrared receptors, too, Rod. At this moment, there are only traces of small animals.''

''Around this way,'' Rod instructed the knight. ''It winds down around the corner.''

It wasn't exactly a crevasse, but it was certainly wider than a man, spiraling down the cliff face and into the ground, its shadows darker than the granite.

"Canst thou not give us light, wizard?" Beaubras hissed.

Rod glanced up. The castle walls blended into the rock without the slightest trace of an overhang, but they were only thirty feet away, and the chances of a sentry looking straight down from the battlements were small. "It's worth the risk." Rod drew his dagger, twisted the pommel, and pointed it at the crack.

Nothing happened.

"Why dost thou wait?"

"I'd, uh, like to be a lot closer before I show a light," Rod improvised, wondering frantically what had gone wrong. He was sure he had recharged the batteries.

Batteries.

He was in a magical realm, and batteries weren't magic. They didn't work here.

However, his own magic did. He cupped a palm and frowned at it, imagining a ball of light in his hand.

The fox fire glowed to life.

Modwis caught his breath, and Beaubras murmured in wonder, "Thou *art* a wizard."

"More than I know, apparently." Rod turned the will-o'-the-wisp toward the crack, cupping his other hand behind it to keep the back-glow from dazzling his eyes.

He wondered why Fess made no comment. Ordinarily, any new phenomenon was enough to send the robot into a tizzy. But the great black horse only paced slowly toward the gouge in the rock, and Rod thrust the ball of light in, looking about.

The crack was about three feet wide, and perhaps ten feet deep.

"That's why the builders didn't worry," Rod murmured. "It doesn't go deep enough to weaken the support."

" 'Tis not a knight's view," Beaubras pointed out.

"No." But Rod was peering downward, his attention caught by the lower depths. "I, uh, don't see any bottom here . . ."

Fess looked down, too, opening his mouth. A bat suddenly fell spinning down the shaft, its ears dazzled by the supersonic the robot had just emitted. "Sonar indicates bottom at fifty feet, Rod."

"Don't the riverboat captains wish they'd had you," Rod muttered. To Beaubras, he said, "It goes down for another fifty feet. Think the face is rough enough to climb?"

The knight, with a full load of armor, looked up into the gloom, frowning.

"There is a stairway," Modwis rumbled.

Rod looked—and, sure enough, what he had mistaken for natural irregularities were indeed a set of rough-hewn, uneven steps. He felt his scalp prickle. "What is this, an invitation to dinner?" He wondered who was supposed to be the main course.

But Beaubras shook his head, smiling again. "Nay, Lord Gallowglass. 'Tis the postern gate. No knight would build a castle that had only one door."

Rod relaxed a little. "But if the castle-builder knew about it, it will be strongly defended."

"Aye, yet only with such wards as he could render harmless—and what one man can knit, another can unravel. My misgivings are answered; it *is* naught that valor and courage cannot meet." He swung down from his horse and clanked toward the cliff. "Come, gentles! Let us walk!"

Rod stared. Then he glanced back at the knight's horse, jumped down, and caught up with Beaubras. "Aren't you going to tether your mount?"

"Nay. He will hide himself, and come at my whistle." Talk about training.

Beaubras smiled. "Wherefore dost thou not tether thy beast, Lord Gallowglass?"

"Oh, he'll, uh, come at my whistle, too." Rod took time for a quick glance back at Fess.

"I shall, Rod," the robot assured him, "and the portcullis can*not* keep me out. Call at the first indication of need."

"Thanks, Old Iron." Rod turned back to Beaubras with a grin, just as Modwis caught up. "Shall we go?"

They stepped onto the rock face, lit by Rod's will-o'-the wisp. He tried to ignore the flat denial his stomach was giving him—it felt as though he were trying to walk up the side of the cliff like a fly, stairway or no. His skin crawled at the thought of the fifty-foot drop just an inch away—it might not look all that bad, but it was enough to kill. It would be more than enough, as they climbed higher. "Uh, you might want to look for handholds, gentlemen." He suited the action to the word, finding a narrow cleft with his fingertips. "Just in case."

"In which case, Lord Gallowglass?" Modwis called up.

Black on black, leathery wings and putrid smell, flapping in Rod's face. He swallowed a cry of fright, emitting only a choked yelp as his body swung back, and he clawed frantically at the cliff face. Then it was gone, and he had to haul himself in while his stomach did backflips.

"Thou hadst but to say," Modwis rumbled. "We do comprehend words."

"Well, you know how it is, actions speak louder, and all that." Rod drew a trembling hand across his brow, removed a fine sheen of sweat, and trudged on up, clawing for fingerholds as he went.

Then it was all over his face, clutching at his arms and

chest, unseen but grasping. The ghost light revealed a vast many-legged monster running toward his eyes. Rod gasped and jerked back. " 'Ware!''

Metal hissed behind him, and Beaubras's sword tip probed past his shoulder. Cobwebs gathered in faint traceries on the metal, and the monster jolted, then swung aside. Perspective returned, and the vast obscenity was suddenly reduced to an ordinary spider, though a very large one, the size of Rod's palm. It scuttled away toward the top of its web, but the sword tip slashed through it, and it tumbled into the abyss.

"It was just a spider," Rod said in faint protest.

" 'Twas as deadly as the greatest dragon," Modwis answered. " 'Twas a Death's-Scythe spider, with venom that can fell an ox in a minute."

Rod went limp with aftereffects. Apparently there were a lot of things about Grandfather's kingdom that he hadn't known.

He wondered if Grandfather had.

"We must press on," Beaubras murmured. "Yet 'ware these beasts, Master Gallowglass—if there is one, there may be many."

"Inspiring thought." Rod hoped he'd hidden the quaver in his voice. He pulled himself together and groped on up the stair, holding his fox fire higher.

They were halfway up when the kobold hit.

It came hopping and leaping down the stair toward them, whooping and giggling with glee, a bat-eared, snub-nosed, fang-toothed obscenity with gorilla's arms and talons for fingers.

" 'Tis a thing of evil!" Beaubras gasped, and his sword snickered out. Rod braced himself to keep from falling back against the knight, fervently reminding himself that *anything in here, the lord of the keep must have known a way to guard against!*

Then the kobold was on him, all teeth and claws, ripping a huge gash in Rod's cheek, another in his side. Rod cried out as fear flared though him, and the knight's sword thrust past him, skewering the kobold neatly—but it only gibbered and cackled, and clawed up Rod's chest as it strove to reach Beaubras.

Anger followed the fright, a searing anger that revealed, in sudden clarity, the impossibility that a member of the elfin kind could be pierced with Cold Iron and not even feel it—and could have claws that could rend but, now that Rod thought of it, brought no pain, nor blood. Suddenly, Rod knew what he was facing, though how it had been made, he couldn't guess.

Beaubras bellowed, slashing, and Rod just barely managed to grab the knight's arm, throwing his own weight back against the cliff, as Beaubras thrust too hard and jolted toward the drop. His weight hauled at Rod, then swung back, while Rod glared at the kobold, willing it away, willing it to appear as it really was . . .

And a huge moth battered Modwis with its wings, upon which were two great ovals suggesting evil-looking eyes. But only the moth was there; the kobold was gone.

With an oath, the dwarf swatted the insect away. It bumbled on down the rock face, bouncing off the cliff, then turned, arrowing back toward the will-o'-the-wisp that floated where Rod had left it.

"I thank thee, Lord Gallowglass," the dwarf gasped, "though how thou didst banish that fell sprite, I know not."

"Easy—it was never really there." Rod took a deep breath to stop his voice from trembling. "Whoever built this castle laid a very thorough illusion-spell on this stair. He knew the counterspell, of course, but no intruder would. Almost did its job, too."

"It would have," said Beaubras, "hadst thou not been with us."

"And I would be decorating the floor of this shaft now if you hadn't speared that spider for me. Hey, maybe the three of us will make it, after all. Want to take the lead, Modwis? The next monster should be yours."

"By thy leave, I'll decline the honor."

"Yeah, it would be a little tough to squeeze past us on this stair. Next monster ought to be in about another twenty feet, gents, if they keep on coming regularly. All ready?"

"Lead on," Beaubras grunted.

Rod toiled upward, trying to look jaunty.

But the attack didn't come, and didn't come, and Rod found himself going more and more slowly, sweat running down his sides, waiting and waiting.

Then, suddenly, the sides of the shaft were gone. Hardly able to believe it, Rod stepped out into a large open space. He stepped aside—carefully, but there were no more stairs—to let Beaubras out. The knight stepped up, muttering, and Modwis followed. Rod thought of more light, and the fox fire brightened. He held it up high, turning slowly. The crack of night sky was gone; they were in some kind of cave.

"We made it," Rod whispered, not quite believing it. "We're inside the keep—and nothing else attacked us."

"Not fully inside yet." Modwis pointed.

Light winked off faceted surfaces. Rod stepped closer, frowning, and saw a large oaken door set in the rock wall, fastened with a large, gleaming steel lock.

" 'Tis enchanted 'gainst rust," Beaubras murmured in wonder.

"Makes sense, if they only want to use the key every dozen years or so." Rod frowned though, and stepped closer to investigate—steel made stainless by any means struck a warning note within him.

But it wasn't the lock he needed to guard against, for, as he bent down to investigate, something flickered through the light, pain seared his calf, and Modwis shouted, kicking and stabbing at something beside Rod, before the light dimmed, and Rod felt himself tumbling into the shaft, down and down, into darkness.

11

Rod seemed to have an affinity for dungeons; if there was one around, sooner or later, he'd wind up in it. It was a convenient place for baring the soul, not necessarily his.

In this case, he found out where he was after he got the aftertaste out of his mouth. The medicine hit him like a jolt of electricity, wrinkling his tongue with the intensity of its sourness and blowing off the back of his head. He levered himself up far enough to free a hand to feel his scalp, reassuring himself it was still there, and perforce opened his eyes.

He saw Beaubras, unhelmed and anxious, frowning down at him. His face lightened with relief when he saw Rod's eyes. "So, then. Thou'rt with us once again."

"So it would seem." Rod wiped his mouth with the back of his hand. "Pffah! What *was* that stuff?"

"A restorative potion. The wizard who gave it assured that it would raise me from any wound, no matter how grievous, provided only that I could still swallow."

"But after that, would you really want to? Though I

have to admit, it works like a charm.'' He frowned. "Wait a minute—it *is* a charm.''

"It hath restored thee most remarkably," Modwis rumbled.

"All right for *you*—you didn't have to take it. Wouldn't recommend it, would you, Beaubras?''

"I know not, friend," the knight said with a gentle smile. "I ha' ne'er tasted it.''

"What!'' Rod stared, appalled. "Your only dose of a magic restorative, and you gave it to me? What's going to happen when you're *really* badly hurt?''

"I will mend," the knight assured him. "I will ever have mine amulet.''

"Oh, yes—the Astounding Amulet of Ambrosius.'' Beaubras wore a magic pendant that could turn into whatever charm he needed, to get him out of any bind that Grandfather had put him in. It had been Rory's standard *deus ex machina,* which Rod had always regarded with amused tolerance, once he had been taught about such things. All of a sudden, it didn't seem so lame an excuse, after all.

Still, Rod felt like a robber. He opened his mouth to protest again, but Modwis laid a hand on his arm. "Let it rest, Lord Gallowglass.''

Rod locked gazes with him, and realized just how ungracious he was being. "I thank you deeply, Sir Knight," he said. "I stand in your debt.''

"Then help me to rescue my lady," Beaubras enjoined him.

Rod looked up, managing a crooked smile. Then he frowned around at the gloom, relieved only by the yellow glow coming in through the grille in the door. "We don't seem to have come up in the world.''

"Not so," Beaubras assured him. "We have come into the keep. Our friend Modwis hath something of a gift with

Cold Iron and its intricacies, and hath managed most wondrously with the lock.''

'' 'Twas a gross old thing.'' There was too little light to tell, but Rod would have been willing to bet Modwis was flushed with pleasure at the compliment. '' 'Twas quick enough work to turn it. In truth, the rust did withhold me longer than the mechanism.''

Rod nodded slowly. "Very good, Master Modwis. Then the two of you hauled me in here, I take it?"

"The knight slew the serpent first," the dwarf rumbled.

Rod had a brief vision of a bisected carcass, and wondered whether it had been Beaubras's sword or his iron boot. "So. At least we're inside."

"Aye," said Modwis, "and with none the wiser, so far as we know."

"We have but to find the stair, and climb up to the hall," Beaubras assured him.

"Oh, is *that* all?" Rod levered himself to his feet cautiously, but was amazed to find not the slightest trace of headache or dizziness. "Say, that potion worked like magic!"

"What else?" Modwis murmured.

"Poor choice of phrase," Rod admitted.

"Here is a better," Beaubras offered. " 'Onward and upward!' "

"I think I've heard that somewhere before—but never mind. Which way is up?"

"Well asked," Beaubras admitted. "There is naught but a barren hallway which doth stretch out before us."

"You can see *that* much?" Rod peered into the darkness. "You've got better eyes than I have!"

"Nay—I went forth to scout, whiles the knight did tend thee," Modwis explained. " 'Tis naught but a narrow hall of stone blocks, with another door at its end."

"Another door?"

"Aye. Who can say where it doth lead?"

"We can, as soon as we've gone through it. Think you can handle the lock on this one, too?"

Modwis grinned. "Can an otter catch fish?"

"So I hear, though whenever they see me coming, they just play around."

"Then let us disport ourselves," Beaubras urged.

Modwis turned and strode to the door. He laid his palm over the keyhole, frowned in concentration, then muttered something under his breath and rotated his hand a quarter of an inch.

The lock groaned like a ghost in mourning, then made a crack like a breaking stick. Modwis grinned and pulled the door open. He stepped aside and bowed them in. "Gentles, will you enter?"

"Don't mind if I do." Rod hurried to jump through the door ahead of Beaubras, expecting a booby trap.

The steel-bound log slammed down directly behind him.

Beaubras stopped, staring in surprise.

"Nay," Modwis said, "they warded well."

"Nice to be right about something now and then." Rod stooped to haul up the log, then frowned. "No, wait a minute. It's easier to climb over it, isn't it?"

"It is, in truth." Beaubras swung a leg over the log. "What is this gin, Lord Gallowglass?"

"We call it a 'deadfall,' where I come from."

"Aptly named," Beaubras judged. "Hadst thou not brought it down, I would have fallen dead indeed, beneath its weight."

Rod had his doubts about that. There were things that could kill Beaubras, but a foot-thick log wasn't one of them.

On the other hand, Rod wasn't Beaubras, was he? Nice to know that the knight's apprehensions, at least, were normal.

Modwis vaulted over the log and trudged ahead. "Thy light, milord?"

"Huh? Oh!" Rod looked back at the fox fire and whistled. It rose into the air and bobbed over to him.

Modwis stared at it for a moment. Then he said, "Yes," and cleared his throat. "Shall we climb?"

"By all means."

The dwarf started up the stairs, calling back over his shoulder, " 'Ware, gentlemen. An there be one trap, there may indeed be others."

But there were no more traps. Small wonder; the stairs were almost enough to finish Rod off by themselves. By the time he came to the top, he was panting and dragging feet that felt like lead—but Beaubras plodded steadily upward, not even noticing the extra hundred pounds in steel plate he was carrying. "Talk about fantasy," Rod muttered.

"What sayest thou, Lord Gallowglass?"

"Nothing worth hearing." Rod leaned against the stairhead and wheezed. "How . . . about this door . . . Modwis?"

"We shall see." The dwarf stepped up and set his palm over the keyhole. He frowned, then shook his head. " 'Tis strange."

"What?" Rod was instantly on his guard. "Is it rigged?"

"There is naught linked to it, no. Yet there is no warding magic, either. I should have thought there would have been."

"Overconfidence?" Rod said, but he felt uneasy.

"There was magic enough in the cleft below," Beaubras pointed out. "I misdoubt me an the builder looked for any to come so far as we have, gentles."

"Good point," Rod admitted. "Who knows? Maybe this door is here to keep people *in*."

"There is that," Modwis admitted. Then the lock groaned, and the door swung open.

Candlelight assaulted their eyes, seeming as bright as noon on a chalk cliff after the glow of the will-o'-the-wisp. Music and laughter swirled about them, punctuated by voices in sneering badinage. Rod squinted against the light and made out a multitude of forms, gaily dressed in rich apparel, milling about a huge open space. Distant walls hung with glorious tapestries, lit by sconces and chandeliers. "We did it," he said, half to himself. "We actually made it. Gentlemen, we're in the Great Hall!"

Then the draft blew his way, and he nearly keeled over from the thickness of the incense. It smelled as though the Buddhists and the Catholics were having a contest to see which of them was in better aroma with God. In his weakened condition, it hit him like a padded hammer. His eyes glazed and his knees buckled.

The steel chest of Beaubras held him up, and the knight murmured, "Courage, Lord Gallowglass. We must face whatever horrors the Lady Aggravate can conjure."

"I'll—adjust." Rod gasped. "I just hadn't expected the keep to be so odorous."

"Yet surely thou thyself did say that they who dwell in High Dudgeon are always incensed!"

"Yes, but I hadn't quite registered the notion emotionally. I'll manage." Rod pulled himself together and stood forth.

Actually, he stood second—Modwis had managed to push past him, so he was first in line when the guards attacked.

They seemed to materialize from each side of the portal, shouting and stabbing with pikes and halberds. Modwis's iron club whirled out, blocking desperately, and Beaubras shouldered past Rod, drawing his sword. Fear stabbed harder than the halberds, with anger right behind it; the adrenaline tightened Rod's sinews and pulled him back into fighting trim. He drew his own sword and plunged into the melee, hacking and slashing, but the only heads he managed to chop off were spear points. Beaubras's sword was a blur, and guardsmen fell back from his blade; their broken weapons littered the floor, and the circle around the companions widened as the guards retreated, step by step. Rod bellowed with joy and followed the knight, hewing mightily, with the fleeting hope that all he was *really* doing was stacking up kindling for the rest of the winter.

Then, suddenly, a low moan went through the throng, and the guards right in front of them drew away. The guards to either side stepped back a pace, holding their weapons at guard, and Beaubras hesitated, glancing up at the parting circle, then looking again as an avenue opened in front of them. He straightened, head high and sword ready, but he left off chopping. Modwis stepped back, too, but with a murderous glare and a ready mace. Rod was feeling a little more ready and lot more murderous, but he held off, anyway.

Fess's voice sounded in his ear. "Rod, why has the fighting stilled?"

"Because," Rod said slowly, "the Grande Dame approacheth."

Down the aisle she came, a walking mound of brocades and velvets, a maze of houppelandes and bustles and panniers. Her lantern-jawed horseface was crowned with a lofty headdress surrounded by a chaplet enclosing a coronet, and the amount of veiling that floated about her would have appalled even Salome.

"Nothing succeeds like excess," Rod murmured.

The lady stalked to a halt in front of them, jammed her fists on her hips, and demanded, "Who art thou, who dost come so unmannerly into my castle?"

Her effluvium hit like a ton of atomizers, and Rod

understood why she burned all that incense. Having nearly fainted once, he was better able to withstand the onslaught, but Beaubras had had no such hardening. The knight staggered back, and Rod had to catch him, throwing all his weight against the knight to shove him upright. Even then, he tilted slowly backward until Modwis jammed a shoulder in under the knight's hip, and the two of them together managed to restabilize him. Unfortunately, Beaubras was still at an angle, and Rod was not inclined to hold up two hundred pounds of knight and a hundred pounds of armor all morning. "The amulet," he hissed. "Pull out the amulet!"

Weakly, Beaubras fumbled at his gorget, pulling the bauble out of his armor. "O magic charm," he gasped, "ward me from this olfactory ambuscade!"

The amulet's outlines softened. It seemed to flow, elongating, then became hard and clear again—as a necklace of bulbous, tissue-wrapped lumps. A reek emanated from it, surrounding Beaubras's head like an invisible shield, and spreading out to enclose his whole entourage, all two of them. The knight's nose wrinkled with disdain, but he managed to clamber back upright, protected from the lady's aroma by a necklace of garlic.

"I am the knight Beaubras, and these are my companions, the dwarf Modwis, and the Lord Gallowglass. Art thou the Lady Aggravate?"

"I am." She tilted her head back and somehow managed to look down her nose at a man a good foot and a half taller than herself. "Wherefore hast thou come?"

"Why," said Beaubras, "to free my dear Lady Haughteur from the toils of this keep!"

"Ha!" the lady cried, and managed to follow the syllable with something approximating a laugh. "Toils? All is lighthearted gaiety, in High Dudgeon! And as for thy leman, she hath not been borne here, nor is held by aught but her own desire!''

"Why," said Beaubras, "then bid her come nigh me."

"I move at no man's bidding, sirrah!''

Beaubras winced at the insult of the "sirrah."

"An she doth wish converse with thee," the dame went on, "she will come of her own accord."

"I misdoubt me of that," Beaubras said, his lips thin, "and I will judge it for myself. In what chamber dwells my lady?''

"Thou shalt not learn of her dwelling, nor shalt thou seek it out!" the dame stated, affronted. "Thou shalt betake thee out as thou didst come in!''

"Nay," said Beaubras, "that shall I not. An thou dost give so little courtesy, thou hast small cause to look for it in others." So saying, he stepped forward, shouldered past the dame, and bulled his way through the guardsmen.

Rod and Modwis leaped to catch up.

Lady Aggravate gave a howl of indignation, and her guardsmen closed ranks with a shout—or tried to. Beaubras slammed into them like a tank with a sword in place of its cannon, all but sending up a bow wave as he plowed through their ranks.

"Where to, O valiant and noble one?'' Rod putted, blocking a halberd and cutting off its head with the riposte.

"To the tower," Beaubras called back. "My Lady Haughteur would seek the highest chamber."

"So would everyone else here." But Rod couldn't say it loudly enough to be heard; he was too busy blocking chops and thrusts, and occasionally finding time to wonder why none of the guards was receiving so much as a scratch. A spear point jabbed at him; he struck it up, caught the guard by the front of his doublet, and tossed him back overhead (he was amazingly light). The guard sailed by with his mouth forming a perfect "O," and Rod stabbed up as he went by, experimentally—but the guardsman rose up just enough to miss the point of Rod's sword. He brought it down in time to chop off a halberd head and, on the riposte, to thrust full into the halberdier's midriff—but the man started to turn back, and the sword tip slid past his tunic without the slightest tear. Rod recovered and called out, "How come I can't stab any of these guys?" Not that he really wanted to, but it was frustrating.

" 'Tis because they dwell in High Dudgeon, and are therefore not of a piece with the world," Modwis huffed.

There was no time to figure out what he meant, because Beaubras smashed through a door at that point (quicker than Modwis's technique, but not advisable for sneak attacks) and charged for the stair. Strangely, they seemed to be going down, not up. Rod and Modwis followed, backing down step by step, fending off thrusts and chops. At least the guardsmen couldn't quite hit Rod and Modwis, either. One missed his footing and fell, shooting upward, with an echoing wail. There was a crash from the landing above, echoed by a low and growing moan from the guardsmen. They lowered their weapons and stopped their advance.

"Can we trust them?"

"Aye," Modwis said with grim certainty. "They have failed in their purpose. They have no need to attack now."

"Well, we're still taking a chance—so, when I say 'Run,' we'll both barrel up the stairs. Okay?"

"As thou sayest," the dwarf grunted. "Save that our 'up' hath become 'down.' "

"Down we go, then. Okay—*run!*"

They turned tail and shot down the stairs like rockets, but the guardsmen made no move to follow.

Rod managed to catch the doorjamb and swing into the room not too many steps behind Modwis, and saw a spectacle of breathtaking beauty and sadness. Beaubras knelt, head bowed, before a lady who stood by the window, clad in a gown of shimmering iridescence—with a collar that rose up in points, along her cheeks to her eyes.

"It's a gown of her own tears," Rod gasped.

"And a sorrow her own making," Modwis explained.

"My lady," Beaubras murmured, "wherefore dost thou weep?"

"Oh, I weep with humiliation, Sir Beaubras! For all here do delight in belittling me!"

"The churls! How dare they!"

"They cry that they are affronted by my effrontery in coming hither," the lady explained, "and do therefore treat me with contempt and condescension. This chamber is of a piece with it—they pretend to exalt me, yet truly place me beneath them. Oh, how grievous is mine error! And how miserable my penance!"

"They who seek to dwell in High Dudgeon must needs beware of finding their places," intoned a gravelly voice, and they turned to see Lady Aggravate in the chamber door.

"Thou shalt rue the day thou didst thus to my Lady Haughteur!" Beaubras cried, springing to his feet.

Lady Aggravate laughed, a harsh and unpleasant bark, but Beaubras's lady moaned, "Oh, call me 'Lady Haughteur' no longer, but rather 'Lady Bountiful'—for surely never again will I think myself above my fellow mortals, nor deny aught that Charity may require!"

Beaubras turned, a delighted smile on his face, but Lady Aggravate screeched as though she'd been mortally wounded. "How durst thou speak so within my keep! Out, out and away! Be gone from High Dudgeon!"

"Thou shalt not so address my lady!" Beaubras bellowed, turning on Lady Aggravate; but she only grinned wickedly, malice and delight competing in her gaze. The knight flushed and stepped toward her, balling one iron fist, but Modwis caught it, crying, "Nay, good knight!

Dost not see? She hath near to caught thee, too, in her net of wiles! For surely, thou dost approach her in High Dudgeon!''

Sir Beaubras blanched, but Rod heard a different voice in his ears. ''Rod! I have detected a disturbance! Come down from that cliff immediately, for your own safety's sake!''

''What kind of a disturbance?'' Rod muttered, though his nerves screamed panic. ''A mob? An upheaval in public opinion?''

''No, on the Richter scale! Come out, quickly!''

''Out!'' Rod shouted. He grabbed Lady Bountiful's arm in one hand and Sir Beaubras's in the other. ''Up the stairs and out the door, wherever we can find it—and *now!*''

''Wouldst thou have me run from conflict?'' Sir Beaubras protested.

''No. You can walk. Besides, there won't be any conflict if you go fast enough.''

He had the right idea, for once—Lady Aggravate saw them coming and dodged aside with an outraged squawk, and the guardsmen were no longer in any mood to argue. They broke before the knight's charge, and the courtiers scattered before them.

''Which way out?'' Rod panted.

''Through the Great Hall, then the antechamber!'' Lady Bountiful answered. ''Yet wherefore must we flee in such haste?''

''You *want* to stick around?''

Modwis was cranking up the portcullis by the time they got to it. Beaubras lent his weight, and Rod blocked off the porter. ''Six feet is enough!''

Modwis locked the winch, and they stormed out. The porter leaped back to his job, and the portcullis clashed down behind them. Rod didn't slow, though—he led the way across the causeway at a pace that he hoped wouldn't tire a knight in full armor. But when he glanced back over his shoulder, he saw he was worrying about nothing— Beaubras was right behind him, Lady Bountiful in his arms. Finally, they reached the far side and the foothills, but Rod called, "Not yet! Keep going! A hundred yards from the causeway, at least!"

"But wherefore do we flee?" Beaubras panted.

"Just a hunch." Rod finally slewed to a halt and dropped down on the grass. "We should be safe here . . ."

You should, with a hundred feet to spare, Fess assured him.

"Yet whence cometh this premonition of thine?" Lady Bountiful sank down to sit beside him.

"You wouldn't want to know," Rod muttered.

"I assure thee, I would." Beaubras stood over him, frowning. "To leave without chastising that vile dame was galling, and to accept her slights thus was woefully less than honorable. Wherefore have I fled, Lord Gallowglass?"

"Because somehow, all of a sudden, I knew this castle didn't have long to stand. Look at the cleft in the cliff!"

They turned back to look, just as the earth began to tremble, and the cleft beneath the castle began to vibrate along its edges. The vibration grew greater and greater, till the whole cleft was in turmoil, tossing and heaving the castle at its top like a load of potatoes on a lumpy road. The rumbling reached them, then the wholesale roar as the cliff abruptly split asunder, and the whole keep of High Dudgeon came thundering down into a heap of rubble.

They stood staring, appalled, as the earth stilled beneath them and the thundering died away.

Then Beaubras said softly, "Gentlemen, uncover," and removed his helmet.

Modwis snatched off his hat, a tear running down his cheek.

But Lady Bountiful jumped to her feet and ran toward the winding downward path.

"Whoa, there!" Rod leaped, and caught her arm. "No, milady! The rocks haven't stopped falling! You could still be crushed!"

"Yet we must search to aid any who may still be living!"

"They couldn't be," Rod assured her. "That was a hundred feet, straight down. No one could have survived it, even without the castle falling on top of them."

"What a horrible death!"

"Yes. It would have been, if any of it had been real."

"How sayest thou, sir! How can they have been otherwise?"

"He doth speak so because all have no substance, who build themselves up through false pride," Modwis answered. "Is't not so, Lord Gallowglass?"

"Or false modesty, either," Rod agreed. "Either way, what little there was of them that might have been genuine is lost. Come away, Sir Knight and Fair Lady—this is no place for such virtuous folk as yourselves."

And slowly, they turned their eyes from the sight of the ruins of High Dudgeon, and came down to a less exalted, but also less spurious, world.

12

Beaubras's horse was as good as his master's word, and came at his whistle. Fess, of course, had already arrived, holding the reins of Modwis's donkey in his teeth. So, horsed again, and with Lady Bountiful riding pillion, they set off into the sunrise.

Unfortunately, the sun never quite made it that morning, and the rooster lived up to his name. The reason hit them in midafternoon, hit them by the gallon—or a gallon a minute, more likely. The wind lashed them with rain and howled in delight at their discomfiture, without the slightest impediment—they were on an open moor, and the wind was bound and determined to drive them out of its domain.

Modwis gasped, "Wizard! Canst thou not find shelter?"

"Yeah—right over there!" Rod pointed toward a dim glow in the murk. "Sir Beaubras! Lady Bountiful! Head for the light!"

They looked up, saw him veering away, and saw the glow beyond him, too. They turned to follow.

It seemed a lot farther than it was, but finally they found

themselves pounding on the door of a ramshackle cottage. Rod waited, then pounded again and, finally, the door creaked open a crack, revealing a suspicious yellowed eyeball surmounted by off-white fuzz.

"We're travelers, caught in the storm!" Rod called. "Can you let us in till it's over?"

The eye seemed to snarl something like, "Into the sea with 'ee," and the crack narrowed; but Rod had shoved the toe of his boot in, and kept enough room to call out, "Our party includes a knight and his lady!"

The pressure on his toe eased, and the yellowed eye widened. So did the crack, revealing a mate to the yellowed eye, a whetstone of a nose, and all around both of them, a wealth of wild, disordered hair that would have been white if it had been washed within the last month. It was hard to tell where the beard left off and the mane began, and the mouth was hidden in a curve between moustache and beard.

The eye locked onto Beaubras and Bountiful, and the door opened all the way, revealing an emaciated, wrinkled form inside a long tunic, almost long enough to be called a robe, with two lumps of rags showing under it. "Aye, then. Come in, come in from the damp."

Rod streamed in thankfully, wondering what the old man considered "wet," and very much misliking the gleam in the eye as Lady Bountiful passed in front of it.

"Blessing on thee, goodman," Beaubras said, taking off his helmet.

"I've no robes to offer ye, but there be fire." The old man turned away to throw some more peat on the single flame. The fire licked up, and the knight and lady came to it. Rod stepped up beside them. "Are there but the three of ye, then?"

"We have another comrade, who said he would take our beasts around to thy shed. Wilt thou permit it?"

"Aye," said the hermit, looking distinctly unhappy about it. "Yet there be grain within; let them not eat of it too greatly."

"We shall pay for whatsoever they eat, and that with gold," Beaubras assured him, and the hermit's eye lit with a gleam that was almost a blaze. Rod resolved to keep his own eye on their host.

The door creaked, and Modwis stamped in, streaming buckets. He saw his friends and moved over toward the hearth, holding out his hands to the flames with a sigh. "Bless thee, goodman, for thine hospitality!"

Rod could have sworn he saw the hermit wince, possibly due to the reminder that he was a host, which in turn reminded him that he was supposed to offer food to his guests. "I've little enough, gentles, yet thou art welcome to what I have." His tone belied the statement. "There is beer and barley, and a sack of turnips. An egg, too, if the fowl is right-minded."

Rod suppressed a shudder, and Beaubras said delicately, "We have provision, goodman. Wilt thou share our provender?"

"Wine." Modwis held up a pair of saddlebags. "Salt beef and biscuit."

The hermit's mouth watered. "Aye, certes that will be welcome! And now that I think on't, I may have a tuber or two laid by. Shall we fill the kettle, then?"

The stew brewed stronger as the daylight faded, and they ate from wooden bowls (from the saddlebags) by firelight. It made the squalid hut seem almost cozy, chiefly by hiding the worst of the grime and filth.

"Meat and drink do ever cheer the heart." Beaubras sighed, setting down his bowl.

"Yes." Rod smiled. "A full stomach and a warm fire always do make the future seem more rosy."

Modwis sighed and leaned back. "Who can look to tomorrow, when the day is long and the body weary?"

"Do ye not ken yer fortunes, then?" asked the old hermit, a gleam in his eye again.

His eye spent a lot of time gleaming, Rod thought—too much time. He sat forward, deciding to give the man all the rope he wanted. "No, I don't, matter of fact. Seeing the future is one gift I lack." Strictly true, on the face of it, though he could have made arrangements . . .

" 'Tis one I do not lack," the old man said, sitting rock-still.

The hovel was quiet for a moment.

Then Lady Bountiful smiled, eyes bright. "Hast thou truly the Sight?"

"In very fact," the hermit averred. "Give me thine hand, and I shall tell thy fortune."

"Tell, then!" Lady Bountiful held out her hand with a merry smile.

The hermit took it, caressed the back long and lovingly as he turned her palm up, then stroked it twice, a rapt smile coming over his face.

Rod frowned and glanced at Beaubras, but the knight was leaning back with a genial smile, apparently seeing nothing amiss. Rod turned again to Lady Bountiful, who was managing not to shudder at the hermit's touch.

"Thou shalt have wealth and happiness," the old man claimed. "See, thy Line of Life is long, and crosses with the Line of Love near to its beginning. Thou shalt wed a man most excellent, and that quite soon."

Beaubras frowned, but Lady Bountiful seemed to find nothing amiss. She turned back to give Beaubras a roguish glance. "Shall we wed so soon, then, my lord?"

"As soon as thou shalt say," the knight returned gallantly.

"And thou." Regretfully, the old man let go of the lady's hand and reached out for the knight's. Beaubras frowned, but held out his palm. The hermit took it, looked, then stared. "How can this be? Thy Line of Life is broke in five places!"

"What meaning hath that?"

"Why, it doth signify that thou shalt die, yet shall live again, and not once, but five times whole!"

" 'Tis but a seeming." The knight smiled, amused. "I never truly die."

The old man gave him a very fearful look, but seemed to be reassured by the knight's open, smiling face. "As thou wilt have it, my lord." He turned to Modwis, dropping Beaubras's hand like a hot rock. "And thou?"

"By your leave, I'd liefer not."

"Wherefore?" The hermit demanded.

"A man lives ill, if he doth know his end."

"I'll second that," Rod said quickly. "But you might tell us of the future of this land."

"Aye!" Beaubras agreed. "what shall pass for our court of Granclarte, goodman? And for the Four Kingdoms that have their union here?"

The hermit stared at him. Then, slowly, he knelt, and splayed his palms against the bare earthen floor. Gazing off into space, he began to mutter. The others fell so quiet that the flames seemed louder than his words. Finally, they became comprehensible.

> ". . . will rise 'gainst Alban.
> She shall not go,
> Yet shall find woe,
> And lovers' plight
> Shall bring a blight
> Upon the land
> And palace grand!
> The Courts of Light
> Shall break in fright
> And portions flee
> Until a sea
> Of darkness shall
> The lands enthrall!"

He thundered the last couplet, then knelt rigid a minute longer, eyes glazed. Finally, he began to loosen, till he sat in the dirt, holding his head in his hands.

"Magnificent!" Beaubras said. "Thou dost conjure a vision that doth make my brain to reel!"

"Do I so?" The hermit looked up. "I cannot tell."

"Why, how is this?" The knight questioned.

"When the Power doth seize me, good sir, it doth speak through my mouth—yet I have no remembrance of what I've said."

" 'Tis not so strange," Modwis rumbled. "I've heard of such aforetimes."

The knight frowned. "Then thou canst not tell us its meaning."

The hermit shook his head. "Was it so senseless, then?"

"Thy words were verse," Lady Bountiful explained, "and grand were they, and awe-bringing. Yet we know not that of which they spoke."

Rod did, of course—he knew the whole story of Granclarte, including its ending. But it wouldn't have been polite to mention it to the people involved.

" 'Twas a tale of doom, though," Beaubras said quietly. "That much of the sense of it, I caught—yet the doom of whom, or how it came, I could not tell."

The hermit nodded, mouth twisting. " 'Tis ever thus." He shrugged. "I cannot say, then, what shall come. Yet I may tell thee this." He looked up, glaring with sudden energy. "An there be doom for Granclarte, it shall come from the foul sorcerer who doth dwell in the castle to the east!"

"We know of him," Modwis said quietly. "He is evil, aye!"

"Evil! He is the source of every evil that may come to Granclarte! Even his apprentice hath left him, and his apprentice is evil enough, I wot! His castle is haunted, and

the evil spirits therein have seeped their vile influence into
his soul!''

''Thou knowest much of him, then?'' the knight asked.

''More than I wish,'' the hermit said darkly. ''If there is
a doom on Granclarte, I can tell thee he shall bring it—yet
how or when, I cannot say.''

'' 'Tis better thus,'' Modwis said, by way of comfort.

''Mayhap.'' But the hermit didn't sound convinced.

He climbed to his feet, slowly and painfully, and sighed.
''Ah, me! But the evening's fled, and wise folk should be
in their beds. I have some comfort that I've set by, to aid
me in my rest.'' He took an earthenware bottle and a horn
from a dark corner. ''Wilt thou drink?''

No one answered immediately, but he didn't seem to
notice. He pulled the cork and poured. A rich amber fluid
streamed into the cup, catching the firelight with ruby
glints. He held it out to Beaubras. '' 'Tis most excellent.''

The knight took it—reluctantly, Rod thought, but courtesy must be paid. He sipped, then looked up, surprised.
'' 'Tis mead, and I misdoubt me an I've ever had a better
drop!''

''A taste.'' Lady Bountiful took the cup and drank a
substantial draft, then passed the horn to Modwis. The
dwarf drank, too, then nodded and passed it on to Rod,
who wet his lips with it only enough to assure himself that
it was indeed mead, then passed it back to the hermit.
''Quite good.''

''I thank thee.'' His eyes were glittering again. He
drained the horn as he turned away—but Rod, watching
closely, was quite certain he'd poured the mead out onto
the floor under cover of putting both horn and bottle back
in their nook.

He turned back with a look of regret. ''I've but the one
chamber, gentles; we must all sleep herein. Yet the lady
and knight shall have the hearth.''

"Nay, we could not deprive thee," the knight objected. "Thy chamber's warm enough!"

The hermit protested, and the upshot was Lady Bountiful sleeping next to the fire on a pallet of old straw, wrapped in Beaubras's cloak. Modwis helped Sir Beaubras remove his armor, and the knight scrupulously piled it between himself and the lady, lay down in his gambeson. Modwis bunked down above their heads, and the hermit hunkered down on his pallet in the corner. Rod lay beside Beaubras on his own pile of straw, wondering how he was going to get the fleas out of his cape and listening to the rain on the roof. "Fess?" he muttered.

Yes, Rod?

"If I sound as though I'm sleeping, wake me up with a buzz, will you?"

You need your rest, Rod.

"I need my breath more. I don't trust this old geezer, Fess. If you could see the look in his eyes, you wouldn't, either. Besides, he didn't drink the mead he fed us."

Very well, Rod. The robot put the resigned tone into it. *I will assure your wakefulness.*

"I appreciate that." Rod lapsed into silence and lay still, very still, listening for the slightest movement from the hermit's couch.

It came after about an hour—an hour of fighting heavy eyelids; it was hard to stay awake when he was taking even, slow breaths, to simulate the sound of sleep—but Rod managed it. At last, his vigilance was rewarded by some heavy rustling in the corner. The old hermit appeared again, crawling out with a breathless giggle, a long rusty blade in his paw.

Rod rolled over with a mutter, still feigning sleep.

The hermit froze.

Rod snored.

The hermit smiled and crept forward again, lifting the knife.

But the fake roll-over had served for Rod to gather himself. He braced against the earth, ready to spring.

The hermit crouched beside Beaubras and raised the dagger high.

Rod sprang.

The dagger flashed down, burying itself in Beaubras's chest with a sickeningly soft, wet sound.

A split second later, Rod's shoulder slammed into the old murderer even as Beaubras cried out and Lady Bountiful sat bolt upright. She took one look and screamed, then screamed again and again.

Modwis was beside her in an instant.

Rod was battling for his life. The old hermit lashed out with the dagger, howling in terror, and Rod barely managed to lean aside from the thrust, then rolled back in, catching the old man's shoulder and pushing hard. He slammed over onto his front with a wail.

Lady Bountiful managed to slacken her scream to low moans, with Modwis's help.

Rod pulled his own dagger and yanked the hermit over onto his back again, blade ready for the death blow.

It wasn't necessary. The old man's own knife stuck out of his belly just below the sternum. His lips moved, almost soundlessly, with his dying words: "Brume . . . mine old pupil . . . he shall avenge . . ." Then he shuddered, his throat rattled, and his eyes glazed as his whole body went limp.

The thrill of victory coursed through Rod's veins, even as something inside him sickened at the sight.

Brume, this geezer's pupil? *This* was the sorcerer Saltique?

Beaubras groaned.

Rod whipped back to him. "Your murderer is dead, Sir Knight."

"It . . . matters not . . ."

"But I was too slow! I didn't think the old lecher could move that fast!"

"The lady . . . is well . . ."

Lady Bountiful moaned.

"Oh, yes. That was why he killed you, of course, and would have killed Modwis and me—but not her. Not until later." Rod's face contorted. "I should have struck sooner!"

"It . . . matters not . . . I shall . . . rise . . ."

And, with the promise on his lips, the knight faded from sight.

Rod stared, unbelieving.

Then he turned to console the lady—just in time to see the last faint wisp of her form, before it, too, vanished.

"Where he will go," Modwis whispered, "she will go."

"And you?" Rod reached out to touch the man, but didn't quite dare. "Will you fade away, too?"

"Nay, Lord Gallowglass. I may diminish, but I shall not cease."

But even with the words, he seemed to shrink, dwindling to a foot-high mannikin, and the whole hut seemed to grow more barren filled with dust and cobwebs, with gaps between the boards and holes in the roof. The rain had stopped, but coals still glowed on the hearth, giving off enough light for Rod to make out a form dressed in peasant garb with the handle of a knife sticking out of its belly—but the beard was neat and well trimmed, the hair was dark, and the form was stocky.

"Fess?" Rod whispered. "Who is this I've killed? Where's the old hermit?"

The door creaked open, and the robot filled the doorway. It looked, and nodded. "This man is indeed the one who admitted you, Rod. The old hermit was of your making, not his own. This hut shows signs of abandonment; I conjecture that the quondam peasant came only a few hours in advance of you."

"Quondam? He's not a real peasant? But . . . the dagger's real . . ."

"Yes, Rod, and he really did try to murder you in your sleep. If he died on his own knife, it is his doing more than yours."

The anger returned then, but nausea followed it. Rod lurched to his feet and stumbled out into the night, catching the saddle to hold himself up. Pain hammered through his head from one temple to the other, and he found that his hands were trembling. "Fess . . . I'm sick . . . very sick . . ."

"Yes, Rod. It seems to follow each spell of delusion."

"They're . . . getting worse."

"They are. You must lie down and rest."

"Not . . . here . . ."

"Then climb on, and I shall carry you to shelter." The robot knelt. Rod scrabbled into the saddle, lay down on the horse's neck, and held on for dear life. Carefully, Fess climbed to his feet and turned away into the darkness and mist.

13

According to an authority (i.e., a survivor) on Nile River black water disease, "The first day, you only *think* you're going to die. The second day, you *wish* you were."

Rod's malaise was something along that line, though it fortunately didn't last anywhere nearly as long. By sunrise, he was beginning to feel better, and when the sun rose, he had pretty much decided he was going to live. Of course, that didn't mean he was happy about it.

"The spells are getting worse," he muttered, "the paranoia *and* the aftereffects."

"You are still restraining your impulse toward violence very well," Fess contradicted, "though your physiological reactions are increasing in severity."

"But what is it?" Rod gasped. "It can't be something I ate—it's going on too long."

"That does not necessarily preclude the ingestion of a substance, Rod."

"If I did, it's one that really lasts. I don't know how much longer I can keep going, Fess."

152

"There is no particular reason why you should right now, Rod."

Rod jolted bolt upright. "You don't mean I should just sit down and die."

"Rod! Of course I mean no such thing! But it would be beneficial for you to lie down and sleep. You have not slept for twenty-five hours, now."

"A telling point." Rod suddenly realized his eyelids were drooping. "Maybe a few winks would help. Find me a cave, would you, Fess?"

Caves were not to be had, but Fess did find a fallen tree whose crown had caught in its neighbor's fork. Rod spread his cloak over a mound of leaves under the trunk as Fess began to drag brush to pile against it.

Suddenly, Rod stood straight. "Fess . . . somebody's on my trail."

The robot was still, then said, "I detect only animal life, Rod."

"Don't ask me how I know, but I do! I didn't say they were watching, but they will be!"

"Have you become precognitive, Rod?"

"Who knows? Anything can happen now! But they're on my trail, and they're going to catch up soon! Ambush stations!"

He disappeared into the brush. Reluctantly, Fess stepped away into the density of a thicket.

The forest was quiet. After a few minutes, birds began to chirp again.

Then a hand parted the brush along the trail, and someone pushed through. Others followed him.

Rod parted the leaves, but in the shadows of dawn, he could only make out three forms. He waited for them to pass, then slipped out onto the trail, sword in hand, and hooked an arm around the throat of the last person in line, yanking him off balance and lifting the sword.

The person gargled, flailing for balance, and Rod froze, realizing that the person was female. Then someone else shouted, "Papa, no!" and the ground slipped out from under his feet. He found he was floating, saw Gregory over the girl's shoulder, and realized he had almost stabbed his daughter. He dropped the sword as though it burned his fingers, let go of Cordelia, and thought *Down!* furiously. Rage kindled as his heels touched ground—slowly, as though he were sinking through molasses. "Damn it, let me *down*! What the deuce do you think you're doing following me!"

"Husband," Gwen protested, "we feared for thee!"

"Who asked you, blast it! Here I go freezing and starving, nearly being drugged and poisoned, just to stay far enough away from you to be sure I can't hurt you, and what do you do? You come sneaking after me without even telling me! Thank *Heaven* I realized in time!"

Geoffrey's lip quivered, but he maintained, "Thou hast enemies, Papa! We feared they might . . ."

"Well, they didn't!" Rod thawed a little. "Your concern is appreciated, but not your interference! I was fighting off murderous sneaks for ten years before I met any of you! Look, if you don't trust *me* to take care of myself, at least trust Fess!"

"Why, so we do," little Gregory said gravely. "Yet thou must needs own, Papa, that on Gramarye, thou hast had more enemies than e'er before."

The kid was right, and that just made it worse. The anger turned hot. "Yes, and I never know how many! Anyone I meet might be a futurian agent, any peasant, any knight, any forester! And how in Heaven's name am I going to be able to fight them off if my family won't at least do as I ask and *stay out of it*!"

"We cannot," Gwen said simply. "We are of thee, as thou art of us!"

"And you! You have never given me a chance to see if I can handle my enemies on my own! Right from the first, you were in there interfering."

"Interfering!" Gwen paled.

But Magnus intervened. "Thou hast told us, Papa, that thy greatest strength is uniting folk to fight along with thee."

"Aye!" Cordelia cried. "Thou didst say thy first great achievement was in winning our mother to thy side!"

It was true, and Rod had virtually bragged of it—but that was not exactly what he wanted to hear at this moment in time. "I can handle them on my own, thank you! Look, just say I'm on leave of absence. It's enemies to myself I'm fighting now, not enemies to the whole kingdom!"

"They are one and the same." Gwen had begun to harden. "They seek thy death, so that they may work their will upon the kingdom."

"Well, they don't have a chance any more, do they? You folks are there to handle things if anything happens to me! And you *can* handle them, can't you? You can handle them just fine! You don't need me at all!"

"We shall ever need thee!" Cordelia protested, and Gregory threw his arms around Rod's waist, clinging like a leech.

Rod felt himself thawing—but he looked at Gwen, and saw that all the walls were up. He hardened his own heart again and gently disengaged his son. "Then stop chasing me. Let me deal with my own demons in my own way. If you need me, then leave me. I'll come back when I'm well. This is one time you can't help—but, boy, can you hinder! Follow me any more, and you'll have me afraid to strike a single blow in my own defense, for fear what I'm fighting might really be one of you! Try to help, and you'll do me in!"

"Husband, thou dost wrong us! We would ne'er . . ."

"Not intentionally, you wouldn't, but . . ." Rod broke off, staring, feeling as though an electric current were tingling all across his back and up into his brain, making his hair stand on end. "Or *is* it intentional?" he whispered. "After all, you really *can* handle things without me. I'm just in the way now, aren't I?"

"Papa, no!" Cordelia cried, and Gwen stared, horrified.

"I notice your mother doesn't have anything to say, does she?" The anger flowed. "Not a thing! I've only been getting in her way, slowing her down all these years! Maybe she's finally realized she could have been the greatest witch in all Gramarye without me, that she could have led the revolution to put the witch-folk in power, and I was the only thing holding her back!"

Tears filled Gwen's eyes, and she shook her head, faster and faster, her lips forming words, but no sound coming.

"See? She can't deny it, even when she tries!" And Rod knew he had paused, more than long enough for Gwen to reply.

"Papa, there is not a word of truth in all of this!" Magnus stepped between his parents, anger beginning to show through a pallor of apprehension. "Mama hath never sought aught but thine happiness!"

"Who are you to speak, Heir Apparent? Who's the next High Warlock, eh? Who will be their king, after the uprising?"

"Thou canst not mean it!" Magnus said, hotly.

"But I do!" Rod caught up a stick and slashed out at them. "Away from me, all of you! Stay back in Runnymede! Run your power play without me! And whatever you do, *don't follow me anymore*!" He turned on his heel and strode off into the forest.

The trees swam past him, not quite in focus; blood

pounded in his ears. He bulldozed through the woods, brush crashing around him.

Then he realized that there was more crashing than he was making. He looked up and saw Fess pacing beside him. "What are *you* doing here?"

"You were unjust, Rod," the robot answered. "They never sought to hurt you."

"Whose side are you on!" Rod whirled to face the robot-horse.

"Only yours, Rod. I cannot be on anyone else's side, while you are my owner; it is contrary to my programming."

"But if you had a different owner, you wouldn't have to stand by me—is that it? Help the heir move up a little faster, eh?"

"Never, Rod, and you know it! Do not pretend to have forgotten your knowledge of computer programming!"

Rod glared back, confounded for the moment. He knew Fess was the one being who couldn't lie to him.

In the real world. Even in Gramarye.

But in Granclarte?

The horse pressed his advantage. "I cannot stand silent when I see induced paranoia distorting your perceptions of those who love you best, and most support you. Your wife and children are as loyal as I am—perhaps more so."

"I don't see how they could be," Rod growled. "*I* wouldn't, if I had to live with me. In fact, I do, and I'm not."

"Hear your own words," Fess advised. "Are you disloyal to yourself, then?"

"So you have to be even more loyal, to make up for it?" Rod's glare narrowed. "Even granting that, there's one big problem. How do *you* know what their motives are?"

"There are semiotic indications . . ."

"Interpreting signs can't let you read their thoughts."

"I can listen on human thought frequencies . . ."

"Yes, and *if* they want you to hear them, you will. But if they slip into family mode, you can't pick up their tiniest scrap of thought."

"I cannot decipher simultaneous multiplexing of decay modulation, it is true. However, I am working on the program . . ."

"But don't have it yet—which means you can't know what my tender chicks and their doting mother are planning in their hearts of hearts."

"Rod, you cannot honestly believe they would conspire against you!"

"Why not? Everything *else* does! Including you! Go ahead, side with them! Cozy up to the heirs! Just don't try to pretend you're still on *my* side!" Rod turned and stalked off into the forest.

"Rod! My devotion has always been . . ."

"Go away!" Rod thundered. "Get out of my sight! *Leave me alone!*"

He stumped off into the snow, and the bare branches closed behind him like whips.

Half an hour later, he had begun to calm down.

Then the nausea hit, and the headache started.

If it had been bad before, this time it was hellish. He cast about, frantic for cover, stumbled into the nearest thicket, and fell to his knees. His stomach turned inside out, but there was nothing there to come up, except a little bile.

When the spasms passed, he tumbled sideways into a mound of dead brush, managing to gather his cloak about him, and lay shivering as pain throbbed through his head. Finally, it slackened, and he fell into an exhausted slumber.

He woke to the glow of coals. Frowning, he started to rise, then remembered the headache and lifted his head very carefully. But there was no pain, so he dared sit up, though slowly. Something fell off him, and he looked down, amazed, to see that he was covered by a fur blanket. Who had thrown it over him?

For that matter, who had kindled the fire?

He stared at it, absorbing the fact that somebody had been close enough to kill him while he lay totally helpless, but instead had made sure he wouldn't freeze. Finally, he decided he would just have to accept the fact that the world really did contain some people who cared about him, whether it was Fess or his family.

Guilt hit, and hard, as he remembered what he had said to them, and the manner in which he had said it. It seemed incredible now, that he could actually have thought they wished his downfall, totally crazy . . .

Yes. It had been crazy. That was why he had gone away from them, to make sure he wouldn't hurt them while he was mired in delusion.

He lifted his head, feeling a little better about it all. There was still guilt about his rage, mind you—but at least he had been right in telling them to stay away from him.

Then he started at a sudden thought. How had his family come to be in Granclarte, anyway?

He thought about that for a little while, and decided that he had had a temporary lapse back into reality—sort of swapping delusions, Granclarte for persecution complex.

Was that to be the limit of his existence—just a choice of delusions?

He thought about it—and the more he thought, the

angrier he became. Oddly, that seemed all right now—maybe because his anger had no one to focus on. After all, who could be responsible for his current state of existence?

Whoever had pushed him into delusions, of course.

Who was that?

Modwis had said it was the sorcerer Brume, from his haunted castle in the east.

But Modwis was part of Granclarte. Who had sent him the affliction in Gramarye?

Maybe the sorcerer Brume.

Why not? So far as Rod could tell, the fantasy enemies who attacked him in the delusion realm of Granclarte corresponded to real enemies—real people, he corrected himself, then corrected the correction, remembering Fess's verification that the man who Rod had thought was a homicidal old hermit had really tried to kill him. If the hermit had been a real assassin in disguise, why not Brume?

It was worth a try, at least—especially in Gramarye, where evil magicians were a definite possibility. For that matter, Fess had identified Modwis as being, in real life, a leprechaun . . .

Rod looked around, frowning. Come to that, where *was* Modwis? He remembered the dwarf shrinking down to elf size . . .

His gaze focused on the flames.

Could it have been Modwis who threw the robe over him and lit the campfire?

Rod stumbled to his feet in turmoil, apprehension coiling through his belly at the thought that a friend might be within striking range. He stood a moment, taking stock of himself. He felt well, though, surprisingly well; the spell had really passed. He resolved not to hallucinate again—the aftereffects were murder.

''Murder''—he didn't like the sound of that. He shrugged

off the thought and started walking. If Modwis were here, he didn't want to see him, though Rod couldn't have said exactly why. There was a lingering distrust of anybody who professed to be on his side right now—or was it a distrust of himself?

No matter. The result was the same—stay solitary. For a moment, he wavered, tempted to take the fur robe, then decided against it; it would have felt too much like theft. Whatever kind soul had loaned it to him didn't deserve to have it stolen. He strode off into the gloaming, feeling renewed and invigorated—and hungry enough to eat a bear. Which might not have been a bad idea, if he'd met one—then he could have made his *own* robe.

14

If anyone was following him, they were smart enough to stay hidden. He trekked through snow-bound country for three days, building campfires when his toes grew numb and building brush huts when the sun went down. Roast partridge wasn't bad as rations went, and neither was the odd rabbit. Rod drew the line at deer, though—he couldn't possibly have eaten one before it spoiled.

Then the game became scarce, the occasional homesteads began to look very run-down, and Rod began to suspect he was in country that the sorcerer had milked dry.

So, replete with chilblains and chapped lips, but strangely refreshed, Rod came to the eastern shore, and found himself looking up at the sorcerer's castle atop a sea cliff.

It wasn't hard to tell it was a sorcerer's castle—the clouds turned dark and thick as they came swirling behind its turrets, and emitted bolts of lightning that always struck the battlements but, strangely, never did any damage. Rod worked his way up the cliff face, climbing higher and higher into constant thunder. Not for the first time, he began to wish he had Fess along or, better yet, Modwis.

Then the first dragon attacked.

It wasn't much for size, only a couple of meters long, but it roared with great verve, and its two-foot tongue of flame was very impressive.

"Shoo!" Rod shouted, trying to bat it away with one hand while the other clung to a fingerhold. The dragon shied away, and Rod yelped, shaking his hand—that beast was *hot*! If it was an illusion, it was a very vivid one.

The dragon circled and came roaring back. Rod drew his sword, sighted along it at the dragon's mouth, and cried, *"En brochette!"*

Unfortunately, the beast didn't know French. It slammed into Rod full tilt, the sword ramming straight into its brain. It died on the instant, plummeting down the height—and dragging Rod's sword with it. He gritted his teeth and yanked back, knowing he'd be lost without the sword—but his poor numb fingers slipped from their hold, and sea reeled about him into the sky as he fell, howling in horror. It took the sight of the rocks shooting up at him to remind him he could levitate. He thought how repulsive the rocks looked and, sure enough, they repulsed him, slowing his fall, stopping him two feet from their hungry, jagged teeth, then raising him slowly back up. With a sigh of relief, he settled onto his former footholds, felt himself start to grow limp, and sternly reminded his body that it had a task to complete. It complied with protest, pulling itself back into semblance of firmness, and started climbing on up the cliff—at which point, his brain came into play and sneeringly reminded him that, if he could levitate to save himself, he could also levitate to get to the top more easily. Astounded, Rod stood still for a minute, then smiled, stepped off into space, thinking *Up!* and silently drifted toward the base of the keep.

Then the next dragon hit.

It came roaring down like a V-1 rocket, flaming out of a

darkening sky like a reminder of doom. Rod swooped aside, but the monster changed course and came flaming up his backside. Rod whooped, did a backflip, and landed just behind the lizard's batwings, shouting, "Hi-yo, Iguanodon!" The dragon took umbrage at the epithet and tried to twist back on itself enough to scorch Rod. Unfortunately, it succeeded; fortunately, he managed to lean aside just enough for the flame to miss him. Its heat fanned his arm—and he twitched a little farther away—a little bit *too* much. He tumbled sideways with a shout, knees still locked on the dragon's ribs, perforce twisting it with him. It bellowed butane, trying to twist itself back upright, and the upshot was a downshot, the two of them twirling and tumbling down through the air toward the jagged rocks below.

This won't do, Rod thought dizzily, and managed to catch the beast under the jaw. The flame cut off with a burp, and the beast fought wildly—but followed its head. Rod managed to get its nose pointed upward and rode, swooping and swirling, back toward the battlements, clinging for dear life, and trying to hold on to his dinner. Rugged cliff face gave way to granite blocks with a five-foot ledge between masonry and precipice; Rod felt a surge of panic as he had a sudden mental image of himself rising up above the battlements and turning into a pincushion as the sentries gleefully took the chance for a little target practice. Inspiration struck, and so did the dragon, as Rod turned its head toward the castle. It roared toward the granite full tilt and slammed headfirst into the wall. Rod jumped off and sagged against the wall as the dragon flipped backward, its eyes rolling and wings fluttering, to coast spiraling down. Rod didn't worry; it was only stunned, and would probably recover before it hit the rocks.

On the other hand, if it did, it might come back for him.

It behooved him to find some way to get into the castle before then. He shoved off and rose once more, then remembered his vision of skewering archers, and decided to settle down to exploring. He cast along the base of the wall, searching for some sort of opening—and, not surprisingly, came to the drawbridge.

However, he did feel surprised to find it down. Rod frowned up at the gate towers. "Got to be sentries," he muttered. "If they're going to be anywhere, they're going to be here."

But there was no sign of a single mortal sentry; the gate towers looked to be completely deserted, not to say ruined . . .

A single *mortal* sentry . . .

Rod shivered. This was Granclarte; what kinds of sentry might a sorcerer employ?

Well, there was only one way to find out—but with great caution. Rod stepped out onto the drawbridge, then carefully let his weight down onto the planks.

The wood crumbled away.

Rod drew back, heart thumping as he watched chunks of rotten wood splash into the greenish oily waters of the moat. Yes, definitely there was more to this drawbridge than met the eye—more threat, less substance. He thought of floating, felt his heels leave the ground, and stepped out onto the drawbridge again, pretending to walk, though he really drifted across. But he let his toes touch the wood for appearance's sake.

Something cold slapped around his ankle and yanked.

Rod toppled off the drawbridge, saw the waters coming up at him, then a long, rubbery arm reaching up from the scum to his ankle. He thought repulsive thoughts in a panic and began to float up, the tentacle drawing out straight. Apparently it didn't like the resistance; it yanked again; hard. Rod was caught off balance and slammed down into the water. He just managed to catch a deep breath before the waters closed over his head, and he reached for his sword.

Something cold coiled around his wrist.

Another one slapped around his waist.

Revulsion filled him, and he thought *Up!* frantically, but the tentacle-owner was ready, and pulled down harder as he pulled up. His chest ached—this was taking too long. In a panic, Rod thought of water boiling into vapor inside a skin.

The tentacle on his wrist exploded.

Rod snapped his sword out and slashed through the manacle around his ankle as something huge hooted in pain and wrath beneath him, its voice filling all the watery world. Fear and horror battled inside him, and he chopped at the tentacle around his waist. Blood spurted from it, deepening the reddish cast of the water. He chopped again, saw another tentacle slamming down out of the murk and slashed at it, then chopped one more time at the arm around his waist. It fell free and he rocketed upward, agonized hooting echoing about him.

Rod shot out of the moat twenty feet into the air before he managed to contain his emotions enough to level off. Then the guilt hit, because the whole crag echoed with the agonized hoots coming from under the water. At least he could put the poor beast out of its misery.

So he did; he opened his mind, searching, winced at the pain coming from under the water but zeroed in on it, and poured every ounce of mental energy into a sudden searing stab.

Three arms lanced out of the water, straight and stiff, then went limp and fell back.

Rod floated in the air, shaken but relieved; the hooting had died, and so had the monster. The air and water were quiet once more. Rod sighed, then turned his attention to the gate before him. Shadows clustered there; below the iron teeth of the portcullis, it was dark and filled with gloom.

Rod screwed his courage to the sticking place and floated on in.

Darkness enveloped him, darkness filled with eerie moans. Not just one, mind you, but a dozen—first one, then another, then a third, then a fourth and a fifth and a sixth, a tenth, a twelfth, each on a different pitch, in a different voice, one dying as another began. Each voice held a different emotion, but the spectrum wasn't narrow—anger, lust for revenge, agony, horror, remorse—filling the whole castle with a droning, heartsick chord.

Something glowed in front of Rod, quickly becoming clear—the gowned form of a young woman with a bare skull beneath long, flowing hair, jaws parted in a wail of despair. Before Rod could shrink back, she faded, and a man appeared off to the side, a man with a sinister, scarred, malevolent face, and a skeletal body clothed in rags. He lifted a hand as though to strike, but faded even as he swung. A third spectre appeared opposite him, cloaked and hooded, baleful eyes glowing from the shadows within, a bony hand reaching out toward Rod.

He stepped right through it. There was a deep chill as the ghost's hand passed through his arm; then it was fading behind him. The next ghost appeared, but Rod drifted straight ahead, ignoring the fear that clamored within him—he was used to ghosts.

Not that he was ruling out a booby trap in phantom's guise, mind you. He was also drifting six inches off the floor, in case of sudden trapdoors or bear traps.

Finally, he grew tired of the phantoms and remembered his will-o'-the-wisp. With an impatient mental shrug, he made the ball of light appear in his hand. It gave off enough light to show him the stone walls and the archway beyond, but not enough to banish the ghosts; they kept appearing and disappearing before him as he moved toward the Great Hall, flanked by an honor guard of phantoms. The fear was still there, but it was contained by a feeling of irritation—after all the strain of getting in, he had expected something more than a trip through the Fun House.

Then he went through the archway, and found it.

The dais at the end of the hall was lighted by fireballs. Between them, on a tall, skinny throne, sat a bald man in a long red robe.

"Who comes against the sorcerer Brume?" demanded a deep and cavernous voice.

It *was* spooky, considering that the old man's lips hadn't moved; but Rod rechanneled the spurt of additional fear into irritation. He frowned. "*Against* you? Why do you automatically think I'm against you?"

The sorcerer sat immobile for a minute, nonplussed (Rod hoped), then answered, "None would come nigh Brume with goodwill. What seekest thou?"

"My right mind," Rod said instantly. "You cast a spell of madness on me, sorcerer. Take it off."

The man's lips peeled back from pointed teeth, and shrill, manic laughter filled the hall. Even though he was braced, Rod was shaken.

"Come closer," the deep voice commanded, though the laughter still echoed. "I would see the worm that dares command Brume."

Rod narrowed his eyes and marched right up to the dais—and wished he hadn't. Here, he could see the man's eyes. They were bloodshot, staring, and unfocused—mad.

Now the sorcerer spoke through his own lips, and his voice was like the wind through a thin reed. "Why dost thou think 'tis I that have laid madness on thee?"

"Who else would?" Rod countered.

"Hast no enemies?" the sorcerer demanded. "Are there none else who would wish thee ill?"

"There are a few," Rod admitted. Privately, he was beginning to wonder to whom the deep voice had belonged.

"Ask of those who have fought thee, then," the sorcerer commanded, and the deep voice proclaimed, "Thou art naught to Brume, mortal man. Why should he care for thee, he who hath ranked demons at his command?"

"Not the only thing that's rank," Rod growled. "As to the 'why,' I think you know who I am, and what I'm capable of. I tell you again: remove your spell!"

"I tire of this game," the sorcerer snapped, and fire blazed up between them, a sheet of flame that quickly ran in a circle around Rod, then began pressing in.

Smoke rose from his cloak, and Rod yelped at the burn. Hallucination or not, this was entirely too convincing for comfort. He fought to concentrate, managed a semi-trance where he thought of an ice cube crunching in on itself at absolute zero—and the flames died down.

The sorcerer stared.

"You mean you didn't know who I was?" Rod set a foot on the step up to the dais. "Now, about that spell . . ."

"Avaunt!" Brume threw a lightning ball.

Rob hopped aside, drawing his sword, dropped to one knee, and leaned the sword against the dais The lightning ball swerved toward him, hit the sword, and grounded out with a huge explosion.

The sorcerer's eyes bulged.

Rod tapped the charred remnant of sword, frowning, to see if it was too hot to touch. He thought of the ice cube again, then picked up the sword, envisioning a yard-long rapier. The blade renewed itself, taking on the sheen of good steel once more. Rod nodded, satisfied, and looked up at Brume. "I get it. You really are a magic-worker—in Gramarye, I mean; there, you're an esper. A pyrotic."

"What fool's words are these!" the huge voice boomed, and a spear detached itself from the wall and shot toward Rod.

Rod sidestepped, parrying with the sword. "Okay, so you're a telekinetic, too! Want me to show you what *I* can do?"

The sorcerer's eyes narrowed and, suddenly, Rod was floating off the floor, turning upside down. "Hey, look! You already showed me you were a TK! Okay for *you*!" He dove at Brume, pushed with his own mind. He felt the thrust of force that tried to deflect him, but bored on through it. The sorcerer shouted in alarm and shot out of his chair, dodging aside from Rod in the nick of time.

Rod sank into a crouch on the side of the throne, turning to follow Brume with his eyes, belatedly remembering that Gramarye warlocks couldn't accomplish telekinesis—it was a sex-linked trait. Only he and his boys were exceptions. So where was Brume getting that ability?

Fantasy, obviously. *That* part was Granclarte.

"Blasphemer!" the huge voice tolled. "Who art thou to so profane the castle of the great sorcerer!"

"It's pretty profane already, really." Rod lifted the point of the sword toward Brume. "If you want to get rid of me, just remove the spell."

But Brume's eyes suddenly flared red, swelling and growing until they filled Rod's whole field of vision, as the grandfather of all aches split his head. Dimly, he realized he'd just been hit with the most powerful blast of projective telepathy he'd ever experienced. He tried to strike back with a mental stab of his own, but his whole head seemed to be burning, and all he could see was red haze, filling the whole Great Hall, obscuring the sorcerer, the dais, the fireballs, and Rod's own sense of who and where he was, filling the whole universe so that there was nothing there but red mist and burning pain, in a present that had no past and no future, but existed and endured without hope of cessation.

But it did cease, finally; it slackened, the pain receding to only a normal headache, splitting Rod's head anew with every beat of his pulse, the red mist fading until he could see again. His ears gave him a hollow boom followed by a metallic grating and clunk, then a gloating laugh fading away into the distance. Sight, though, seemed to be limited to afterimages in brilliantly colored geometric patterns. Finally, he began to be able to make out stripes of orange through the afterimages. Then the colors darkened down to purple and blue, and through them, he could see the stone blocks that the orange stripes revealed. He frowned, turning his head, and saw a rectangle of orange light across from the stripes, a rectangle that was itself striped with black lines.

Iron bars.

He was in a dungeon again.

Rod let himself go limp. He might be in eventual mortal peril, but he was safe for the instant. He found himself wondering why he was still alive. If the sorcerer had been able to knock him out long enough to put him down here, why hadn't he just killed Rod outright?

"Because he wants to use you for bargaining."

Rod frowned, looking up, staring through the darkness, trying to see to whom he was talking.

It wasn't hard. The person in question provided his own glow—a very ruddy glow. He had a black moustache and goatee, with red horns and a barbed red tail. All of him was red, actually, except his black cloak, and he looked very familiar.

"Ready to think about that contract now?"

Rod sank back with a groan, and braced himself to resist a sales pitch. He made a valiant try to forestall it. "I think I'll hold out a while longer, thanks."

The devil shrugged. "It's your choice. Take him, boys!"

With a howl, a dozen demons swooped down at Rod, batwinged, scarlet-skinned, and horned. Rod yelped, "No fair!" and thought of an invisible shield.

The air glimmered in front of him.

The foremost demon splattered against an invisible windowpane, lay spread-eagle for a second, then peeled off backward and fell.

"What in hell do you think you're doing?" the debonair devil cried.

"Wrong origin." Rod tried to think holy thoughts. Who was the appropriate saint in charge of this sort of situation? Saint Vidicon? Saint Jude?

The other demons put on the brakes, but they didn't quite make it; they piled into Rod's invisible barrier like a stack of animated dominoes.

"All right, remember your duty!" the devil called. "Let's get about the torturing now!"

"But, boss," one little demon said, "how can we torture him if we can't get at him?"

"Think of something! Find a way!"

"I thought that was your department."

At a guess, Rod decided, none of them was particularly long on brainpower.

"Yes, it is." The big devil scowled. Then he grinned a devilish grin. "I have it! You can't reach him—but he can see you and hear you."

"So?"

"Tell him about himself." The grin widened, revealing shark teeth. "Start with the truth."

"The *truth*?" the little devils cried, appalled.

"You heard me, truth!" the big devil snarled. "You want to hurt him, don't you? Tell him about his *real* self!"

Of course, Rod reminded himself quickly, the big devil could have been lying.

Not a moment too soon, either. The first little devil pranced up to the unseen barrier, eyes alight with malice. "You've got a vicious temper, you know that? Oh, you're slow to boil, but when you do, you don't care *who* you burn!"

"I know that," Rod growled, but even so, he winced within.

The demon ignored him; it turned to one of its fellows, whose form had melted into something approximating a female in skirt and bodice. "Gwen, you're vile! Always after me, always nagging, never giving me a moment's peace!"

"*Me* after *you*?" the female demon shrilled. "Who came after who in the first place, huh? You think I made all these brats by myself? Let me tell you, monster . . ."

Rod kept a stony face on it, but inside, he was quailing. He didn't really think that about Gwen, did he? And he *hoped* she didn't think that about him. Though she had reason enough, Lord knew.

Then the "female" demon pranced aside, and the others stepped back into the shadows, leaving the one who was impersonating Rod—and looking more and more like him all the time—alone in the darkness.

Eyes open, yellow and glowing. Something snarled in the night.

"Oh, no!" the demon cried. "Get me *outa* here! Somebody help me!" His knees began to knock, and the trembling spread to his whole body. "I'm *scared*, damn it! He-e-e-e-l-p!" He turned to run, but more yellow eyes blinked open, and he backed up, moaning. "Oh-h-h-h— what'm I gonna *do*?"

Rod lifted his head in indignation. Whatever he was, he wasn't a coward. Fearful, yes, there were a lot of things that scared him—but he didn't run from them.

They'd just catch up with him, anyway.

"I'm gonna *kill* 'em!" the demon wailed, and it whipped out its sword. "If I can't run from 'em, I'll cut out their hearts!"

"They might be innocent," the big devil suggested. "They might be harmless."

"They will be when *I* get through with em!"

Rod emptied out inside. They had him pegged; he realized, with a sick sense of certainty, that the charge was true. He *did* strike out from fear—and, frequently, out of all proportion.

The Rod-demon seemed to shrivel as his clothes shredded into rags, darkening with filth. His shoulders slumped, his knees bent, and he moved toward the real Rod with a dispirited shuffle. He lifted his head and Rod saw rheumy, bloodshot eyes and a dirty, unshaven face. An icicle seemed to impale Rod.

The beggarman clasped the shreds of his cloak about him with his left hand and held out his right, cupped. "Got a coin, bo? Anything'll do . . . Alms, goodman! Alms!"

A prosperous couple brushed past, and the beggar swiveled toward them, hand out. "Spare me a penny, kind sir!"

Somewhere, someone was moaning.

The lady gave him a furtive glance, then turned to her escort, but he rumbled, "He isn't worth it, my dear. If he was, he wouldn't be begging."

"If you say so . . ."

Another prosperous gentleman pushed past him with a snarl. "Out of my way, human garbage!"

Someone was moaning, and Rod realized it was himself.

"Worthless," sneered another passerby. "Not worth a damn."

"No-o-o-o!" Rod howled. "It's not true! Not a bit! I *am* good! I *do* work! I *am* worthwhile!"

But the prosperous passersby were gathered around him now, pointing and gesticulating, sneering and spitting, and laughing with malice and sarcasm, laughing, laughing, and Rod was shouting now, wailing, "No-o-o-o-o! No, no No-o-o-o . . . "

"NO!" a deep voice bellowed, and the word stretched out into an inarticulate roar of anger. Something small swelled hugely as it swooped toward them, roaring down on them like an express train, hollow eyes narrowed in rage, mouth a circle of thundering wrath, bulking huge over the little demons. They fled screaming, and the apparition turned on the big devil, who stuttered in fear and turned to flee, but the spirit of wrath seized it in huge ham-hands, tore it in shreds, and threw it yammering away. Its wails faded; the devil and his demons were gone, and Rod cowered in abject terror as the huge spirit turned toward him.

Then he froze, unable to believe his eyes. He reached out toward the spirit and whispered:

"Big Tom."

15

Rod stared, galvanized. He knew that face, that form, even as the anger left it for a mordant grin.

"They'll not bother ye more, that ragtag horde," the spectre assured him.

"Big Tom," Rod whispered.

"Aye, 'tis me. Wherefore dost thou look so grim?"

Rod's mouth moved, but he couldn't force the words out.

The ghost frowned, then lifted its head as understanding came. "Thou dost feel guilt for my death, dost thou not?"

"I should have prevented it," Rod whispered.

"Thou couldst not. 'Twas done in battle, and 'twas an enemy's blow, not thine."

"But you were my man."

"I was mine own man, never aught else's. An I served thee as squire, 'twas for mine own ends—as well thou didst know."

"Yes." The reminder of deception helped; Rod got his voice back. He cleared his throat and spoke aloud. "Yes, you were trying to manipulate me for your totalitarian buddies.''

"There! 'Tis easily said, is't not? And as I sought to maneuver thee, so thou didst seek to make use of me.''

Rod twitched uncomfortably. ''Well, I wouldn't put it that way . . .''

"Thou didst not seek to sway me to support thee? Thou didst not seek to recruit me to fight for the Queen?''

"There! I *knew* I was responsible for your death!''

"Thou art not, and thou dost know't!'' the ghost snapped. "I did join in the fray to advance mine own cause, not thine! 'Twas my doing, never thine! What! Art thou so arrogant as to claim all achievement for thine own?''

"Of course not! You know me better than that!''

"Aye, and therefore know that 'twas mine own fault, not thine to steal! An thou wilt not steal credit, thou must needs not steal blame! So, an thou didst not wish to make me thy pawn, what didst thou seek?''

"To make you my ally.''

The ghost was silent, a glow kindling in its cavernous eyes. Slowly, it nodded. ''In that, thou didst succeed. Yet couldst thou have sustained that alliance, an I had lived?''

"I'd like to think so,'' Rod said carefully. ''We'd shared quite a few dangers together, not to mention a dungeon other than this. I had hoped that I could have persuaded you to stay my friend.''

The ghost smiled, and said, ''Thou hast.''

Rod just stared.

Then, slowly, he smiled, too. ''So. That's why you chased away my persecutors.''

Big Tom dismissed them with a snort of contempt and a wave of his hand. ''That pusillanimous crew? They were not fit to torment a merchant, much less a doughty agent!''

Rod smiled. Gramarye born or not, Big Tom had had a modern education—very modern; he was from hundreds of years down the time-line—and was a devout totalitarian. To him, the capitalist, not the criminal, was the lowest form of human life. "They were doing a good enough job on me just the same." He shuddered. "I didn't know I was like that."

"Thou didst, or thou wouldst not say so. Thou didst, yet thou art not—for each of thine evil impulses is controlled so tightly it ne'er can force action."

"Not now, it's not." Rod turned somber, remembering. "I'm hallucinating and attacking anything that moves, almost."

"Thou art, and hast therefore sought the wilderness, where thou hast the least chance to hurt any soul. If thou canst not control thine impulses, thou canst control thy body so as to minimize aught chance of damage."

Rod looked up. "You make me sound better than I am."

"I think I do not." The ghost sat down cross-legged and leaned forward, elbows on knees, looking into Rod's eyes with orbs of fire. "Thou art a good man, Rod Gallowglass, and a most excellent companion. Be mindful of that. Be ever mindful."

"I am," Rod said in a small voice.

The ghost raised an eyebrow.

"Well . . . I'll try, Big Tom. I'll try."

"Do." The ghost straightened up. "And know that this madness is not of thine own making."

Rod frowned. "My own making? How can insanity be 'made'?"

"By slipping a drug in a glass of wine," Big Tom returned, "or, in thy case, in a chestnut."

Rod stared.

Then he said, "You've been talking to Fess."

"In a manner of speaking." The ghost leaned back,

smiling. "What he hath said is in thy memory, is't not? And I am thy hallucination, am I not?"

"Well . . . I suppose, if you say so." Rod looked forlorn. "But I had kinda hoped you were real."

"Thou dost believe that I am, but in an Afterworld," Big Tom reminded. "If thou'rt right, it may be my spirit speaks to thee through this seeming—or it may be 'tis thine own unconscious mind that doth speak through me, for surely 'tis of that unconscious that thine hallucinations are made."

"I've heard that, that hallucinations are projections of your unconscious mind, as dreams are."

"To be sure thou hast heard it, or I could not say it."

"So you're the voice of my subconscious." Rod sat back, too. "Okay, tell me—what has my subconscious figured out?"

"Why, that the robot's computer brain hath the right of it, as it ever doth in problems of reason, and thy Futurian enemies did taint the old woman's chestnuts with some substance that doth induce hallucinations."

"And paranoia?" Rod nodded. "Yes, I've heard of drugs that will do that. But how about my family, Big Tom? How come *they* didn't start hallucinating?"

"Why, for that the drug given thee was summat which did affect them not at all, yet did wreak havoc within thy brain."

Rod shook his head. "Mighty picky of it. Do you know offhand of any substance that could discriminate that way?"

"Aye—witch-moss, the fungus that doth respond to telepathic projection."

"Witch-moss? But that's poison!"

"Would thine enemies be concerned therefore?"

"Well . . . no," Rod said slowly. "And come to that, I don't *know* that it's poisonous; I had just naturally assumed it was."

"Ask the elves—mayhap they know."

Rod looked up, his brain making connections. "But it wouldn't be poisonous to them—they're *made* of witch-moss!"

Big Tom sat there and nodded.

"And Gwen's father," Rod said slowly, "is Brom O'Berin, who's half elven. So Gwen is a quarter elven, and each of my kids is one-eighth . . ."

"No great amount," Big Tom agreed, "Yet mayhap enough."

"Yeah, enough so that the witch-moss responds to their subconsciouses, and molds itself right into their DNA! Of course it wouldn't hurt them—it would give them a little more psi power, if anything! But me . . ."

"It would magnify thy subconscious," Big Tom said, "out of all control of thy conscious mind—and here I am."

"Yes, here you are," Rod murmured.

He was silent for a few minutes, trying to get used to the idea. Finally, he said, "But why give me something that would make me see monsters?"

"Why," Big Tom said, "dost thou think thine enemy would leave thee to wander whole?"

"Yes, while he makes hay at home—or at least an insurrection." Rod stiffened as he caught Big Tom's meaning. "Hey! You don't mean the agent who masterminded this little scheme is still following me, do you?"

"Wherefore not? Would he not wish to be sure of thee?"

" 'Be sure' sounds uncomfortably like 'execute.' "

"It doth, and 'tis like to be uncomfortable in the extreme."

Rod wondered whether it was Big Tom talking or his own paranoia.

What was the difference?

Nothing—if Big Tom really was a product of Rod's overactive imagination.

If.

"Of course," Rod said slowly, "you *could* be a real ghost."

"There are no ghosts." But Big Tom was smiling.

"Oh, yeah? How about Horatio Loguire and his corps of courtiers that I met in the abandoned quarter of Castle Loquire?"

"They were witch-moss constructs," Big Tom said immediately.

Rod nodded. "Possible. Very tenuous, but nonetheless crafted unwittingly by some ancient bard who had known the originals while they were alive, and sang of them after their deaths. Probably shocked him as much as anyone when they 'came back.' But . . ."

"What else?" Big Tom leaned forward with professional interest.

"I have this son," Rod said slowly, "who has lately turned out to be a psychometricist. He hears thoughts people left in the objects around them, and if he isn't careful, he starts seeing the people, too."

"He doth wake the dead?"

"I always said he made enough noise to, when he was a baby. Now, let's just say some innocent who didn't *know* he was a psychometricist happened to walk into the haunted part of Castle Loguire . . ."

"Was his name Rod Gallowglass?"

"If it was, he didn't know it at the time. Besides, the first one who had that little 'accident' was probably several hundred years ago—and the scare story he brought back was reinforced by a few others down through the centuries. Who knows? Maybe they did it so often that they set up a psionic standing wave, and after a while, the ghosts existed without them. Or maybe I just did a little bit to raise their spirits, after all.''

"Mayhap thou didst. And if their spirits, why not mine, eh?''

"Right. Got an answer?''

"Aye—my bones are not here, nor did I haunt this castle whilst alive. In truth, I knew not of it.''

"A point,'' Rod admitted, "but not an insuperable one. You seem to have caught the popular imagination, Big Tom. I still hear beggars who were at the battle tell of the giant Tom who fell fighting the lords, and died blessing the High Warlock.''

Big Tom answered with a mordant grin. "I would not call it 'blessing.' "

"In your death, you gave me words for life.''

"I but enjoined thee not to die for a dream.'' The ghost's gaze sharpened. "I see though hast not.''

"No,'' Rod said slowly, "I'm still alive.''

"As I am dead. Yet I would die thus again, if I could be sure 'twould bring greater happiness to the poor folk for whom I fought.''

"Yes,'' Rod said softly. "They knew that. That's why they still tell your story, all over the country.''

"And doth greater happiness come to them?'' the ghost demanded, an edge to his voice.

"They're better off than they were,'' Rod said. "Fewer of them die in the lords' civil wars now, because Tuan enforces the peace. And more of them have enough to eat, and clothes to wear.''

"Yet not all?''

Rod spread his hands. "I'm doing what I can, Big Tom. After all, I can't spring modern farming methods and medicine on them all in one instant.''

"Nay, nor would I have thee do so—for to bring it to them from off-planet would mean they would collapse when thy government withdrew it. Then would there be great famine indeed, and pestilence with it.''

"There would," Rod agreed. "We have to help them build it up on their own, so it'll be self-sustaining. But we're making progress."

"And thou dost not seek the welfare of thy children in this?"

"Of course I do. But my kids' welfare is tied up with the people's welfare, Big Tom. Modern technology doesn't come in one generation. Who will be their teachers after I'm gone?"

"There is no shortage of volunteers."

"Yes—the futurian anarchists."

Big Tom turned and spat. "They would abandon all technology, and have my people scratching the dirt with a stick once more!"

Rod nodded. "Can't support the current population level that way, no. But do you still believe your futurian totalitarian pals would do any better?"

"Mayhap," Big Tom said, scowling, "yet they've little concern for the people themselves. Their devotion is to the idea, not the folk. Nay, I will take the cash, and let the credit go."

"Nice to know I'm coin of the realm," Rod grunted.

"Hast not wished to be a medium?"

"A medium of exchange? No, thank you. I don't even want to be a channel for ghosts, though I'm finding present company quite acceptable. Why—were you wanting me to broadcast your spirit to your peasant followers?"

" 'Twould be pleasant," Big Tom admitted.

"Then enjoy, because it's happening—and without any assistance from me. You gave the poor people the notion that they're worth something in their own right, not just in terms of how valuable they are to their lords—and the idea seems to be catching on."

" 'Tis good to know I have been busy."

"What do you mean, 'good to know'?" Rod frowned. "You've been walking this land ever since your death, haven't you? A guest at every peasant's fireside, and a nemesis at every lord's bedside."

"Why, how could I be?" Big Tom asked with a sly grin. "I am but thine hallucination."

"I wonder," Rod murmured, eyeing his old henchman and friendly enemy. "I really wonder . . ."

"Do not. 'Tis superstition."

"But there's nothing wrong with wishing the dead quiet repose. What keeps you awake, Big Tom?"

"Why, certes, the people, dost thou not see? I cannot rest till all are free from want and fear, till all are masters of their own destinies."

"Then you'd better get to working on some mental health schemes, not just economic and political. You're not exactly scot-free yourself, are you?"

"The people are my tyrant," Big Tom agreed. "An thou dost wish me sweet repose, do all thou canst to raise them up."

"I do," Rod said. "I will."

"First thou must needs win back thy wits. Thou knowest that any who have offered thee hospitality have been false, dost thou not?"

Rod stared.

Then he said, "I thought that was my own paranoia."

"Thinking that they seek thy death? Aye, that was false. Yet think—each hath offered thee food or drink."

Rod lifted his head slowly. "It *was* drugged!"

"Aye, though not with extract of poppy. There was witch-moss in the bread and water of thy hostels."

"Modwis? Even the dwarf?"

"I think not, or he'd have ne'er abided thy making meals at campfires."

"Well, he did make some remarks about my cooking . . ."

"Truth will out. This is why thou hast not shaken these hallucinations—because thou hast taken more witch-moss brews as thou hast traveled."

"That's it! I'm going on a diet. No food or drink unless I collect it myself!"

"The game thou didst slay was untainted, aye. Yet I would not bid thee eat such wildlife as thou wilt find within this dungeon."

"Don't worry—low cuisine never caught my fancy. But who's going to all this trouble, and why?"

"Wherefore dost thou ask?"

"Because I can't trust my own hunches right now. I'm paranoid, remember?"

"And am I any less? Be mindful, I'm the voice of *thy* subconscious."

"More likely my conscience. Of course, you *could* be a real ghost—in which case, you could give me an unbiased view."

"Scarcely unbiased—yet I'll tell thee that thine old enemies, and mine, did thus taint thy food, and thy mind, and do reinforce the dose whene'er they can, to keep thee crazed and disabled."

"The anarchists? Then there's an uprising going on back in Runnymede!"

Big Tom nodded, eyes glowing.

"How about your old buddies? Don't tell me the totalitarians are letting a chance like this slip away!"

"As thou dost wish—I shall not. There's no need, sin that thou hast said it thyself."

Rod scrambled to his feet. "I've got to get back to Runnymede! Tuan and Catharine must be going crazy." He stopped, jarred by the sound of his own words.

"Crazed, in truth," Big Tom murmured. "What of thine own mind?"

"With a rebellion going on, what's a little paranoia more or less?"

"And thy wife and bairns?"

"I'll stay far away from them, of course."

"Thou canst not; they'll be working in aid of the King and Queen."

Rod froze.

"And what of thine hallucinations?" Big Tom demanded. "Shalt thou see an enemy knight, when 'tis truly thy son?"

"So I can't go help fight." Rod turned slowly, eyes narrowed. "Did you come here only to gloat?"

"Thou dost know I did not. Yet I bid thee cure thyself ere thou dost return."

"Look, I don't know how long it will take for these chemicals to pass out of my system, but by the time I've purged myself, the war will be over!"

"Mayhap," Big Tom said judiciously, "or mayhap thou canst learn to master the witch-moss."

Rod stilled, gazing at him intently.

" 'Tis witch-moss, after all," Big Tom explained, "and thou hast crafted the stuff aforetime. Canst thou not assert dominion o'er it even now, when 'tis within thee?"

"I might be able to learn," Rod said slowly, "but how will I know if I have or not? It *could* just be hallucination!"

Big Tom shook his head. "Thou dost speak as though thou art truly crazed. I tell thee, thou art not. 'Tis but a substance in thy system."

"A substance that has changed my ability to see the world as it really is. No, Big Tom—that's a description of a crazy man. Just because the madness is artificially induced doesn't make it any less a madness."

The ghost shrugged. "Mayhap. Yet an thou art beset by delusions, mayhap thou canst counter them with illusions."

Rod pondered. "Why, how do I do that?"

"I cannot say." Big Tom sighed and shoved himself to his feet. "Thou must needs find those who know the manner of dealing with such unbonded imagery."

"A poet, you mean?"

"A poet, or a priest—or both. A doctor of the arts who is also a doctor of the soul."

"Great," Rod said with a sardonic smile. "Where do I find somebody with *that* combination?"

"I ken not. Yet thou canst, at least, take arms against the illusions thou dost know to be false."

"Wait a minute," Rod protested. "You're saying that I'm not really crazy—I'm just going to have to learn a new way of thinking?"

"In some fashion. Thou must needs learn to think in lifelike images, to oppose these false illusions with counterillusions. Thy wife and bairns were born to this mode of thought, and have no difficulty in dealing with it—yet to thee, 'tis alien."

"Then I'm not so much poisoned, as simply having had my mind fouled," Rod said slowly, "and I have to learn to deal with the foulness in its own terms." He squeezed his eyes shut and shook his head. "That doesn't make sense."

"Then strive until it doth," Big Tom said. "Thy subconscious hath emerged into the perceptions of thy conscious mind, which cannot deal with its wild and rampant nature. As a beginning, take arms against those illusions thou canst be sure are only that—or are truly evil things."

"You mean Brume." Rod nodded. "Yes, I think I can go up against him with a clear conscience. He's either a total hallucination, or an esper who's out to victimize the whole countryside."

"Therefore," said Big Tom, "let us strike."

Somewhere there was a banshee howl, and a myriad of imps descended on them out of some nameless dimension.

Big Tom looked up with disgust. ''The sorcerer Brume hath heard my thought, and hath called up his minions.'' He turned, setting his arms akimbo, and bellowed, ''Avaunt!''

The imps halted in a hollow globe around them, shocked. Then their faces creased with anger, and their mouths opened in yowling.

''I bade thee hold!'' Big Tom thundered, and their tentative advance halted. The yowling took on a definite half-hearted tone.

''They dare not strike whiles I am nigh,'' Big Tom said aside to Rod. ''Do thou ope the door, whilst I hold them at bay.''

''Good division of labor,'' Rod agreed, and he turned to the door, letting his mind drift into a trance, reaching out to the lock, probing, finding, pulling . . .

The bolt slid back.

Rod hauled the door open. ''Care to join me?''

''Aye, and gladly.'' Big Tom stepped up to the doorway with a grin. The gibbering chorus started up again behind them, and the big ghost called back, without even looking at them, ''Follow, an thou durst.'' And to Rod, ''I doubt me not Brume hath penned them in here, to torment his enemies. Let them now come loose!''

16

A lone torch burned in the hallways outside the cell, illuminating a curving stair that rose up into gloom. As they started climbing, the gibbering behind them grew louder. By the time they'd reached the top of the stair, it was turning into yowling again, with the occasional manic giggle.

They came out of the stairwell into the Great Hall, and the imps spilled free in their wake, filling the hall with batwings and howling.

The sorcerer was ready for them—whatever kind of psionic warning system he had, had worked perfectly. The first fireball hit before they were five steps from the stairwell. Rod dodged aside, but the fireball swerved to follow, and swords yanked themselves off the walls to come arrowing toward Rod.

He saw them through clear syrup, for he was in a trance, willing entropy—and the fireball faded and died before it reached him. His own blade was out, parrying, and with a thought, he wrenched a shield off the wall. It flew to interpose itself between Rod and the other two swords, hovering as he slipped his arm through the old, stiff straps.

Then the floor heaved under his feet and, on top of everything else, he had to frantically levitate. The distraction was enough—one sword shot past his guard. He parried frantically, but it nicked his chest before he could swat it down.

Then the imps hit Brume, and the swords fell to the floor as the sorcerer shifted his attention to the little devils. They burst into flame, filling the air with shrieks of agony.

Rod set himself and marched toward the throne.

Brume glanced up, saw him, and a knife flicked itself from his belt, flying straight toward Rod.

Rod caught it on his shield, batted it out of the air—and the other knife he hadn't seen flashed before his eyes. He recoiled, falling back, and the blade shot by—but it opened his forehead on its way, and blood welled up. Rod bellowed with anger and leaped back to his feet, charging toward Brume through a rain of charred imps.

Brume turned to glare at him, and Rod quickly averted his eyes—he wouldn't be caught with the projected migraine again! But flame exploded all around Rod, and every nerve in his body screamed with pain. He ran toward the sorcerer, trying to break through the wall of fire, but it stayed with him, and he couldn't breathe, the flames had swallowed the oxygen . . .

Through the sheet of fire, he saw Big Tom's ghost towering over the sorcerer, fist slamming down toward the bald head. But the sorcerer's hands were sawing the air, and Big Tom disappeared like a soap bubble on the breeze.

Rod shouted in rage; a huge surge of anger tore out of him, and his envelope of flames scattered in shreds. He leaped up to the dais, his sword high . . .

Brume turned, hand flashing out as though throwing something, and a ball of force slammed into Rod's belly, knocking him down. For a moment, the world turned dim, the sorcerer's mocking laughter rang in his ears . . .

The laughter turned abruptly into a scream of pain and fear. Rod caught his breath, could see again—and saw a living torch, darting here and there at the sorcerer's head. Brume fended it off, but it came again, and again—and while it did, a lean young wolf clawed at his midriff, jaws snapping for his throat. A broadsword flashed through the air, cutting and slashing as it sang a song of bloodlust, filling all the room with its high, clear tone. The sorcerer had gained a shield somehow, but was hard put to block the sword cuts, the more so as a ball of lightning danced and dodged about him, seeking for an opening through the magical screen that he had managed to build, that glimmered about him like an aura.

Behind them stood their animating force—a fairy lady, impossibly tall, impossibly slender, an elongated woman with a coronet binding her silver rain of hair, her eyes hard and pitiless.

Brume fell back before her onslaught. He couldn't do anything else; he was barely able to keep his guard up, let alone strike.

Rod closed in, narrow-eyed but silent.

The sorcerer glanced his way, saw him, and howled in anger and frustration. Suddenly, flames sprang up around *him*—a veil of green fire, billowing up to hide Brume, then slackening and thinning into a green fog. It dimmed and diminished, thinned, and was gone.

So was the sorcerer.

Rod stood staring, amazed. "That is one trick that no esper has ever been able to do!"

Or had he? Brume might have teleported, under cover of his green fire. That was why it had dimmed and thinned, instead of dying down.

Or had he seen nothing but what really happened? That

was the tricky part, the word "really." "Am I in Gramarye or Granclarte?"

"What is Granclarte?"

It was the fairy lady who spoke. Her voice was rich and melodious, and her eyes had become more human, but were still guarded and remote.

"Why, it is a fancy," Rod said slowly, turning to her, "or is at least just a figment of imagination. I thank you, lady, for your timely rescue. I doubt that I could have lived through that onslaught, without your aid."

" 'Twas given gladly, Lord Warlock—yet thanks is also due these instruments of mine." Her hand rested on the young wolf's head, her other hand cupping the ball of lightning. The torch flared by her side, and the singing sword balanced itself before her.

"Thanks due to things of enchantment, to your creations?" Rod frowned. "Well, if you say so. Sir Wolf—I thank you." Rod inclined his head and shoulders in a small bow. "And you also, Lightning, Torch, and Sword—I thank you all. Without your aid, I might have been a cinder."

The ball of lightning crackled in approval, and the torch flared brighter. The sword's pure tone rose to a high, clear pitch that rang on through the hall after the sword itself had ceased to sound.

"Though I greatly appreciate your assistance," Rod said, "I cannot help but wonder at it. What am I to you, milady, that you should aid me so?"

The wolf's jaw lolled as though it were laughing, but the lady only said, in cold, clear tones, "This vile sorcerer did cast awry the balance of Water, Earth, Air, and Fire within my domain. Therefore did I wish to move against him. Yet with all my force, I still could not break through his wards. Then thou didst come into his castle as though naught did prevent thee—and when thou didst come out

from the dungeon, why, thou wast already within. Thou
didst then so catch and hold the sorcerer's mind that I
could come in past his wards, and these mine helpers.
Thus did we come; thus were we right glad to aid thee.

"Yet he hath escaped," she went on, face hard, "and
therefore must we beware. He will come again, I doubt
not."

"He will," Rod agreed, "or I'm totally wrong about
what he is."

The faerie tossed her head impatiently. " 'Tis plainly
seen."

"Quite," Rod agreed. "Still, I don't think we should
wait here for him to return. We should leave, milady,
before he can bring back reinforcements."

The wolf sniffed and wrinkled its nose as it peered about
into the gloom.

"Well said," the faerie agreed, "and the more so for
that there may be all manner of venomous spirits that the
sorcerer hath called up, but left here without restraint or
ward, now that he hath fled. Aye, certes we should be out
from this place."

Rod turned toward the portal. "And since you're leaving, could I ask a favor of you? Would you go to
Runnymede, and see how Their Majesties fare? I'm afraid
the rebellion might be too much for them, without supernatural aid."

The wolf stopped, staring, and the sword hummed with
surprise. The faerie asked, "How didst thou know of the
uprising?"

Rod shrugged. "Stood to reason." He didn't say whose.
He ushered them out under the portcullis and came after
them over the drawbridge. "It's *probably* nothing they
can't handle—but they have some enemies who keep
springing some nasty surprises on them."

"We shall go, then." The faerie frowned. "Yet I must

profess concern for thee, mine ally. How wouldst thou fare an the sorcerer should come upon thee alone?''

"Oh, I have another ally who will forgive my last outburst, and come back to protect me, never fear. His patience and forgiveness are unlimited.''

"Thou hast most amazing trust in thy deity.''

"Only ultimately—I don't see much of a guarantee for immediate needs. But I had a different ally in mind.''

"An thou sayest it.'' But the lady hesitated. "Still, an thou hast need, but cry aloud my name, and we will come.''

"What name is that?'' Rod asked politely.

"Mirabile.''

"I thank you, Lady Mirabile.'' Rod bowed. "Be assured that I will call.''

"Then for thy sake, I shall rescue thy monarchs.'' Mirabile drifted up into the air. "Farewell!''

Rod waved as she sped south, flanked by the ball of lightning and the torch, sword arrowing on ahead of her. The wolf looked up at Rod as though doubting his sanity (animals can be very perceptive), then gave a snort and turned away to lope south after his mistress.

Rod watched them go with a smile.

Then he turned back, to say goodbye to the one spirit that he was sure had not been raised by the sorcerer.

Mirabile and her ensemble flew down into a stand of pine trees. The faerie looked back over her shoulder, saw that Brume's castle was hidden from view, and said, "Well enough, children. We may come down to earth, and shed these forms.'' She suited the action to the word, drifting earthward like thistledown. As her toes touched, her form wavered and shimmered, and the faerie turned into a mother. She hopped off her broomstick with a sigh as the torch settled down beside her and turned into Cordelia. The ball of lightning resolved itself into Gregory; the singing sword keened down the scale to a snort, and turned into Geoffrey.

"Ere thou dost wear thy guise again," Cordelia told him, "thou must needs learn to hold a pitch."

Geoffrey's eyes narrowed. "Dost thou truly wish to burn?"

"Where is thy brother?" Gwen said sharply.

They looked up, startled. "We know not, Mama," Cordelia said after a moment. "How should we?"

"Belike hot afoot," Geoffrey said, scowling, "sin that his guise could not fly. He need not have stayed within it, though."

"An he had flown," Gregory pointed out, "Papa would ha' known him on the instant."

Before Geoffrey could think up a comeback, the lean and hungry one leaped out of the evergreens, came bounding up to Gwen, and sat up and begged, whining.

"Oh, be done with thy jesting!" Cordelia said crossly.

" 'Tis no matter for mirth, my son," Gwen agreed.

The wolf sighed. His form blurred, stretched, flexed— and Magnus stood before them. "And I thought the form became me, too."

" 'Tis thy very self," Cordelia assured him, "and that shall I tell all the lasses of the county."

Alarmed, Magnus started to answer, but his mother's forefinger got in the way. "Hush. We must think what to do in regard to thy father."

"He *would* make the matter so involved," Cordelia pouted. "Wherefore could he not simply have accepted the fairie's company? Wherefore had he need to send her away?" A shadow crossed her face. "Mama, now and again I wonder . . ."

"Do not," her mother assured her. "He hath the urge to hermitage within him, aye, but would not long abide the state."

"Doth he seek after holiness, then?" Gregory asked.

"Nay," Magnus answered. "In his heart, he doth think himself unworthy—and the greater we grow, the lesser doth he feel himself to be."

"Magnus!" Gwen gasped, scandalized, but Cordelia scoffed, "How couldst thou know such of him?"

"I am his son," Magnus answered simply.

His sister frowned, and his mother looked worried.

Then she shook her head and said, "Enough. His soul's his own, to care for. How shall we ward his body?"

"I was too slow," Geoffrey said with chagrin. "I should ha' slain the fellow outright." He turned to Magnus. "He cannot truly be a knight, can he?"

"Nay," Big Brother assured him, "and I doubt me not the King's Herald will ne'er have heard of his device. As to his armor, why! Any squire may wear a breastplate 'neath a robe, and carry a shield."

"What did Papa see him as?" Gregory wondered.

"He spoke of a sorcerer," Geoffrey reminded.

"Small wonder," said Cordelia, "sin that he is a warlock."

"A traitor!" Magnus's face was grim. "Would that I could ha' caught some shred of thought, of whence he did teleport himself!"

"He warded his mind well," Geoffrey agreed. " 'Tis no hedge-witch we face."

"At least, his henchmen will not follow Papa—they're affrighted." Cordelia sighed, shaking her head. "Thy husband is too good, Mama. I could wish he'd left them dead."

"Do not," Gwen assured her. "The master may be an agent of thy father's enemies from Tomorrow, yet I doubt me not his henchmen are but poor, unlettered peasant men, who, like as not, followed a promise of riches. Still, some stay in the royal dungeons may enrich their souls."

Magnus looked up in the castle's direction anxiously. "The soldiers should ha' come within the palisade, ere now."

"I doubt me not an they have," Gwen assured him. "Despite his troubles, the King was good as his word; his soldiers came as soon as we summoned, and have reaped a rich harvest of felons as they have followed in thy father's wake."

"As should we." Magnus's face was pinched with anxiety. "This false knight, Brume, may spring upon him at any moment."

"Not without an army at his back; he hath too much fear of Papa for that." But Geoffrey didn't exactly look sanguine, either.

"Here's a true how-de-do!" said Magnus. "His delusions are too deep for him to fare safely alone—yet an we throw over all to follow him, his enemies will hale down the Crown."

"And thy father's life's work with it," Gwen agreed. "Nay, that we cannot permit, either."

"Nor the grief that would come to all the poor folk, in the turmoil that would follow such a catastrophe," Cordelia added.

" 'Tis indeed a dilemma," Gregory agreed. "Yet are there not enough of us to do both?"

"Aye," Gwen said. "There is no aid for it. Magnus, thou shalt go back in thy guise to follow thy father, and protect him from any who seek to abuse him in his madness."

"And to protect any he might chance to abuse?" the young man returned.

"How now!" Geoffrey protested. "Wherefore doth this honor fall to Magnus, and not to me?"

"For that he's the eldest," Gwen said in a voice of steel that softened amazingly for the next sentence. "Bide thy time, my son. When thou art come to thy young manhood, thou, too, shalt undertake such a quest alone. Yet for now, thou art still a boy. Come away!'' She turned to kiss Magnus on the forehead. ''Fare thee well, my son—and call at the slightest sign of peril; thy brother Geoffrey, at least, may come to aid thee on the instant.''

''I shall be glad of his strong right arm, to ward my back,'' Magnus returned. ''Godspeed, Mama—and thee, my sibs.''

Cordelia took a quick peck at his cheek, too, while Geoffrey made a face, and Gregory watched, frowning faintly, as though he were puzzled. Then Magnus turned and loped off toward the forest, and Gwen turned to her younger three, saying, ''Let us fly,'' and hopped on her broomstick. It wafted up and streaked away south, with Cordelia behind her and the boys to each side.

''Fess?''

''Here, Rod.'' The great black horse shouldered out of the underbrush and onto the road.

''I knew I could depend on you.'' But Rod felt very sheepish. ''Sorry about that last outburst.''

''There is no need for apology.''

''But there is—my own need, at least. Will you accompany me again?''

''Surely, Rod.'' The robot stepped up beside him.

Rob mounted. ''That was nice of Gwen and the kids, to disguise themselves like that.''

The robot was still for a moment, which, for him, amounted to major shock. ''You saw through their disguises, Rod?''

''Not really—so they did serve their purpose; they allowed me to accept their help, before I figured out who they were. But it didn't take much deduction, after the fighting was over.'' Rod smiled. ''It gives me a very warm feeling, to know that they insist on watching over me—especially when I'd just been so vile to them. Doesn't say much for their confidence in me, though.''

"It does, in its way, Rod. They understood that you were ill when you spoke.''

"I don't deserve them. Or you, for that matter.''

"Or myself?''

Rod looked down, startled, and saw the dwarf striding along beside him. He grinned. "Hey, Modwis! Good of you to find me again! How'd you manage?''

"I but followed the sounds of clashing magics,'' the dwarf answered. "An thou wouldst wait for me, Lord Gallowglass, thou wouldst ease my toil.''

"I will, I promise. Sure you want to come along on this quest, though?''

"I am still wroth that I missed my chance to battle Brume,'' the dwarf answered. "Whither goest thou?''

"North,'' Rod said, "until Brume finds me again. Feel like baiting the foe?''

Modwis looked up quickly, then slowly smiled. "Aye, that I do. Let us march.''

17

By midmorning, Rod was becoming acutely aware that they had set out on this jaunt without food or water. "Y'know, Modwis, I'm getting a mite peckish."

The dwarf took a sling from his pouch and unwound the strings. "Shall I seek us a brace of partridges?"

Rod's mouth watered. "Sounds good. Know how to cook 'em?"

"Aye. 'Twill be some time, though—I must seek and bait them first."

"That's okay, I can use a break. Say, can I help?"

The dwarf flashed him a grin. "I shall hunt more quickly alone—yet I thank thee."

"However you like." Rod reined in by a stream. "I'll get the fire going."

"An thou wilt." Modwis dismounted and tied his donkey to a bush. "Ere noon, we shall dine. Wish me a hunter's luck."

"Hunter's luck!" Rod called, and waved a hand as Modwis rode away into the wood. Then he went down to the stream.

"Be careful, Rod."

"I will, Fess—but I'm thirsty enough to drink water now." Rod took up a fallen branch and brought its end down sharply on the ice. It cracked through; water welled up, and Rod knelt to drink.

And froze—for he saw the top of a shaven head with a knot of hair in the center, floating just below the water. He backed away, but the head rose up out of the ice, with a bull neck and a massive torso beneath it. It was a face with hard, narrow eyes, high cheekbones, and long, drooping black moustaches. Adrenaline tuned Rod's system *What's a Mongol doing here?*

Then he realized he could see through the man.

"I am come again." The apparition's voice was thin and whispery, but had the echo of a rotund basso.

"For the first time, as far as I'm concerned! Who the hell are *you*?"

"Aye, feign innocence! Thou knowest well I am the warrior Pantagre, whom thou didst most treacherously slay in battle—and am come now for revenge!"

The ghost suddenly lashed out with an arm, and Rod had no doubt that, if he'd really been the guilty party, that mean left hook would have managed to drag him down into the water. Because he was innocent, though, the ghost's hand went right through him.

The spectre stared at his palm. "How can this hand fail me!"

"Because I'm innocent," Rod explained. "Look, I don't know who killed you—but it wasn't me."

"Thou dost lie! 'Twas thee, or thy very likeness!"

"That's not impossible—I seem to have a lot of duplicates running around—but it wasn't me."

The ghost's eyes narrowed. "Art bold enough to prove thy claim?"

"Generally, yes."

The ghost reached up to a low-hanging branch of the oak tree above them, and plucked a sprig of mistletoe. He pulled off one of the little white globes, then held the sprig out to Rod. "My hands cannot grasp thee, yet thine can serve. Take thou this berry, and eat, as I eat. Whiche'er doth lie shall sink."

"Sink?" Rod asked. "I can understand what that means for you—but what does it mean if *I* sink?"

"That thou wilt die, and become a ghost, as I am—whereupon we may fight on equal terms."

Rod's scalp prickled as his hair tried to stand up. It might have looked like mistletoe, but the berry he held was poison.

"Art afeard?" the ghost jeered. "Dost own to thy guilt?"

"Never," Rod snapped. He opened his mouth and lifted the berry . . .

With a howl, a wolf shot from the brush and leaped on him.

Rod shouted and rolled aside—and the wolf caught the berry in his mouth and barreled on past Rod. He landed and wheeled toward the ghost with a manic growl.

The ghost wailed in dismay and sank from sight.

Rod stared. What kind of ghost was afraid of a wolf? And what kind of wolf would charge a ghost?

A young one. The beast turned to Rod, tongue lolling out—and Rod could have sworn he was smiling. Slowly, he let his own mouth curve, too. "So. Mirabile left a guardian over me, did she?"

The wolf nodded and came right up to Rod, sat down, and held up a paw.

Rod took it with a grave bow. "Delighted to have the opportunity to further our acquaintance, Sir Wolf." Then he looked up in alarm. "Hey, wait a minute! If that berry was poison, we'd better take you and get your stomach pumped!" Every protective instinct in him screamed—he might play along with the charade, but he *knew* who the wolf was!

But White Fang shook his head, still smiling, and Rod realized, *Of course*. If Big Tom was right, the berry was made of witch-moss—and if the wolf was who he knew it was, then the berry wouldn't hurt it. Just the opposite, if anything.

Either that, or the wolf meant it had had the sense to spit the berry out. For a moment, Rod was tempted to ask it, then decided he didn't want to hear the animal speak. Why weaken the illusion? "Okay, Fang—and thanks for the vote of confidence. I knew I was innocent, but it's nice to have somebody confirm it."

When Modwis came back, he stepped into the clearing and dropped the partridges, staring in alarm.

Rod looked up from the fireside and smiled, resting a hand on the wolf's head. "Hi, Modwis. Meet my friend."

He hoped he was right.

They traveled together all the next day, and Rod and Modwis found the young wolf to be remarkably good company. But when the sun's rays were stretching the shadows of the trees halfway up their neighbors' trunks, Rod finally admitted, "We're not going to find an inn tonight."

"Even so," Modwis said.

Rod sighed. "Time to find a campsite." He turned to the wolf. "Want to run ahead and find us a clearing?"

The wolf grinned, then loped off ahead among the trees.

"Art thou certain 'tis safe to have him with us?" Modwis asked.

"That particular young wolf, I would trust with my life," Rod answered.

Fess, of course, said nothing.

The wolf came loping back, still grinning, slewed to a

halt on its haunches, and jerked its head back over its shoulder, as though pointing.

"Right ahead, huh?" Rod nodded. "Well, let's see."

The clearing was only about twenty feet across, and would have been fully roofed with leaves in summer—but now the darkening sky showed clearly through the bare branches. Modwis tethered his donkey and hung its oat bag over its ears. Rod watched him, muttering under his breath, "Just how conspicuous should we be, Alloy Ally?"

"So far as Modwis knows, you have already left me to graze once, Rod—as Beaubras left his horse, outside High Dudgeon."

Rod nodded. "Good point." He dropped the reins and strolled away to hunt for firewood.

"There are pine boughs." Modwis took out a long knife. "I shall make our beds."

"Great," Rod called back, "and I'll get the fire going. Then it's my turn to hunt." He turned to the wolf. "I'll find dinner for Modwis and me, but you'd better go dig up a rabbit for yourself."

The wolf grinned up into his eyes, then turned and trotted off into the underbrush.

Rod watched him go, reflecting that he was being mean—but he had to play along with the boy's charade, didn't he? Either that, or reveal his own knowledge of it, which would no doubt dampen Magnus's spirits like an autumn rain.

Of course, he *could* have been mistaken—the wolf might have really been a wolf, though a fairie's pet. What then?

Well, then the wolf might not be back until late, or might not come back at all, for that matter. Rod felt a chill, and hoped it would come back.

Out of sight of the camp, the wolf's form fluxed; it turned back into Magnus. He slipped from trunk to trunk until he could see the camp clearly through a screen of

branches, waited until Rod and Modwis were both facing
the other way, then stepped out where Fess could see him,
and waved. The great black horse lifted its head, and
Magnus nodded, then stepped back into cover, satisfied
that his father's other guardian knew of his own presence.
He leaned back against a trunk and reached into his pouch
for some dried beef. It wasn't going to be much of a
dinner, but he didn't intend to let Papa out of his sight.
Like father, like son—only now, it was *Magnus's* turn to
be overprotective.

Rod lay awake, listening to Modwis's deep, even breath-
ing, and trying to imitate it. He kept telling himself he was
being silly, that there was no way Magnus could come to
harm. Nonetheless, he knew there was equally no way he
was going to sleep until the wolf came back. He'd even
saved him some stew, too . . .

Then he realized that the shimmering through the trees
wasn't all moonlight.

He tensed even more, staring off toward the south,
weighing his worry about Magnus against the possibility
that the boy might have run afoul of whatever was shed-
ding that eldritch light—and wishing heartily that his son
had not insisted on coming along into the wild.

He finally decided that knowledge was better than worry.
If Magnus came back while he was gone, Modwis would
waken to take care of the lad—assuming the wolf disguise
didn't bother him too much. Even if it did, there was
always Fess. "I'm going to investigate that light," Rod
murmured to the robot-horse. "Stay here and take care of
the 'wolf,' will you?"

"Rod—the only light is that of the moon."

Rod shook his head. "No. I thought so, too, but I took
a closer look, and there's another kind. It *looks* like moon-

light, yes, but it's different. Hold the fort, Fess.'' And he slipped off into the forest.

The robot hung poised between obedience and concern for his owner—but Rod had ordered him to stay, and there was no sign of an external threat, only Rod's own hallucination . . .

Which could be dangerous enough; but Rod had given an order. Fess heaved white noise and settled himself to wait—but he opened the channel to Rod's maxillary microphone, and boosted the gain.

Magnus's head nodded heavily, and the jerk woke him from his doze. Blinking, he glanced toward the campfire—

And saw Rod's bedroll empty.

Instantly, the boy was alert. He scanned the campsite and saw Rod slipping into the trees on the far side. Magnus pulled himself together and set off around the clearing, being careful where he stepped, moving almost silently through the winter wood.

He was a quarter of the way around when something hard and blunt cracked into his skull just behind the ear, and he dropped, senseless.

18

The ground sloped up, and the light grew brighter, until Rod found himself thinking dawn was near. But that was silly, of course—it couldn't even be midnight; Magnus wasn't back yet, and he never stayed out that late.

Then he came out of the trees into a hilltop meadow, one not made by nature—for in its center was a castle, glowing with its own inner light. The walls were translucent. It looked like a child's night-light, or a Christmas-tree ornament.

An ornament sixty feet high and a hundred yards square.

He came up to the drawbridge warily, but with determination—his son might be in there. After all, if it had drawn him, why might it not draw Magnus?

As he neared the drawbridge, the sight of the stone caught him. He stopped to take a closer look—and gazed at it, fascinated.

It was marble, all marble. By the subtle variations of shading, he could tell it was made of several different kinds of the stone—but all without a trace of grain. That was why it glowed—because it was completely pure.

No, not quite unmarked—there was something there, within the stone. He stepped nearer, went across the draw-bridge to look more closely—and saw a man's torso and face, looking back at him. The stranger was surprisingly good-looking, and wore a doublet and cloak identical to Rod's own.

It took him a few minutes to admit that it was his own image.

But not himself as he had ever seen himself, for every mirror had always showed him a homely stranger who looked very competent, but strangely lacking in self-confidence. This image, however, wasn't homely at all, but was very good-looking—and if the modesty was there, it was balanced by a certain hardness, almost ruthlessness. In fact, Rod found himself recoiling—this was a very dangerous man!

But dangerous, he saw, not just because of his abilities, but because of his morality. He was safe to anyone who followed his moral code—but to anyone who lived far enough outside that code, he could be a ruthless and efficient killer; for if anyone broke the Law this man lived by, that person was completely outside that Law's protec-tion, and the murderer before him felt justified in unleash-ing the fullest of his mayhem.

Rod felt himself cringing inside, even though he couldn't look away; he had always thought of himself as a nice guy.

And not without reason, he saw—there was mercy in that man's eyes, and his savagery was tempered by humor. Yes, he could be sudden death to anyone who lived out-side his own ethical code—but very few people lived so completely within that code that they could knowingly break it enough to give the murderer his moral excuse. Only occasionally did he encounter such a person, a man or woman that he could truly say was evil, and then . . .

He enjoyed what he did.

Rod felt his soul shrivel, but there was no denying it. This man before him was a cold-blooded killer who enjoyed practicing his craft. That was the spectre that had been haunting Rod since he left Maxima; that was why he had felt the compulsion to chain this beast in morality; that was why, in his heart of hearts, he knew he was unworthy of Gwen, and of the children.

His children. What would happen if one of them ever broke that man's rules? Not just broke them—but smashed them, trampled on them.

A fierce surge of paternal protectiveness swept him. Never, he vowed silently, never would he risk a single one of them coming to harm. He swore to himself that he would kill the lizard before he could raise a hand against those kids.

But how could he kill himself?

Easy.

But he could see, behind the reflection, images of his children growing and striving in their own right, and felt reassured. They had been raised within his fence, and Gwen's. They might kick against it, they might break a rail or two in anger or resentment, but they would never try to tear it down. It was their protection as much as their prison.

But now that the scenes had begun, they continued—scenes of Rod's youth, not of the children. He saw himself again, among the mercenaries attacking a city guilty of no more than the urge to be free; he saw himself, a year later, struggling to atone by helping another band of patriots overthrow an off-planet tyranny. He watched himself duel with and kill the tyrant's bodyguard, while the locals swamped the tyrant himself. He saw himself between the stars, studying the history of the next planet Fess was taking him to in their asteroid-ship, saw himself struggling, manipulating, again and again, and all the time searching, hunting, for the love he knew he did not deserve.

He couldn't take his eyes off the pageant. Spellbound, he watched the scenes he remembered, but not *as* he remembered them; they were shown objectively, impartially. What he saw made him proud one instant and ashamed the next—exalted his spirit, but also left it humbled.

As he watched spellbound, his enemies stole up behind him.

Rod couldn't have said what it was that warned him—a creak of leather, a heavy tread—some signal that filtered through to him and broke his trance. He spun around, whipping his sword out, just in time to see an ogre followed by a handful of trolls, all advancing across the drawbridge. The ogre was ten feet tall, with legs a foot and a half thick, foot-thick arms, massive chest and shoulders, and nothing but a twist of loincloth for clothing. He was hairy and filthy. His eyes were tiny and bright with greed, peering out from under shaggy eyebrows. His nose was a blob, and two long fangs thrust up from his jaw. His trolls shambled behind him, their faces brutal, their bodies formidable, their fingers sprouting talons.

The ogre gave a little gloating laugh and slammed his club down at Rod.

Rod shouted and leaped back; the club spun by him. Then he leaped in again, slamming a kick into the ogre's solar plexus; but the monster only grunted, and swung from the hip. Rod was just landing as the blow struck, still a little off balance; he leaped to the side, but not enough; the club caught him a glancing blow on the shoulder, and his whole right arm went numb. He tumbled into the snow on the drawbridge and saw a troll pouncing on him, claws winking in the castle's glow. Rod scrabbled frantically for the sword and managed to get it up between the troll and himself, clumsily, left-handed.

The troll couldn't stop; he skewered himself on the sword, knocking Rod backward onto the drawbridge. The monster screamed and died, but his flailing talons flexed in death, shredding Rod's doublet and chest. Blood welled, and his whole front blazed with pain. He yelled and struggled up, barely able to wrench his sword free in time to see the ogre towering over him, club high in both hands, trolls pressing in all about him, and the dead troll's scream still rang in his ears . . .

Only the scream was coming from behind the trolls, and something struck the ogre hard in the back. He stumbled and turned with a roar, and Rod saw Fess, reared up and lashing out with hooves and teeth. He lunged at a troll; the monster stumbled back and fell into the moat with a howl, where it began to dissolve. Another troll grabbed at Fess, bellowing; steel teeth reached for him, but the ogre was smashing out with the club, and Fess was trying to hit him with a hoof, rearing high and slamming down . . .

Down stiff-legged, knees locked, head swinging between the fetlocks. He had had a seizure.

And the ogre's club was slamming down.

Rod bellowed and barreled into the ogre with his full weight, driving into the small of his back. The ogre wobbled, swung around, and lashed out at Rod with a roar. Rod fell back, but the club caught him alongside the head, and his ears rang while stars danced before his eyes. He struggled to clear his head, waiting for the blow to fall, knowing he was doomed, hearing the roaring still . . .

Then the stars were gone, but the bellowing was still there. The ogre had turned away from him, and was battling something on his other side. Then one of the trolls lurched and fell into the river. Modwis rose up where he'd been, buckler on his arm, mace in his hand—and behind him, Beaubras battled the ogre with axe and sword while his charger guarded his back, lashing out at the trolls with hoof and tooth.

Gasping for breath, Rod limped toward them. He couldn't let the knight die in his defense without at least helping, though Heaven only knew what Beaubras was doing alive again.

The horse struck out, and the last troll fell into the moat with a wail of despair—but the ogre's club finally battered down Beaubras's guard, and a huge blow slammed the knight's own axe flat against his head. Beaubras reeled and fell, and the ogre swung up a huge foot, to stamp on him.

Rod finally got there and stabbed the foot.

The ogre howled, flailing for balance on the edge of the moat. He almost recovered—but Modwis was there, throwing all his weight against a huge kneecap, and the ogre tottered and fell, with a roar of wrath that changed to terror. He hit the water with a huge splash, and his howl cut off. The moat heaved, and was still.

"Allergic to water, too, I guess," Rod muttered, and turned back to the knight, his own head whirling.

Modwis was there before him, kneeling beside Beaubras, cradling the knight's head in the dwarf's arm. The knight looked up at him, and Rod saw the slick of blood that covered the whole side of his head. "Do not weep for me, friend," he whispered, but Modwis's eyes were filled with tears, anyway.

"Hang in there," Rod grated. "You'll make it—somehow."

Beaubras turned back to him with a sad smile. "Nay, Lord Gallowglass—though I thank Heaven I . . . came in time."

"But how did you . . . I mean, you were . . . "

"Dead?" The knight gave him a weak smile. "Only gone—as I go now. You must act for both of us, Lord Gallowglass, for both of us together, in this world and your own. Yet fear not—for I shall come again. I shall always come again.''

Then he sighed, and went limp.

Rod stared, aghast.

The knight's form rippled, thinned, and was gone.

Modwis looked at his empty hands in disbelief, then looked up at Rod in mute appeal—but the light glinted stars off the tears in his eyes, and the stars grew and dazzled, filling Rod's vision with a fall of light. Dimly through it, he thought he saw a beautiful lady, with long, blond hair bound by a coronet, followed by several nuns. But that couldn't have been, there weren't any nuns on Gramarye, and Rod found himself tumbling again, into a world of light.

The leprechaun crouched over the Lord Warlock's body, hammer in his hand, glaring at the tall woman.

''Peace, Old One,'' she said. ''We come to aid your friend, not to hurt him.''

''Who be these women by ye?'' Modwis demanded. ''Wherefore are they garbed in monks' robes?''

''Why, for that they *are* monks—though with ladies, they are spoken of as 'nuns.' ''

''We are Sisters of Saint Vidicon, Old One,'' the first woman said. She was plump, with kindly eyes peering from under the white headband that separated her face from her hood. ''We have dedicated our lives to the worship of God, and the service of our fellow sinners.''

The leprechaun winced at the name of God, but held his ground, and his suspicion lessened. ''Ye are healers, then?''

''Aye, and we could not help but see what befell at our very gate. Dost know who was that half-armored fellow in the red robe?''

''A fell knave hight Brume, who hath followed this man through half of Gramarye, to plague him. Beyond that, I know only that his peasant band fled as soon as they were struck. Will ye mend my companion, then?''

"We will that," the lady replied. "Sisters, take him up."

Two of the nuns unrolled a stretcher, placed it beside Rod, set themselves, and heaved him onto the canvas. Then they rose and carried him in through the Gothic arch, past the low walls.

The lady with the coronet turned back to Modwis. "Thou art welcome, an thou dost wish to enter and rest."

"Nay," the leprechaun returned, "for thy holy places are bane to us. Yet I will abide in a hollow tree nearby. An thou hast need of me, lady, but call out, 'Modwis, come hither!' ''

"I shall, friend—and fear not; my friends shall care for thine. Canst thou tell me his name?"

But the leprechaun was gone, vanished like a dream. The lady smiled sadly and turned away, going into the convent. The porter closed the oaken shutters behind her.

19

In the darkness, a spot of light appeared, dim and nebulous, but growing, until Rod realized he was looking at the moon through a heavy haze. But it kept growing, larger and larger, until it was swollen greater than the harvest moon—and it kept on swelling.

Finally, Rod realized he was moving toward it.

In a panic, he looked about, trying to see the spaceship that contained him, the scooter, even just the space suit . . .

. . . and saw an old man drifting beside him in the void. His long white hair flowed down around his shoulders; his beard streamed down over his chest, held there by acceleration, not gravity. He was wearing a long white robe with a golden chasuble over it, and had a huge, thick book under one arm—

And no space suit. Not even a helmet.

"Be at peace, my son," he intoned. "Thou art in a realm of magic; thou shalt not want for air to breathe, nor heat to thee. Aye, and if thou dost hearken, thou mayest hear the music of the spheres."

Rod swallowed an automatic protest and listened. Sure

enough, he heard a harmonious chord of clear, crystalline tones, each beginning and dying in a staggered progression, so that the music kept changing, but never ceased.

He turned back to the old man, amazed. "But these are things that cannot be!"

"Save in a realm of magic," the old man reminded him. "Thou art not in the Earth of Mankind's childhood now, nor on the Isle of Gramarye, nor even in thy grandfather's Granclarte. Thou art in a realm of magic, pure magic, and naught else."

Rod began to suspect his schoolboy memory was working harder than his subconscious.

"You are a knight, after all," the old man said, as though reading his thoughts. "Where would your soul find rest, save in a realm enchanted?"

"Not really a knight—I only have a title." But Rod felt a certain sick certainty that the old man was right. "Still, if I am a knight, what are you?"

"I am only a watcher now," the old man said, "and mayhap a guardian. I was a writer of books once, but my work in that is done, and therefore have I time to journey here and there for pleasure, now and again. And thou, sir, are not only a knight but also a wizard, art thou not? For unless I mistake, you are the Lord Gallowglass."

"That is my real name, I guess," Rod said slowly. "And you, honored sir—whom have I the pleasure of addressing?"

"I am that John whom men call the Evangelist," the venerable father returned. " 'Twas I who beheld the visions of the end of Time, and set them forth for all to read."

"The Book of Revelation? *That* John? The saint?"

The old man smiled, amused. "There are many saints named John, praise Heaven. Yet I am one among them, aye."

And probably the first one, Rod noted. "I am honored, Father." Well, after all, he had been a priest, hadn't he?

Or was he still?

"Thou hast honor because thou dost give honor," the old man replied.

Rod thought about that for a minute. "How is it that I am so fortunate as to meet you? And why are we going to the moon?"

Saint John laughed gently. "Thou art in my company, Lord Gallowglass, *because* thou must needs go to the moon—and must needs go there to recover thy wits."

"My wits?" Rod asked. "How'd they get to the moon?"

"The celestial beauty doth draw men's minds," Saint John explained, "and those whose hold upon their wits is feeble do yield them up unto her."

Rod remembered an old tradition that the full moon could bring madness. In fact, he believed that was the origin of the term "lunatic."

"All that is lost from men's hearts or minds doth come to the surface of the moon," the Evangelist explained, "and is there transmogrified, into shapes that the eye can perceive, and the hand can touch. But come—the Sphere draws nigh."

And so it had, Rod realized with a start—the face of the moon had grown to fill their whole field of view. Under the strange magic of planetary approach, he suddenly realized he was falling toward the surface, not sailing through space.

But they slowed as they fell, swinging around to the dark side of the moon—only it wasn't dark here, not in this universe. Rather, it was suffused with a strange, muted, sourceless light. They drifted down past the huge, rugged peaks of Luna. But, in the strange fashion of this magical universe, those slopes were no longer barren rock, but clothed with brush, then with somber evergreens. Looking down, Rod could see a few people wandering over grassy plains and by dark, still pools—but all the colors were muted, as though seen through a haze. "Good Father," said Rod, "who are they who wander this bleak plain?"

"Poor, lost souls, my son," the Evangelist said sadly, "who have lost their way in Life, and lost the Faith that might give them purpose. They wander here, without direction, waiting for death. But come—the land awaits."

They swung their feet down and touched, not dust, but gray-green turf. Rod looked up and saw a mound of paired circlets, attached so tightly they must have been cast-joined—but each circle was broken opposite the joint. "Good Father, what are these?"

"Promises of love," the old man said, "broken and forgot. Anon some lost soul may come and sort through this heap, find a promise made and broken long before, and with it find his way again—but few are they, and rarely come."

Rod saw a broken heart engraved on one, and felt a stab of guilt, remembering a few liaisons in his younger days. He reached for the pile, wondering whose names were engraved on the circlets nearest him, but the Evangelist took his arm and ushered him firmly on. "Enough, Sir Knight. 'Tis lost wits we seek, not their cause."

They went around the pile, past an azure pond whose brim was encrusted with salt, through a meadow of pale valentines that were drooping for lack of light, and into a grove of willows. "What trees are these, good Father?"

"Ones that weep, my son. They are fed by the springs of remorse and pity that should soften every human heart— yet some have lost each drop of compassion, and their hearts are hard and sere."

Rod saw names and pictographs engraved on the trunks of the trees. He recognized a bar of steel on one, and a sail from a ship on another, but the old man kept him moving too fast to read.

On they went, past a giant honeycomb holding crystal glasses of muted luster, through a tunnel lined with sealed caskets, and out onto a plain of dust. This, at least, looked a little like the Luna with which Rod was familiar—only an endless, flat plain of shifting particles, with stark crags rising in the distance.

But in the middle of that plain rose a mountain of shields made of darkened metal.

The saint took Rod's arm and stepped out onto the lake of dust. Rod followed, with a sinking stomach—he knew that the dust-pits of Luna could be worse than quicksand. But the saint walked that treacherous surface as lightly as a dove borne up by Faith, or by the magic of that world— and Rod walked with him. "What is this pile of shields, Father John?"

"Blotted escutcheons, my son. Here are arms of honor, made of brightest silver, but tarnished now with disdain or neglect. Their number has always been legion, yet never more so than in these darkened, latter days."

Rod leaned close as they passed, and saw a lectern on one, and a tall hat with a puffy top on another, but he couldn't make sense of the icons.

They rounded a huge mound of shredded paper, through which two pale shadows sifted wearily.

"What are they looking for?" Rod hissed to Saint John.

"A Seal of Confidence, my son," the Evangelist answered, "yet they are doomed not to find it, for it was a thing of their own devising."

Then the rugged peaks loomed closer, and Rod saw that one of them was composed of millions of shards of glittering glass. "Father, these are not merely lost, but broken also."

"Aye, my son, and wondrous would be that soul who

could find all the pieces of any one cup, let alone weld them back together. Yet those who have lost these vessels have no such interest—for this is the resting place of broken integrity, where those who have fragmented themselves, seeking to give a bit to each who can aid them, will end their days. Yet sadly, they've often much of life to live ere death.''

Rod craned his neck as they went by, and made out a compass with its needle pointing upward, a playing card with a knave holding an antique pistol, and a sort of rusty machinery jack. Beyond that, there were a few initials, some in the Roman alphabet, some in Cyrillic, some in Arabic, and many in Oriental ideograms. He wondered what was at the bottom of the pile.

Then, finally, they came to a huge mound of stoppered test tubes. A few lay open; all were engraved with people's names. On some, the letters had been so thoroughly eroded by time that only the initials were clear; on one, Rod could make out something that looked like the word ''AH.'' Some were so old (or so new) that they had, not writing, but pictograms; one had a picture of two elks with wide, spatulate antlers. Rod could even see one with a picture of a Buck Rogers–style blaster. ''What artifacts are these, sainted Father?''

''These vials hold the wits of men and women, my son—the reasoning faculty of they who have lost the power of logical thought.''

Rod could see a very large test tube that read, ''Conte Orlando,'' and decided that he had come in in the middle of more stories than one.

That tube, at least, was unstopped. ''Why is that vial still here, if it's empty?''

''It awaits the return of the wits it held,'' Saint John explained.

It would wait forever, Rod knew. ''Am I in there?''

"That part of thee that doth lend clarity and judgement to thy thinking, aye—that aspect of thy mind that doth see the material world about thee as it truly is."

"Only the material world? What about that part of my mind that discerns the intangible world?"

"That, at least," said the saint, "thou hast not yet lost."

Rod was about to ask about the "yet," then decided against it. He turned to start sorting through the test tubes. "This could be a long search, Father."

"Not so," said the holy one. "Thy wits are only a few days' fled; thou wilt find them near to the top."

Then a large tube caught Rod's eye—one of the ones that was stoppered with rubber, instead of being sealed with wax. Engraved on it, in large, plain letters, was the name "Rod Gallowglass, né d'Armand."

Beside it, of course, lay Rory's. Rod was surprised to see that it was empty.

He lifted his own test tube, frowning at the murky vapor inside. "How come everybody else's is clear?"

"Ask, rather," murmured the Evangelist, "why thine is beclouded."

Rod noticed that he didn't answer.

"Hold it 'neath thy nostrils," the old man urged, "and ope it."

Frowning, Rod did as he was told—and the mist curled up out of the tube, shrouding his whole head in fog, then streaming into his nostrils, his eyes, and his ears. A tendril brushed his lips, leaving a trace so tantalizing that Rod opened his mouth before he could think—and the vapor cascaded over his tongue and down his throat.

"The cloud of thy wits hath entered thine head through each of its orifices," the Evangelist explained.

Rod's senses reeled; he suddenly felt that he was tasting color, and feeling flavors. He listened to warmth for a moment, as the world went fuzzy; then the mist rose up and obscured it all. Only sound remained, the sound of the old man's voice right next to his ear, to each ear, intoning, almost inside his head, "Remember this—and, whensoe'er thou dost begin to doubt what thou dost see, or to suspect that thou dost see things that are not there, only close thine eyes, recall this moment and this place. Find thy vial again, if need be—and thou shalt have thy wits about thee once again."

Someone was asking, a long way away, "How can this work, good Father?" and the old man answered, "Through manipulation of symbols, my son. Through signs of what is not, thou shalt awaken to what truly is . . . to what truly is . . . truly is . . ."

Somewhere in the distance, Gwen was crying, "See the world as it truly is, I implore thee! Husband, awake!"

Rod blinked, and the murk thinned. He squeezed his eyes shut, then opened them, and saw daylight on a whitewashed wall.

20

Rod woke with the familiar nausea upon him. He moaned and clasped his belly; all he wanted to do was lie down and die.

Then he realized that he *was* lying down. He was staring at whitewashed walls, a low rough-made table beside his narrow cot, a similarly rough-hewn chair by the table, and a crucifix on the wall. He contemplated the crucifix and decided he could bear the nausea.

Something cold and wet touched his forehead. He recoiled automatically—and saw a plump lady with a kindly face and a no-nonsense manner, in a brown monk's robe, cowl thrown back to show a sort of white bonnet covering her hair, with a broad white band standing up above her face.

"Be easy," she said softly. "The pain will pass. Thou hast been wounded sorely, gentleman, and hast lost some blood; thou must needs rest."

"I . . . I think I can do that," Rod moaned. "And . . . don't get me wrong, I really appreciate all this, especially the fire, but . . . where am I?"

"In our convent," the nun answered, "and I am Sister Paterna Testa. Hast pain in thy belly?"

"Nausea . . . " Rod gasped.

The lady took an earthenware bowl from under the table and set it on the boards. "Use it, an thou hast need. Hast thou but now awaked with nausea, or hath it been with thee afore the battle?"

"Battle? That's right, the ogre . . . No, good woman. I . . . well, I've been . . . seeing things that aren't there, for a few days now, and . . . well, afterward, I feel weak, and dizzy, and nauseous . . ." Rod bit down against the pain, closing his eyes. When the spasm passed, he gasped, "Cramps, this time, too."

Sister Paterna Testa reached down under the table again and took up a bottle of pink fluid. She decanted a little into a vessel that looked for all the world like an eggcup and held it out to him, commanding, "Drink. 'Twill ease thy stomach."

Warily, Rod took it. He was tempted to think he was still hallucinating, but the nausea usually came after, not during. He swallowed the potion and frowned. "Odd. That almost tasted good."

"Give it a moment to work." The nun took the eggcup, then leaned back in the chair. "How long hast thou seen things not truly there?"

"Since I ate a chestnut sold by a stranger. You said I've just been in a battle?"

"Aye."

"Then you saw it, too. Who was I fighting?"

"A warrior with five peasant men-at-arms at his back."

"Hm." Rod shook his head. "I saw an ogre with a handful of trolls. Say, did you see a tall, blond knight help me out?"

The nun shook her head. "Only a tall, black horse and a

leprechaun—yet thou didst lay about thee as though there were two of thee.''

So. Beaubras, at least, had not been real.

Then the first part of her sentence bored through, and Rod sat up, wide-eyed. "My horse! I've got to go help him!''

He scrabbled toward the edge of the bed, but the woman put a hand against his chest and said firmly, "Thou must needs rest. As to thine horse . . .''

Here, Rod.

Rod stared, startled to hear Fess's voice. "He's all right!''

"Aye," Sister Paterna Testa said, unperturbed. "A young man came to the gate, did summat to the horse, and it did lift its head and follow him. He knocked at our portal, and we took him in, for he was yet dizzy from a knock on the head that had laid him low.''

"A knock on the head!" Rod bleated. "Good grief! Did you check for concussion?''

"A cracked pate? Aye—and be assured, the lad hath sustained no injury, though his head aches as badly as thine, I warrant.''

"Wait a minute.'' Rod protested. "You're not supposed to know what 'concussion' means.''

The nun shrugged. "A monk taught me of it, long years ago; 'twas his knowledge showed me my calling to this House.''

"You mean you started the convent?''

"Nay; it hath been here nearly two hundreds of years, and hath several buildings; thou art in our guesthouse. We call ourselves the Order of Cassettes, belike from our call to healing, especially the head and the mind it contains. Thou dost know that 'casse tête' doth mean a broken head, dost thou not?''

Rod did, but the woman obviously didn't know what a

cassette was. "You're not officially of the Order of Saint Vidicon, are you?"

"Nay; we have no formal charter, though we do have our Rule. We are only a group of women who wish to live apart from the world, yet to go out and give aid where we may."

Rod nodded. "Who's the abbess?"

"None; we are not so clear in our ranks and standing as that. We are, as I say, but a group of women who live like sisters; yet the others do call me 'Mother.' I know not whether they jest, yet am honored."

"Mother Paterna Testa, then." Rod had a notion the appellation was anything but a joke. "Then I'll call you 'Mother,' too, while I'm your guest."

" 'Tis not needful."

"Yes, it is." Rod frowned, pressing a hand against his forehead; the ache was dulled, but still there. "I wonder whether I've stopped hallucinating or not—the monks never mentioned a convent to me."

"They wot not of it, I trust; we ha' ne'er sent to tell them, nor have we wish to. We desire only to be left to do our work in peace."

"Without having to take orders from the abbot, eh?"

"There is that," Mother Paterna Testa admitted, "though I've more concern that he might bid us disband. Yet whiles we are not truly a convent, but only call ourselves such, we cannot come under his authority, to make or break."

Rod nodded. "I can understand that—and although the present abbot's a good and understanding young man, his successor might not be. No, I can see your point."

"Yet I assure thee, we are nonetheless real for all that."

Rod shrugged. "That's what the other hallucinations thought, too."

"Aye, but did they know that thou didst see things that were not there?"

"I never told them," Rod admitted. "But I have told you—so why don't you vanish?"

"Because I am real, whether thou art here or no."

The last statement had an uncomfortably philosophical ring to it. Rod eyed Mother Paterna Testa warily.

"Yet now tell me," the good woman pressed, "why thou dost roam the wild wood, an thou dost know thou art ill in thy mind."

"Why, that's just the reason, don't you see? I start feeling my hallucinations are out to get me, so I fight back—and I might hurt someone real that way. Especially my wife and children." He struggled to sit up. "That reminds me—my boy. The young man with the horse. Where . . ."

The room lurched, and he found himself staring up at the ceiling with a chill wet cloth on his forehead again. "Thou must needs rest for some hours yet," Mother Paterna Testa assured him. "We shall bring thy son to thee presently—yet first I must speak more of thine illness."

Rod shrugged. "It's only chemical—at least, according to the ghost of an old friend I met along the way." He glanced at her out of the corner of his eye, but Mother Paterna Testa nodded, unruffled. "What said this spectre?"

"Why, that the chestnut I ate was made of witch-moss, and my system didn't know how to handle it."

" 'Tis likely true," the nun agreed, "for look you, there are many who are witch-moss crafters unbeknownst, even to themselves—and the eldritch substance, when in their blood, doth shape itself to the forms that come from that part of our minds that doth dream. Thus do they see waking dreams, and cannot rule them."

That did pretty much agree with Big Tom's hypothesis. "So how do I get well, Mother?"

The nun reached under the table again and produced a little jar. She took a parchment cover off it and dipped her finger in, saying, "This is a fairy ointment, brought to us by the Wee Folk, for no better reason than that they did applaud our healing. They use it themselves, that they may see through the glamours they shape, and not thereby be entrapped." With a quick, deft movement, she touched Rod's eyes directly above the lower lid, so quickly that he was just pulling his head back as she was sitting up, the pot in her lap, smiling like the Mona Lisa. "Thou wilt now see all things as they truly are."

Rod suspected the cure was mostly psychological, if it did any good at all—why else the tale about the Little People?—but he was ready to try anything. "Thank you, Mother."

"I am glad to do it," she said simply. "Wouldst thou now see thy son?"

"I would," Rod said emphatically.

The Mother Paterna Testa bent over to put the jar away and stood up, drawing out from underneath the table a pouch that she slipped over her shoulder. She turned away to the door, still with her gentle, enigmatic smile, and opened it.

The princess stood there, clad in pastel clouds, coronet glowing. "I greet thee, Mother. What of our patient?"

"He doth mend," the nun answered, and turned to Rod. "This is our most constant patron, gentleman—the Countess Bene."

"My pleasure, Countess." Rod struggled up on one elbow, but the countess crossed to him with a quick, lithe stride, saying, "Do not rise for courtesy, I prithee. Thou hast need of rest."

"So." Rod sank back. "You weren't a hallucination, either."

The countess raised her eyebrows. "Thou didst think me a dream?"

"Yes, and the Mother, here. I've been seeing things, you understand. For example, I thought your convent was a castle of marble so pure that anyone looking into its walls would scc himsclf as hc truly is."

The countess raised her eyebrows. "A puissant charm would that be, and a blessing."

"Not completely," Rod assured her.

"Is any blessing unmixed?" But the countess didn't give him time to answer—she turned away toward the door. "I must be about my lord's affairs, yet let me first usher in one who did speak of thee. Young man, is this the father thou didst seek?"

Magnus stepped in through the door, tense as a lute string. When he saw Rod looking back at him, he almost sagged with relief. Then he was beside the bed, kneeling, holding his father's hand in his own. "Thy pardon, sir! I did seek to mount guard over thee, but some churl whose mind was hidden did come upon me unawares and smite me senseless!"

"No pardon needed, I assure you." Rod clapped the boy on the shoulder, and couldn't stop the grin. "So. You thought it was *your* turn to guard *me*, huh?"

Magnus flushed and lowered his eyes.

"Nice to know," Rod said gently. "Very nice to know. But then, I always have been glad to have you by my side."

Magnus looked up again, saw the unmistakable look of pride in his father's eyes, and smiled again.

"And thanks for taking care of Fess," Rod added. "I wasn't quite up to it."

"Nay." Magnus's face darkened with anxiety. "What struck thee, sir? The elf did speak of thy battling six, with no aid."

"He underrates himself," Rod grunted, "and he forgot about Fess." But he wondered—had Beaubras's deeds really been his own?

There was a knock at the door again.

Mother Paterna Testa opened it. A younger nun stood just outside. "Mother, there are men come before the wall, and they call for thy patient."

"I shall come."

"Me, too." Rod struggled up.

"Nay," Mother Paterna Testa commanded.

"I tell you, I can walk!" Rod felt the surge of adrenaline. "Give me a hand, son." Rod didn't wait; he grabbed Magnus's shoulder and hoisted himself up.

"Thou hast lost blood, good gentleman! Thou must needs rest!"

Rod exchanged a glance with Magnus, then turned back to Mother Paterna Testa. "Can you take a shock? Without thinking I'm some sort of monster, that is."

The nun frowned. "I am a healer; I can accustom myself. Of what dost thou speak?"

Rod let the outside world go hang, and paid attention to rejecting the floor. He drifted upward six inches.

Mother Paterna Testa's eyes widened. Slowly, she nodded. "Thou art a warlock, then."

"Sorry about that."

"Rejoice—'tis a gift from God." The nun turned away to the door. "As thou wilt have it, then. Come with us."

She followed the nun out, across the cloister to the chapel, went in, and climbed up into the steeple. The top chamber held a large bell. They went around it to look out a high, thin window.

Below them, in front of the convent gates, a half-dozen men-at-arms leaned on their spears. Actually, they looked like well-to-do bandits—each wearing different colors and garments, but none ragged. Before them, a tall man in a red robe paced impatiently. His head was bald, and he was in his prime, with a sword at his waist, but Rod would have known that face anywhere.

"Brume!" Rod cried.

"Thou dost know him, then?"

"You bet I do! He's the sorcerer who cast this whole madness on me!"

Magnus stared; then his eyes narrowed.

Mother Paterna Testa nodded. "And behind him?"

"I see a dozen mercenaries," Rod answered. "What else could I see?"

"An ogre and trolls," the nun answered. "These are they who set upon thee last night."

Rod's gaze whipped back to the men. Then he said, "Well. Nice to know I'm in touch with reality again." He didn't say whether or not it was a pleasant sensation.

Mother Paterna Testa smiled with satisfaction. "Thou didst lay about thee like a veritable demon, like two men or three. The ointment has cured thy sight, then."

"It certainly has. But how could a simple paste do so much?"

" 'Tis that part of thy mind that doth make dreams," the nun reminded him. "The witch-moss doth lend it strength, doth enhance its power, so that thy waking mind doth perceive the dreams it doth show. Yet now thou hast had fairy ointment on thine eyes, and whatsoever the Wee Folk did place in it hath convinced thy mind that thou wilt no longer have waking dreams, and thereby doth banish any vision that the witch-moss within thee doth show."

Rod frowned, wondering about residual effects, but he didn't want to know—that word "enhance" worried him.

The man in the red robe turned toward the gate with a gesture of exasperation and called, "Wilt thou speak or not? We know thou hast ta'en the High Warlock within thy wall, sore wounded! Surrender him now, or it shall go hard!''

Mother Paterna Testa looked up at Rod in mild surprise. ''So, then. Thou art the High Warlock.''

''Sorry not to mention it,'' Rod muttered. ''It's just that some clergy have strong ideas about people like me.''

''We know that magic is a gift from God, and that on this Isle of Gramarye, those whom the simple folk call 'warlock' are no more like to be wicked than any other men. Why doth this man seek thee?''

''To kill him,'' Magnus grated. ''My father doth stand between him and the power he doth seek.''

Rod stood immobile.

'' 'Tis true, what the lad doth say?'' the nun asked quietly.

Rod nodded. ''This man is part of a crew that seek to overthrow the King and Queen. So far, the only thing that's been stopping them is me and my family.''

The nun stood quiet for a moment. Then she turned and called out, ''The High Warlock hath claimed the sanctuary of the Church! He shall have it! And thou must needs honor this sanctuary; it must not be violated, at thy soul's peril!''

The men behind Brume stirred and muttered uneasily, but he turned on them, crying, ''What! Wilt thou be frightened by a nurse's fable? Dost truly think thou hast souls to imperil?''

The men stopped stirring, but they glared at him, stone-faced.

Mother Paterna Testa relaxed.

Brume tossed his head, exasperated. ''Well enough, then! Bring the stake, and the woman!''

This, the men were willing enough to do. They ran into the forest and ran back a moment later with a post and some bundles of wood. They jammed the stake into a hole in the ground that they had already dug and piled sticks around it. Then another pair hustled a woman in pastel robes and a coronet out of the forest.

Mother Paterna Testa gasped. "The countess!"

"She rode out a half hour since," said the nun beside her, pale-faced. "She did say her lord did need her ere noon. We begged her to take escort, but she would not hear of it!"

The countess fought them every inch of the way, kicking and biting, but the bandits brought her up onto the pile of wood and bound her to the post. Brume turned back to the convent, a sneering grin on his face. "Send out the High Warlock, or thy patron shall go to her ancestors!"

The nuns' faces were pale, but the countess herself cried, "Do not! Thou must needs not violate sanctuary!"

"That's right, you mustn't." Rod turned back to the stairwell. "So I'll go."

"Sisters!" Mother Paterna Testa called, and two nuns stepped together, to block Rod's path. He turned back to Mother Paterna Testa, his face thunderous. "I'm not that important."

"Thou hast had thy warning!" Brume shouted, and threw a torch into the kindling. Flame billowed up, and smoke rose in a shroud.

"See!" Brume gestured. "Her ancestors come to escort her!"

And as they gazed, the smoke formed itself into amorphous heads with empty eyes and moaning mouths, surging up toward heaven.

The nuns cried out, but Rod called, "Don't let him scare you! We know he's a projective—and smoke is even easier to move around than witch-moss! *He's* making those heads, not her ancestors!"

"But she will burn!" moaned one of the nuns.

"Not if I go," Rod answered, and dove out the steeple window.

"Papa!" Magnus protested, and plunged out after him. "Thou hast not thy full strength! Thou shalt fall!"

But Rod had leveled off and was flying nicely. He looked back over his shoulder. "What was that?"

Magnus gulped and said, "Naught."

Rod landed with a jolt, right in front of Brume, sword out and thrusting. Brume parried, riposted, and returned the thrust. Rod leaned aside and thought, *Fess!*

The monastery gates burst open, and the great black horse charged out with a screaming whinny.

21

Rod was rather busy cutting and parrying, but he did manage the occasional glimpse out of the corner of his eye. Fess was knocking over bandits with his front hooves, then reaching out to grasp a collar with his teeth and toss the man aside. They were coming at him from all directions, of course, which would ordinarily have given him a seizure—but Magnus was on his back, keeping three captured swords busy, two with his hands and one behind him with his mind, fending off culprits until Fess could take care of them.

Then a flying squad charged out of the underbrush and hit the convent wall. Since it was only eight feet high, they were up and over in a matter of seconds.

Magnus whirled, appalled.

In the steeple, Mother Paterna Testa narrowed her eyes. "Aid me, Sister Lynne."

As the bandits hurdled the wall, their feet shot out from under them, and they kept hurdling, slamming down to the ground on their backs.

Then Modwis rose up with his mace.

The Mother Superior squeezed her eyes shut, then shook her head sadly. "Pray God they may live!"

"Amen," murmured Sister Lynne.

But Magnus's concentration had flagged, and bandits hit Fess from all four sides. Magnus shouted and lashed out with his right and back swords, and the bandits there danced away as Fess reached for the one in front while he tried to strike a hoof at the one on the left, then caught the one in the front while he lashed out with his hind legs—and went stiff.

Magnus gave a cry of anger and exasperation, and the soldiers in front of him shot bodily off the ground and went flying toward the trees.

Meanwhile, Rod was cutting and thrusting with panic and anger, afraid for the poor, innocent countess. Already she was coughing in the smoke of her bogus ancestors.

Then a brisk breeze whipped up and blew the ghosts away to her right.

Rod didn't want to know where the breeze had come from, but he was afraid he knew, anyway. He blocked a cut, parried a thrust, riposted, and thrust, scoring Brume's shoulder. The sorcerer shouted an oath and leaped back, then narrowed his eyes and growled.

Yes, growled—and right about then, the elves' ointment must have worn off, because he seemed to grow and swell, towering eight feet above Rod with a fanged mouth and a huge club.

The ogre was back.

All about them, trolls shambled, stabbing with crude spears—and the young wolf danced about them, leaping in to slash with his teeth, then darting out before they could strike.

He was in horrible danger, and Rod's heart lurched. "Magnus! Get out of here, quick . . ."

The instant's distraction was enough. The huge club

smashed down. Rod saw it coming, too late to more than lean away, and the bludgeon smashed into his side, sending him flying. He landed with cracking and crunching, and extra pains shot up his back and sides. Flame danced by his head, and he realized, with horror, that he'd fallen into the pyre around the stake. He struggled to rise—but even as he did, he realized the flames hadn't grown, and were even now dying. He scrambled to his feet, racked with pain, the world swimming about him, and staggered toward the ogre, aiming his sword at its navel . . .

Modwis was there in front of him, mace slamming into the ogre's kneecap.

The ogre howled and fell back, clasping at its collarbone.

"Back, quickly!" Modwis tugged at Rod.

"But . . . but . . ." The scene swam in front of him, but Rod remembered priorities. "The countess . . ."

"She is freed, and safe! Quickly, back through the gate!"

Rod turned, startled. Sure enough, the stake was empty, and the flames were dead.

He didn't ask—he yielded and backed in through the gate.

The ogre roared and charged.

Flame exploded, filling the gateway.

The ogre scrabbled to a stop, and the trolls fell back, muttering fearfully.

Rod had a second to think. What was he supposed to do when the hallucinations hit again? And who had told him . . . Oh, yes, Saint John. And he was supposed to remember opening the vial, that was right. He closed his eyes for a second, and the vision was there, clear and vivid, a huge pile of test tubes, and one of them right under his nose, its fumes wreathing his head . . .

"Lord Gallowglass!" Modwis cried, and Rod looked up through the flame to see the ogre shrink and diminish, becoming Brume again. Behind him, only four bandits stood, and they were looking distinctly nervous.

" 'Tis naught but illusion!'' Brume shouted with contempt. "Walk boldly, and thou shalt not even feel the heat!''

The bandits muttered to one another. They didn't look convinced.

"See! I shall go to root out this vile warlock!'' Brume called, and marched boldly into the flames.

He made it through, all right, but he came out howling, beating at his burning robe. His men stared; then they turned tail and ran.

But they skidded to a halt as they hit the treeline, then backed up slowly, their arms out and away from their sides—for a singing sword whipped figure eights in the air before them, and a firebrand and a ball of lightning drifted out of the wood on their flanks.

Not that Rod saw any of that—he and Modwis were too busy beating out the flames on Brume's robe. When they had it down to a smolder, Rod looked up at the steeple— and, sure enough, the Mother Superior stood there, face stony, staring at the fire. Rod felt his stomach sink; apparently these nuns had something in common with the monks of Saint Vidicon, after all.

Then Brume snarled and lashed out at him.

Rod fell back, startled, but Brume scrambled up and thrust with his sword. Rod managed to bring his own blade up in time to parry—but just as he did, Modwis struck, and Brume's thrust went wide as he pitched forward. Rod rolled to the side, and the sorcerer landed, out cold.

Rod knelt over him, staring, panting, unbelieving.

Modwis, much more practically, unwound a coil of rope from his belt and started tying Brume up.

"He's—he's a psi,'' Rod croaked. "The rope—won't do much good when he wakes up.''

"He shall not waken."

Rod looked up, startled, to see his wife standing over them.

"Thou hast done well," she said to the leprechaun. "I cannot give thee sufficient thanks."

"The knowledge that I have aided thee and thine husband, lady, is thanks enough," Modwis muttered, clearly awed.

"Yet we stand in thy debt," Gwen insisted, "and the enchantment that bound thee is broke now, is't not?"

"It is." Modwis confirmed. "I have, at least, made reparation."

"And brought down another villain betime." Gwen turned—just as the countess came in over the scorched threshold accompanied by Cordelia and Gregory, and Mother Paterna Testa approached from the chapel.

First things first. "What of the bandits?" Gwen demanded.

"They sleep, Mama," Cordelia assured her, "and will not waken, whiles Geoffrey doth guard them."

"They had best not." Gwen's tone hinted at mayhem. "He doth know better than to let one awaken for sport, doth he not?"

"Aye!" came a voice from the other side of the wall, clearly disappointed.

The countess stared. "What manner of dame art thou, that hast the ordering of such terrors?"

"Their mother," Gwen said shortly.

"And my wife," Rod said, senselessly proud. He turned to the other Mother present. "I take it you and your sisters know a little bit more about magic than you led me to believe."

"We are healers," Mother Paterna Testa said noncommittally, "and where there's power to heal, there's power to harm." With that, she knelt, lifted Brume's head, and poured the contents of a vial down his throat.

"Do not wake him!" Modwis cried, alarmed.

"I do not." The nun stood again. "The draught I've given will assure his sleep for a day and a night, at the least." She looked up at Gwen. "How didst thou come to be near when we had need of thee, lady?"

"We had finished some business my husband bade us see to, in Runnymede," Gwen answered, "and mine eldest did cry for aid. We came quickly."

"Aye, thou didst that!" said the Countess. "And I cannot thank thee enough, lady, for loosing me from that stake!"

"Thou hast aided these good sisters, who did aid mine husband," Gwen returned. "An we could do more for thee, we would." She turned to the nuns. "And for thee, sisters."

"We are glad to aid," said Mother Paterna Testa, but she turned to Rod with a frown. "Yet we bade thee rest."

Rod shook his head. "I couldn't see an innocent lady burned for my sake."

"Yet thou shouldst not have been able to lift thy sword," said the nun, "for the loss of blood, and need of rest. How hast thou raised thyself to fight?"

"Sheer adrenaline," Rod answered, but even as he said it, he realized it had ebbed. His weakness suddenly hit him redoubled, and the lights went out again.

22

Remarkably, Rod's head felt totally clear, so clear that he couldn't believe he hadn't noticed how muzzy it had felt.

"What happened to the castle of Brume?"

"Is that what thou didst see?" Geoffrey asked, amazed. "We saw naught but a log house, with a palisade of sharpened stakes."

"That was enough for my subconscious to build a horror-show castle," Rod explained.

Gwen was riding beside him on a Fess-drawn sleigh, heading south on a winter road, escorted by a self-propelled sled with four children aboard.

Rod asked, "How about the sorcerer, Brume?"

"Ah. He, my husband, was real enough," Gwen said, "though his powers were no more than those of any other warlock of Gramarye. Stronger, yes, but no more numerous."

"Yet he did have henchmen," Geoffrey said darkly, "and queerly clad were they."

"Aye." Cordelia frowned. "They went all in black, even to hiding their faces amidst black scarves, and slashed at thee with swords of strange design, and keen-edged stars which they hurled.''

Rod recognized the descriptions and nodded. ''My mind just didn't see anything draped in black, just as the Oriental theater intended. Less seen, less guilt. Tell me—how many of them did I kill?''

''Only one,'' Geoffrey said, wooden-faced. ''Mama lulled the rest to sleep.''

''Where are they?''

''Taken, by a squadron of guards,'' Gwen assured him.

''Guards? How come there just happened to be . . .'' Then Rod turned to her, understanding dawning. ''They've been following me ever since I went berserk, haven't they?''

''Aye,'' Gwen admitted, ''though somewhat tardily, for we knew thou wouldst not wish to be seen.''

''So all the bandits are headed for Tuan's dungeon?''

''Even so, with the squadron of guardsmen who did follow thee.''

''And the sorcerer will wake to find himself bound with silver,'' said Magnus, ''in the midst of a dozen warlocks and witches.''

Rod wondered if even that would hold him. ''Tell Tuan to make the trial short.''

''If he doth feel need of a trial at all. A dozen peasants have cried mercy, and blamed him for their subversion— and Granny Ban did gush forth all her tale when we came upon her, so glad was she to be delivered.''

''Yeah, from me.'' Rod felt guilt weigh him down. ''Was she innocent?''

''She was sore affrighted, Papa,'' Cordelia explained, ''yet unhurt.''

Rod's mouth tightened with chagrin. ''Thank Heaven I had a vestige of self-control—Heaven, and Fess. So I scared an innocent old lady half to death?''

"Well, not so innocent as all that," Magnus hedged.

Rod turned, eyes widening. "The stew *was* drugged?"

"There were vegetables of witch-moss in't," Gwen confirmed, "though there may be truth in her claim that she knew not what they were."

"She had been terrified by men she did speak of as bandits," Geoffrey explained, "foul villains, who did bid her feed thee so, under pain of death!"

"And the one of them," said Magnus, "did come clad in a red robe, with a bald head."

"Brume himself, huh? Well, there's evidence, anyway. So she didn't really want to do it."

"It may be so," Gwen said carefully. "Her neighbors speak well of her, at the least. All do bless her for her cures and midwifing."

"And she did rejoice that thou hadst caught her out," Cordelia added, "so that she had not slain thee."

"What did the bandits do to her?"

"Naught; the Crown's men did take her first, and I misdoubt me an ever a woman was so glad to see a dungeon," said Gwen. "There will be no danger to her now, sin that we have ta'en Brume and his henchmen."

"Been busy, haven't you? Not that I've left you much choice. How about Modwis?"

"He is a true leprechaun," Gregory explained, "who doth dwell in this wood. The King of the Elves bade him watch o'er thee, and he was sore distressed when he woke from his enchanted sleep in Brume's keep, to find thee gone."

"So that's why he seemed to dwindle away." Rod frowned. "What was this reparation you spoke of? Was his guarding me a sort of punishment?"

"Nay; 'twas a chance to redeem himself. The Wee Folks have laws, too, husband, and Modwis slew a man without leave of the Elfin King."

Rod stared. "Modwis? Sentimental, good-hearted Modwis? What had the man done?"

Gwen glanced at the children. "That which we may speak of at another time; yet I think he may have told thee some part of it."

Rod nodded; he remembered Modwis saying something about a damsel, and another wicked sorcerer named Gormlin—but apparently, Gwen didn't want to be specific in front of the children. "So the man he killed was a real villain?"

"Aye," said Gwen. "No elf could truly blame him— yet he had broke their Law."

"So he undertook the dangerous task of escorting a mad warlock, to win his way back from exile. Lord knows he deserved it. Nice to know he was real, if not really as I saw him."

"But where did Modwis get such good information? No, strike that—the elves always do have all the answers, don't they? And you say you found the old lady who sold us the chestnuts?"

Gwen said grimly, "We have learned that the Lord Mayor of Runnymede did go homeward with his wife just before us, and did not see her by the roadside."

"No wonder nobody else started seeing things! Nobody else ate them—except you five; but a witch-moss chestnut wouldn't bother *you*!"

The children exchanged startled glances and backed their sled off a little. Gwen stilled. "How couldst thou know that?"

"Sheer deduction." Rod felt the heat on his face, and hoped he wasn't blushing. "How did you confirm it?"

"The warlock Toby did track her thoughts, and we did seize her basket. When Gregory did make the chestnuts turn to apricocks, we knew them for what they were."

Rod nodded. "What did you do with the old lady?"

"Call her not a lady," Gwen said with asperity, "and her age owed more to skill with paint, than to years. Nay, she doth abide in a dungeon cell, awaiting thy testimony, and judgment."

"So she came by just for us?"

"Solely," Gwen said sourly.

"I never did like special treatment," Rod groused.

"Thou wilt have to abide it, for some time," Cordelia informed him. "Thou hast fearfully abused thy body, Papa."

"Yeah, well, that's what happens when you let it get out of balance with your mind," Rod answered. "Don't worry, though—I'll rest."

Cordelia and Gwen exchanged looks.

"We rejoice that thy mind, at least, is healed," Gregory intervened.

Rod frowned. "Well, don't be too sure of that, son. Once something like this gets into your body, it may never get out. For all I know, I might have a relapse. If I start talking about demons, duck."

"Of demons, at least, thou hast no need to be anxious," Gwen assured him. "Those thou didst see came from the twisted mind of the the sorcerer Brume."

"Give the fellow his due," Geoffrey said. "He is a thought-caster of amazing strength."

"He *is* a top-notch projective," Rod agreed.

"He did cast into thy mind only the embodiments of the terrors and rages that did fill his soul."

Rod nodded. "Just as the monsters I saw were really only projections of my own secret fears."

Geoffrey started. "Hast thou so many fears, then, Papa?"

"Oh, yes," Rod said softly. "Oh, yes—though I usually keep them locked away in the dungeons of my mind. It *is* nice to know that the only reason they were able to get out was that someone fed me the wrong chemical—but that has its bad side, too.'' Rod winced; the worst of the nausea and headache was gone, but there was still enough left to make him wish for a Dramamine.

''Thou must not be so anxious,'' Gwen scolded. ''Thy bairns and I shall handle thee with such care, thou wilt think thou art made of porcelain.''

''Well, if I get too bad, you can always send me back to the Mother Superior,'' Rod said with a smile. ''Say, why do you suppose she looked so horrified when I told her I'd put in a good word for her with the abbot?''

Gwen smiled, amused. ''She did take me aside, and beg me to dissuade thee. She doth fear that the good they do would be sorely diminished an folk did know of them, the more so since the abbot might disagree with them as to the nature of their mission.''

''Oh? And just what do they see their mission as being, pray tell?''

''They have taken it upon themselves to aid in keeping all of Gramarye from madness,'' Gwen explained, ''by discovering the worst of the monsters that do haunt people's nighttimes, and taking action against them.''

''What kind of action?''

''Prayers, most often—yet their prayers do seem to be most singularly effective.''

''I'll bet they are,'' Rod said. ''A bunch of projectives and telekinetics, focusing their powers on a common goal by means of communal meditation? I'll just bet they're effective!''

''I rejoice that they are, my lord, so that they were able to heal thee.''

Rod looked up at her in astonishment. ''You mean it wasn't just an accident that I wandered toward their gates?''

"I can get you a really good deal on favorable accidents," somebody said.

Rod looked up, and saw the debonair devil leaning against a tree just ahead of them. Rod smiled. "No, thanks. I can make my own."

Then he made a circle of his forefinger and thumb and let the forefinger shoot out as though he were flicking away a fly.

And the devil disappeared.